Code Blue

Marissa Slaven

Happy Reading!

Code Blue

Printed in the USA
Publisher: Moon Willow Press, moonwillowpress.com
Coquitlam, British Columbia, Canada

Dedicated to my mother, Marcia Slaven

Acknowledgments

Many people helped me along the amazing journey to see this project through to completion. There are four without whom it would never have been possible.

Noah, my oldest child, who for many years, before I ever imagined that I had the potential to be creative, was a living example. His commitment and passion for music showed me what was possible.

Nick, my middle child, whose confidence in my ability to do this didn't waver. He never thought it was silly or impossible that at mid-life his mother, who had not studied anything but medicine, would successfully write a novel. His steadfast confidence in me was there to shore me up when I had none.

Anna, my youngest, who was my inspiration for writing this story. Her presence permeates and transcends the characters and the story.

Fred, my husband, who has always been there for me and who has supported me in pursuing my passions.

NORTH EAST SCIENCE ACADEMY

ENTRANCE EXAM

VELLE EST POSSE

Please Turn Over This Page and Begin

Question 1:

What is the total length of the United States coastline?

a) 1,000 miles
b) 28,000 miles
c) 88,633 miles
d) 1,040,559 miles
e) None of the above

Answer 1:

c) 88,633 miles

The USA has 88,633 miles of coastline. Approximately 70 percent of it is fenced for public safety.

JUNE

My fingers clutch the metal wire of the chain-link fence until my knuckles turn white. I know the fence at the Edge is meant to keep people safe, to protect us, so why does it feel like a prison? I still find it hard to understand how it is even possible that the same fence that I am hanging on to stretches almost 28,000 miles on the East Edge alone. I look to the top of it, some fifteen feet above me, at the barbed wire. You can always go to a gate if you want out, as long as you have authorization anyway. I've only been out twice. Once was on a school field trip to Boston, and the other time I, well, that time I didn't have authorization, but I did have wire cutters.

I press my forehead against the fence links and strain my eyes against the sunlight bouncing off the water. I can just about see where Uncle Al came in his old red canoe to "rescue" me on November 1st three and half years ago. It was my thirteenth birthday, and I was desperately curious to get out and visit the "island" in the distance after staring at it for years. I had been begging Mom for months to let me take a short canoe trip, saying that she or Uncle Al could come with me and that I wouldn't even be out of sight of the Edge, but she just kept refusing. I know that it was hard for her. I know she was worried because of him. But really Dad's accident was a totally different situation. He was doing research in the North Atlantic and the weather turned. I promised I would only go on a day with clear skies, and only for a few hours, but she kept saying no. And then the weather was perfect on my birthday and she was supposed to be at work all day. I thought I had plenty of time. How was I supposed to know she would get off early?

Looking at it from here, if you didn't know any better, it looks like hundreds of seagulls are standing on the water, walking around on it and building nests, but really they are on the roof of a submerged building. It's a big roof, almost one million square feet. It's the roof of what was once the largest shopping mall in New England. I know from watching old videos that it would have been a place where teenagers like me would have met, shopped, eaten, gossiped, hooked up, broken up…in other words spent a lot of time. Unbelievably, there were two hundred and fifty shops there all selling new things!

Since the Change, that type of consumerism would be socially unacceptable, even if it were possible. Using so many natural resources to excess isn't really an option anymore. Even though we have tons of clean energy, what is most accessible to folks is refurb clothes, refurb furniture, refurb anything. Luckily R-dubs sells everything refurb that anyone could need or want, and they do such a great job that even though it's all second-hand and mostly salvaged the stuff looks new. New Hope Town is a ridiculously dinky town, and even we have an R-dubs. It's a big concrete bunker at the west end of town with no windows and stale air. It's built to withstand any natural disaster, and so clearly is not a place for teenagers to go hang with their buds.

A warm wind carries the gulls' cries to me. They sound harsh and mournful and all too familiar. No one should live as close to the Edge as we do, but so far our luck has held.

"Not thinking about going over again are you?" a man's voice growls, startling me.

I look over my shoulder and see Uncle Al, who raises his whiskered chin and winks at me. He is in a pressed plaid shirt and clean jeans. I unclamp my fingers from the fence and rub them. I didn't realize how tight I had been holding on. I force a smile onto my face.

"Nah, I'm not going out on the water today anyway."

"You don't have to do this if you don't want to," he says.

"Yeah I pretty much do."

I have, after all, chosen to spend every free minute for the past two years studying science instead of having hobbies, having friends, having a life.

"C'mon then or we'll be late," he says as he turns and heads towards the house.

Uncle Al is our neighbor and not my actual uncle. He's a farmer, and he's used to being up "at the crack of dawn" as he likes to say. Today he's taking a day off from running his cows around to take me up to Rock Haven High School so I can sit the entrance exam for North East Science Academy.

I run and catch up to him quickly. We walk quietly side by side. His stride is long and even; mine is a series of quick steps, a trot I have learned over the years in order to keep pace with him. I look down at my feet. My shoes are muddy, and I know I'm not looking my best. I didn't even run a brush through my hair this morning. I pull it up into a bun, slipping an elastic from my wrist over it as we walk. I only slept for a few hours last night and I feel tired and jumpy at the same time. I am a bundle of nerves. Usually, looking out at the old mall helps fire me up and focus my attention, my intention, to be a part of the solution. I need to focus today more than ever before. I have to get into NESA.

***

Question 2:

This is a Remote Associates Question (RAQ). It measures your ability to see relationships between things that are only remotely associated.

Look at the three words below and find a fourth word that is related to all three.

Dew Comb Bee

Answer 2:

Honey

Bees were almost extinct at the time of the International Change Agreement. With the re-settlement of all agriculture to indoor facilities, bees have had significantly less exposure to neonicotinoids and scientists have seen a slow but steady rise in the bee population.

***

The drive up is quiet, which isn't surprising. Uncle Al is not much of a talker, and I am extremely nervous and preoccupied with thoughts about the exam. We make good time and we get to the high school parking lot just after eight. The exam won't start until nine. Uncle Al passes me an egg sandwich Mom made for me, but after two bites I fold the brown paper carefully back around the sandwich and put it on the seat between us. He pulls two mugs out of nowhere and pours us each a cup of black coffee from an old, green thermos. He's looking straight ahead, his gaze tracking a few wisps of clouds, "figuring the sky" for what kind of day it will be.

"Weather seems good," I venture, my hands wrapped around my mug. I hold it close to my face so I can breathe in the sharp, bitter smell.

"We'll see," he answers, making me wonder if he senses something I don't.

Soon the parking lot starts to get busy with more cars dropping off students. My peers. My competition. I pass my mug to Uncle Al. "I guess I should go in now," I say.

"Right," he says. My hand is on the door handle. "Tic?" Something soft and low in the way he says my name makes me turn and really look at him. There are more crow's feet in the corners of his milky, blue eyes lately and his stubble is like speckled ash after a fire. "No matter what happens in there, your mom and I are proud of you."

"I know…" I shrug, get out of the car, and walk to the school entrance without looking back. I let myself become a part of the herd of students being shepherded into the gymnasium and then straightened into one of several neat lines of students waiting to sign in. While I wait, I count off ten rows of ten desks, I shift my weight from one foot to the other and I sneak peaks at the students around me. The girl in front of me keeps twisting and untwisting a piece of hair around her finger. A boy in the next line over is drumming his fingers against his thigh. No one is talking although they haven't said that you can't.

"Name?" says a woman when I get to the front of the line.

"Atlantic Brewer." I watch as she runs her finger down the list on her clipboard, stopping and pinning it firmly on my name.

"ID?"

I pull my New Hope Town High student card from my front pocket and hand it to her. She inspects it carefully for what feels like too long and finally passes it back to me. I start to breathe again. I must have been holding my breath without knowing.

"Take any seat that's available. Tests are on the table." She is staring over my left shoulder as she recites, "Do not turn them over until you are told to do so. Next."

While I wait for everyone else to sign in and take a seat, I look around at the gym. Blue mats lean against a wall, bleachers are stacked at one end of the gymnasium, and a clock has been placed up in front of the desks. Basketball and football pendants hang from the rafters, sporting a yellow-and-black bee on a green background. Handmade signs hang on the walls with illustrations of cartoon bees saying, "Bee Kind" and "Bee at the Fun Fair." School just let out for summer vacation a week ago, and the gym still smells of rubber balls and metal and sweat.

"Attention students," a tall, bald man with glasses calls from the front of the gym. "The entrance exam for North East Science Academy is about to begin. Topics covered include all of the physical sciences as well as recent history and questions that will test your creativity and originality. Please do not turn your tests over until I give the signal to do so. You will have three hours to complete the exam. If you finish before that time, turn your test back over and exit as quietly as you can so as not to disturb your fellow students."

I glance at the girl to my right who is chewing the end of her pen and staring straight ahead.

"Until you are finished with your exam, do not leave your seat or speak for any reason. There will not be any invigilators in the room with you, but I will now draw your attention to our four video cameras." He points to the corners of the room and our heads swivel in unison to see where the cameras stand on tripods. "The entire exam is being recorded, and all of the tapes will be thoroughly reviewed by a team of experts. Any student suspected of cheating will be disqualified. Entrance to the Academy is a privilege, and it is your responsibility to make sure your behaviour is beyond suspicion." He stops his monologue and adjusts his red bow tie. He runs his hands down the front of his tan sweater vest as if brushing off invisible dust. "Let us now stand and recite the Declaration."

Feet shuffle, chairs scrape, and we all stand, placing our right hands over our hearts. We recite the words we have said every morning at school since we were four years old:

We the people of the world
acknowledge and accept responsibility
for and to the Earth
and all creatures that dwell upon it.
We agree to no longer participate in ecocide
and to commit all of our financial, social, and intellectual resources
to creating a sustainable planet
for all living beings.

I exhale into the collective sigh and sit. Complete silence reigns for a long minute before Mr. Red Bow Tie's voice rings out. "Begin."

I am confident about many, but not all, my answers; some of the remote association questions are tricky. I am well-prepared for the chemistry, biology, and physics questions, no thanks to my teachers. New Hope Town High is a public high school in a small town. Its football program is better than its science program, and the football team only won two games last year. Most of what I know I taught myself. My dad was a hydrologist, and he is my inspiration. If only he had been around to help me prepare for this...I might be the top student at New Hope Town High, but I know that means I'm just a big fish in a small pond. The pool of applicants writing the NESA entrance exam is the ocean, and I know for sure I am not the smartest here.

I keep sneaking glances at the big clock up front. I read on blogs by students who have taken the entrance exam that time management is critical. The consensus seems to be that there is just barely enough time to finish the exam. Even though I'm not sure about some of my answers, I think I am making decent progress. The very last time I look up from my test to check the time it is 11:23.

***

Question 3:

"The Change" refers to _____.

a) Rising temperatures and sea levels
b) Increased frequency and severity of natural disasters
c) Exponential loss of species diversity and human life
d) The dogma embraced by the Declaration
e) All of the above

Answer 3:

e) All of the above

"The Change" refers to our understanding and acceptance of the inter-relatedness of all of these crises.

***

I am an idiot!

Really, I am such a total idiot.

I pretty much just threw away my whole future. We barely have enough money to get by each month, which is why we live so ridiculously close to the Edge. This exam was my only hope of getting a higher education so that eventually I could become a scientist and maybe, in some small way, I could make a difference.

Idiot! I hit my forehead with my palm and too late I remember that I am not alone. I steal a glance at the boy sitting next to me in this silent hallway. Of course, they didn't let either of us back into the gym to complete the exam. Why would they? I watched the other students file out of the gym after the exam was done, until one of them looked our way and made eye contact. After that I looked down at the floor until the last shuffling sounds had died out.

I sneak a glance at the boy. He has blond, wavy hair hiding some of his face but not so much that I haven't noticed how hot he is. Get a grip, Tic. You just ruined your life and you're checking out a boy you don't know and will probably never see again. I sneak another look anyway and confirm that he has strong arms, big biceps. It makes sense that he was able to scoop up the fallen girl with ease. My eyes stray to his muscular chest, and for the first time I notice a scarlet splash of blood on his white T-shirt. Shit! I wonder how that girl is.

"Hey, are you okay?" the boy asks.

"Um, yeah. I guess. You?" I answer wondering if he caught me looking.

He shrugs and sweeps his hair back from his aqua eyes. He sighs.

"Do you think we blew it?" I ask. It suddenly feels like a great release to talk to someone about it, but I decide to keep my eyes safely on the floor between my feet.

"I hope not," he says, and I detect what sounds like desperation in his voice. He looks as upset as I feel, and suddenly I feel responsible for him too. I know it's not rational. It's not like I forced him in any way, but...

"Me too," I say and manage a small smile in the hopes of making him feel better.

"I can just about hear my mom's voice in my head telling me to *think before you act Tic*, because you know she must have told me that a million times already."

He smiles back at me and I feel dizzy.

"I'm sorry if," I start to say.

"No, don't apologize," he says, and his left hand closes around my right. My breath catches.

"You were really brave to..." he says, and before he can finish a woman's voice rings out down the hallway,

"Atlantic and Lee, the Board of Examiners are ready for you."

We stand in front of two women and a man who are seated behind a long table. The woman in the middle has straight, white hair that frames her oval face. She narrows her eyes and stares at us, tilting her head slightly. The other two look irritated, bored, judgmental, as if they have already made up their minds and this is all a waste of their time.

"I am Ms. Hunt, the director of NESA," says the woman with white hair. "Years ago, the World Council began to meet annually to make recommendations to try to stem the incredible loss of life caused by the Change. It was at their fifth annual council that they recommended the formation of academies around the world where the brightest young minds would receive the best in science education that the world has to offer. Every year, thousands of grade ten students apply to each academy. Based on school reports, letters of recommendation, and personal essays, six hundred applicants are invited to sit the exam for NESA. The top sixty are offered a chance to complete four years with us, during which time they will earn the equivalent of a university degree and after which they will be placed in internships."

I want desperately to believe that I haven't completely blown it. I figure that if there was no chance at all of me getting in they would have just sent me away. So maybe there is something I can still say or do.
Ms. Hunt turns to look at the man to her left, Mr. Red Bow Tie. "You informed them of the rules?"

"Of course," he says smugly, folding his arms across his chest.

She sighs. "Of course," she repeats.

I steal a quick glance at Lee, who looks serious but calm. My own stomach is doing flips, and I am glad I passed on the egg sandwich earlier.

"We will review all of the tapes in great detail, of course. For now, we have had a preliminary look at one of them. Can I ask that you two start by telling us, in your own words, please, what happened in there?"

I breathe deeply and close my eyes, trying my best to remember everything. It all happened so quickly that it seems like a blur. The first thing I seem to recall was seeing the chewed-up pen drop and bounce on the floor, but that can't be right if I was looking at my test. I saw the girl to my right slump forward and hit her head on the corner of her desk as she fell to the floor. Did I, though? I open my eyes and speak. "I heard a thump and then a second louder, clunky noise. The room was so quiet it caught me off guard, and I looked to see what it was." I pause, weighing my words, trying to go slow in my description to get the details right. "I saw a girl on the floor to my right. She was in an awkward position, and she wasn't moving. I got down on the floor next to her." My heart is pounding, and my mouth is dry.

"Go on," says Ms. Hunt.

"I tried shaking her shoulder and whispering to her to wake her up, but she didn't respond." The memory of my fear is building in me now, wringing my stomach like a wet rag. "Then I saw a puddle of blood spreading on the floor from under her head, and I guess I panicked. I started calling for help. I was still trying to wake her up, too. I…"

"She was seated a ways back from me." Lee picks up the thread of our story. "So I'm not sure if I heard her fall. I don't think so. But I heard someone yelling *help* over and over. I jumped up, ran down the row, and cut across two others until I saw her on the floor. I have my BCLS certificate, so I had an idea of what to do. I checked quickly and could see she was breathing. I could feel a weak pulse in her wrist. She was unconscious and needed medical attention, so I scooped her up in my arms and walked as quickly as I could to the gym door." He is doing a good job, I think. He sounds confident and reasonable, and we are almost finished telling what happened.

I jump in. "I was following and was going to open the door for him, but just as we got there, the doors opened and people were there, taking her out of his arms," I finish.

"Well," says Ms. Hunt, tucking her hair behind her ears, "now that we know what happened, and I am assuming that further review of the videos will confirm your account, I guess the relevant question is why you both would disregard the instructions you were given before the exam started. I assume you both want to attend NESA?"

"Yes." Lee's voice is hushed and urgent. "I very much want to attend."

"Me too," I say. I wipe my sweaty palms on my jeans. "When I saw her lying there, I didn't think about rules, or NESA, or my future, or anything. I just saw someone who needed help and I reacted." I hear Uncle Al's words from this morning in my head now—he and Mom are proud of me no matter what—and I hope I haven't disappointed them. "That's just how I was brought up, I guess."

Lee is nodding his head. "We did what we had to," he says, as if it is just that obvious.

"I see." Ms. Hunt puts on a pair of small, silver glasses that were hanging on a chain around her neck. She begins to straighten some papers on the table in front of her. "This is a very unusual circumstance, as I am sure you can appreciate. We will have to consider your files, the videos, everything, before we can come to any conclusions. We will keep you informed."

It seems pretty clear they are finished with us but—"Excuse me," I say, and when Ms. Hunt looks at me I am as surprised as she is that I spoke. "It's just that I was wondering if you had any news about the girl who fell? Is she going to be okay?"

"I believe she will be fine. When the paramedics arrived she was just beginning to regain consciousness. They took her to the hospital where she will be looked after."

***

Question 4:

Look at the three words below and find a fourth word that is related to all three:

House   Thumb   Pepper

Answer 4:

Green

A greenhouse was an antiquated structure made primarily of transparent materials such as glass for the purpose of growing plants. Current Grow-Houses are not technically greenhouses as they are made of opaque materials that are strong enough to resist natural and man-made impacts. Although they use artificial light they none-the-less serve the same purpose and provide upwards of eighty percent of all food. In indoor farms, the sun never shines, rain never falls and the climate is irrelevant. Indoor farms are automated, hydroponic, climate controlled, vertical growing systems that allow maximum production capacities to be achieved.

JULY

The hot, dry air has crowded in again under the rafters of my attic bedroom, and I wake up sweaty and restless this morning. I kick off my light blanket and flip my pillow to the cool side. It's Monday, my worst day of the week. It's the only day that Mom works at Maplewood Nursing Home and I don't. Usually I am up early even though it's my day off. Because it's my day off, I can get in a few hours of studying, do my chores, and still have a little time left over to do stuff I enjoy, like hiking in the wood looking for wildflowers and checking out animal tracks or scavenging along the Edge for anything that may have washed up. Usually it's just sea glass, but I have found other things: shoes, toy ships, candles, and once a tiara. Some stuff I manage to sell, some is useful and, yes, a lot of it is junk. But I haven't heard anything since the exam last month, and I have cut way back on my studying, so now time alone is just time to worry about my future. If I don't get in, it's back to New Hope Town High for another two years to work my butt off in hopes of getting a scholarship to somewhere half-decent. My dad went to Midhurst College and was a great scientist, but that was before the academies existed. If you look at the bios of scientists who are doing great work now, most are Academy alumni. Did I blow it? The day hasn't even started, and I am already obsessing.

I reach for a book on my bedside table. It was a birthday gift from Mr. Kisway, a client at Maplewood. He is tiny and ancient and has more wrinkles than hair, but he never complains. He has a collection of actual paper books and even though I could read any of them on my tablet he enjoys lending them to me. I have grown to like the weight of them in my hands, the soft feel of the paper, even the smell. I have read this one so often I think I must know parts of it by heart. I stare at the cover. The book is called *Walden,* and its cover has a drawing of a sweet, small cabin sheltered under tall trees. It's a real place, or it was anyway, and not all that far from here. I haven't been there since it is beyond the Edge, but I searched current images of where it should be. If the cabin is still there, you would need diving gear to see it. I press the book to my chest, close my eyes, and try to imagine it the way Thoreau describes it, before all of the destruction: a peaceful, natural oasis.

That lasts for a few minutes before I am back to thinking about NESA. I stand up and stretch, my fingers touching the slanted ceiling overhead. Mom says it's a good thing I am only 5'2" and seem to have stopped growing, otherwise I'd have a hard time standing in my own bedroom. A hazy light is filtering through the lace curtains, which hang limp. I wonder what time it is anyway. I go to my little desk and power on my tablet, surprised that it's almost eleven. My inbox shows one new message and I freeze. The message is from NESA.

I want to open the message, but my finger hesitates, hovering over the message, waiting, considering. I imagine Mom and I celebrating, whooping, laughing, and hugging. I also imagine falling into Mom's arms, sobbing and devastated. What I don't imagine is me opening the message and then, either way, being alone for hours until Mom gets home. For the millionth time I wish I also had a dad to share this day with.

When I can finally breathe again I turn off the screen without opening the message and head downstairs.

Our home is cramped but cozy. It is a clean, crowded mess of treasures that Mom and I have found, fixed, and repurposed. The main floor has only two rooms: the open kitchen and living area and a small room sectioned off in the back for Mom's bed and bedside table. The length of one wall has the sink, stove, counter, and cupboards. There is the kitchen table Mom and I built and two chairs: mine is painted turquoise and Mom's is yellow. Near the largest window are two large, mismatched, and overstuffed chairs. A red-and-grey rug in front of them has seen better days. The whitewashed walls are stippled with bent nails from which hand-knit rainbow sweaters and dried herbs hang. Window ledges are strewn with interesting rocks and sea glass of all shapes and sizes.

I busy myself with making breakfast. I scramble two eggs in a pan on the stove and add a little cheese to the mix just before they are done. I put on the kettle and pace. When it whistles I put in my favourite lemon tea and turn off the flame. I pace some more, waiting for it to steep. When it feels like five hours have passed, though it has only been five minutes, I pour tea into my mug. I eat without tasting anything and sip my tea while it is still too hot, scalding my tongue.

I keep looking at the door as if Mom might unexpectedly walk through. She doesn't. I decide to make myself useful. There is always plenty that needs doing here. I like being outside and figure I will see which garden beds need weeding today. I open the front door to find Ruthie, our massive 120-pound French bull mastiff, determined to get inside the house. Ruthie charges past me, knocking me to the floor. I want to scold her, but she is busy trying to fit her big self under the small table, her favourite hiding spot. I go over to her instead and scratch her behind her ear. "Good dog," I whisper. I wonder what has her spooked as I step out onto the front porch into the day's still heat. Looking around, nothing seems out of place. Maybe she got into a fight with the raccoon who is living under our house this summer.

I pace the rows of the garden Mom and I tend together like a daily sacrament. We have added one garden bed after another until the entire half-acre yard is a grid of three-foot by twelve-foot beds with paths in between. Mom told me that in the old days when she was growing up you could only grow in the northeast for part of each year. In the last decade, though, it's been warm enough to grow all year long. Our garden overflows with riotous green leaves, tendrils stretching up and out in every direction. As much as it sucks to live by the Edge, I know we are lucky to have space to have our garden. Not only does it save us money on our grocery bill but stuff from our garden and Uncle Al's farm just tastes so much better than what you get at the store. Indoor farms have helped secure food supplies, no doubt, but I can taste the difference between fruits and veggies ripened in the sun and those grown in a bunker. I believe I can anyway.

I stop at a tomato bed and my hand rests on a fragrant, bright-red beauty. I feel the warmth from its skin seep into my own palm, and I am off, daydreaming again. Thinking about NESA. Thinking about Lee too. I would be lying if I said I hadn't thought about him these past few weeks. After our interview with Ms. Hunt and the team, he and I walked out together. I wanted to ask him how he thought the interview went, but he seemed lost in thought, staring straight ahead. The parking lot was empty except for Uncle Al's red pickup truck and a shiny, black car. Everyone else had finished the exam and was long gone. Instead of heading right for the cars, we stopped just outside of the school door. I guess I didn't want the day to be over yet. Once I left, everything that had happened that morning would feel so final and fixed in place, in the past. There would be no going back; there could be no do-over. Nothing but waiting.

"Tic," Lee said, "I just want to say that you…that I think it was really brave, what you did during the exam, I mean. You risked your future to help someone."

"Thanks." I flushed, looking down, looking at our shoes, his a deep blue, mine so dirty it was hard to tell what color they were. I bit down on the inside of my cheek hard, not sure what expression my face wanted to make, just sure that I couldn't ever remember anyone telling me I was brave before that.

"I hope you get in," he whispered stepping closer to me.

Anxious about what I would see if I looked up at him, I stared at the girl's blood on his shirt instead. I let my hand bridge the small distance between us and I touched the red stain on his chest.

"I hope you do too," I said, meaning it with all my heart.

31

He covered my hand on his shirt with one of his own, pressing it into him so that I could feel his chest rise and fall with each breath. With his other hand he reached for a strand of my hair that had escaped from my bun and carefully tucked it behind my ear. I looked up and our eyes locked.

"We did the right thing" he said and then let go of my hand. Before I knew it, he had gone down the steps. A man in a black suit and cap stepped around from the driver's side of the car to open the back door for him and closed it quickly behind him.

I have goosebumps even now, remembering it, and I wonder if Lee got a message today too. Unless we both got in, I guess I will never see him again. I hardly know him, really. I don't even know his last name, never mind where he lives. As far as my research has turned up, students can come from anywhere in any one of up to five surrounding states to take the entrance exam for NESA.

I don't notice the stillness that has descended around me until it is too late. No chattering squirrels, no birds calling to one another, and no wind rustling the leaves and branches. Nothing until—

REEEEE-REEEEE-REEEEE

Three splintering blasts followed by a short pause, repeated twice more. My ears are still ringing and, shading my eyes with my hand, I scan the blue sky above. Far to the north I see a dark tide of clouds rushing in.

Question 5:

Name as many possible uses for a stick as you can.

Answer 5:

Answers include, but are not limited to, the following: walking stick, spear, fishing rod, garden pole, firewood, baseball bat, bow, digging tool.

***

I take off running up the little hill to our house. It sits on the highest point of our half-acre property, at the top of six-foot concrete risers. I fly up the steps, leap onto the porch, and tear open the door. My phone is playing two lines from the song "Big Yellow Taxi" over and over again, and I know Mom must be frantic with worry on the other end. I grab the phone from the table and accidentally knock over my mug. Cold tea pours out and rushes off the side of the table. I press talk and her worried face fills the small screen.

"Tic, did you hear it?"

"Yes, Mom," is all I can manage to get out as I catch my breath.

"I was so afraid when you didn't pick up right away!"

"I was just out in the garden. Three, right?"

"Yes, three. I'm at work still. Maybe I should try to come home. I don't want you there all by yourself."

I go over to the front window while we talk and see that the branches and leaves of my tree, the maple that Mom planted when I was born, the one I love to sit in while I read, are all waving frantically. I turn away from it. "No, Mom, it's fine. You need to stay there. It takes too long to get home, and the wind is picking up already."

"But—"

"Don't worry about me. We've been through plenty of threes before. There's nothing to be nervous about. I'll be safe here, I promise. It's not like it's a four or a five." I reassure Mom even as I wipe a sweaty palm against my thigh. I have never actually been alone during a three. I've been at school or work with other people or here at home with Mom. It's like she can read my mind.

"Tic, I can't stand it that you are there alone. I want you to run next door to Uncle Al's house. It shouldn't take you more than five minutes to get there and I'll feel better knowing you're with him."

"Really, Mom," I start to object half-heartedly, but she's not having it.

"Tic, it's not up for discussion." The next round of sirens blast over anything else I might want to say and we hang up. I shove the phone in my back pocket.

I make sure that all the shatterproof windows and doors are closed tight. Ruthie watches me from under the table. I think about leaving her here—I am sure it's safe—but she looks so pathetic that I just can't bring myself to. I stand by the front door calling her, but she stays put. The big beast is terrified. I hunt desperately for her leash, which could be anywhere since we usually just let her run around outside without it. Uncle Al is our only neighbor, and he doesn't care. No one else is crazy or desperate enough to live way out here so close to the Edge. Finally, I find the leash in the knitting basket, of all places, and hook it to Ruthie's collar. I wrap the other end securely around my left hand. Then I yank hard, meaning business, and she reluctantly gets up.

Once outdoors, I look at the sky. I'm not sure how much time has passed since Mom and I hung up, but the heavy dark clouds have already blanketed the midday sky and it's as dark as dusk. I consider going back into the house but figure I have enough time to get over to Uncle Al's if I'm quick. My first thought is to go up to the road, but the speed the storm is moving makes me reconsider. There is a shortcut through a grove that separates our garden from Uncle Al's back pasture. It will be even darker in there and I don't know when the path was last cleared, but I still think it will be faster. It will bring us out closer to the barn than the house, but if I don't think we can make it to the house, the barn is a good, safe option. Ruthie stays right up against my side, her head rubbing my hip as we jog. The siren continues at regular intervals, and loud shots of thunder echo in the empty space in between. Blue flashes of lightning split the ominous grey sky and cast long, bizarre shadows around us.

I have to push against the wind, leaning into it. Leaves and branches tear free and tumble through the air around us. We are almost to the grove when I am smacked on the cheek by something the wind has picked up, a broken branch or a garden stake probably. It happens so fast that I don't really see. My cheek stings, and when I touch it my hand comes away with blood. I stop for a second and gently touch the sore area around the cut on my cheek, probing for further damage with my fingertips. Ruthie barks and starts to strain at the leash trying to pull me back towards our house.

"Okay dog, okay. I get the message. Being out here's not safe, but Mom wants us to go to Uncle Al's so that's what we are going to do," I tell her trying to sound confident.

The next bang of thunder brings the rain. It pounds down from the sky, soaking through my clothes. It is relentless and furious, and we sprint for the trees. The smaller bushes grab at my shirt and scratch my legs as I stumble beneath the leafy canopy. Here at least the wind does not exert its full force, and the chaos of the storm is muffled. I catch my breath, and I feel tiny under the towering beeches and pines whose tops have disappeared into the storm clouds. When I was little I nicknamed this thicket *the dark woods* and thought it was a deliciously scary place ruled over by a goblin king. The "woods" is no more than one hundred yards straight across, but straight across would be impossible in this dense, tangled copse where vine maple criss-crosses skunk bush and ghostly lichen coats fallen branches and stumps. Years ago, Uncle Al cleared a path through it so that we could cross between our properties more quickly. Every few months he comes out with an axe to hack away the plant life that wants to reclaim our path.

It's black as a starless night under here. I pull my phone from my pocket and turn on its flashlight. Holding it in my right hand, I point it at the ground in front of me and am able to make out and skirt the vines growing onto the path and the branches that have already fallen across it. We make steady, careful progress. I figure we are about half way through when a violent boom tears the air in the trees overhead, followed by a splintering sound. A crashing noise rushes at me, and suddenly I feel a searing pain like nothing I have ever known before surge through my right shoulder. I sink to my knees, my left hand clutching my right arm, which now hangs throbbing and limp. A thick, splintered branch lies beside me, its jagged end stabbing the earth. I pull myself away from its leafy embrace and kneel soaked, shivering, and caked with mud.

My breath is coming out in raspy, choked sobs. Ruthie licks my face with patient concentration. I let go of my right arm and wrap my left arm around Ruthie instead, pulling her into me. Her warmth and steady breathing help, and I know I have to get up. I have to push on. It's dark and I realize that my phone is missing. I must have dropped it when the branch fell on me. I grope around with my left hand hoping to feel its smooth, familiar form but find only sharp rocks and sticks. Resigned to darkness, I pull myself up using a nearby birch tree and stand uncertainly. I let Ruthie guide me as I cautiously shuffle my feet.

We come out of the strand to a familiar, wide-open field where I once more feel the full force of the wind slamming into me. Rain pelts me viciously, seeming to fall horizontally, trying like mad to get in my mouth and nose and drown me. I know Al's north-west pasture well and though it's muddy we cross it quickly. At the far end is the hill. On the highest point of Uncle Al's property is the barn where he keeps his prize-winning cattle. Even as I struggle forward, I can picture the ocean, whipped by the storm, pouring through the high mesh fence of the Edge. The rainwater rushing down the hill to meet us is nothing by comparison.

We climb up the hill towards the barn, every step a battle against the wind, water, and mud. Finally, my feet shuffle onto the lip of an angled metal ramp and the barn towers over Ruthie and me on its risers, its grey, weathered wood a sanctuary against the dark sky. Flooded with relief, I practically launch myself at the barn door. The door stubbornly stays closed as I rest my bleeding cheek against the smooth, worn wood. I gather my strength and push off from the door, pulling the handle as hard as I can with my left hand. Nothing. It doesn't budge. I force myself to slow down, to calm my rising panic, to breathe, and to think. I look closer now and see that a four-by-four oak beam rests on iron U-hooks on either side of the door effectively blocking it should the cows panic and try to get out. I unwind the leash from my left hand and drop it. I try to lift or slide the beam with my left hand alone but it's too heavy and I can't get it to budge.

Tears mix freely with rain on my face, and I put both hands under one end of the beam. I scream with the effort and the agony as I raise the beam a few inches, just over the top of the hook, before letting it crash down, sending vibrations shimmying up through my feet, my right arm on fire. The beam lies diagonally, one end still in the hook and the other resting by my feet on the metal ramp. A few quick, one-handed tugs on the door shove the beam down the slick ramp enough and I am able to slip into the barn. I collapse in a heap on the dry wood planks. The cows chew their cud and look at us as Ruthie lies down beside me. Everything hurts and I long for Mom's soothing voice. I can almost hear her singing softly as I fall into an exhausted sleep.

***

Question 6:

The Heretic Wars were fought chiefly in the United States between which two groups?

a) Scientists and the government
b) Religious fanatics and scientists
c) Religious fanatics and government forces
d) Scientists and civilians
e) Different religious factions of Christianity

Answer 6:

c) Religious fanatics and government forces

Religious fanatics in the United States began attacking scientists and researchers working on climate change. Initially these attacks were few, but by the time the United States ratified the International Change Agreement militant zealots had formed groups and attacks became more numerous and more deadly. These groups, by and large claimed that scientists were trying to interfere with God's will. The government declared war on these terrorists in a campaign that involved all levels of law enforcement as well

as intelligence agencies and that came to be known as the
Heretic Wars.

AUGUST

The day of the storm was my lucky day, though you wouldn't think so to look at me. I stare at myself in the mirror in my bedroom, examining the cut on my cheek and the surrounding rotten-fruit-coloured bruise from different angles. I have gotten so used to the sling holding my right arm to my chest these past few weeks that I hardly even notice it. Still, in the mirror it is another reminder of that day. Even though my shoulder doesn't hurt anymore, the doctor said I should wear the sling for another two weeks, just to be safe. As she pointed out, my first piece of luck was that if the tree branch had fallen just a few inches to the left, it would have cracked my skull instead of my collarbone.

Later that day, when I was released from the hospital, I finally opened the message from NESA. When I read it, my mouth went dry as hay and I couldn't speak or even breathe. Mom flew to my side, asking if I was okay. I'm sure she thought I was having a stroke or something. I pointed at the screen. It said that they had reviewed the exam as far as I had completed it and my results looked "promising." Then they explained that because of the unusual circumstance at the exam, my case had undergone a process of careful deliberation and the examining board felt that although I had acted impulsively, having a strong tendency towards compassion might be considered an asset in the ongoing battle to fight the Change. I was in! When Mom read the message she started sobbing and laughing at the same time. Then she called Uncle Al who came over with a bottle of champagne, and we all got a little drunk.

Over the next few weeks there were more messages from NESA, including the Academy handbook that I have pretty much memorized. Studying at NESA is going to be big-time different from classes at New Hope Town High. In fact, as far as I can tell, there are no classes at all. Each student is responsible for listening to a minimum of four assigned podcasts daily and for posting questions, thoughts, or ideas on topical message boards regularly. First-year students are assigned fourth years as mentors, and second-year students have third years for mentors. We will work on different projects in independent or group study with our mentors, pursuing areas of individual interest, and our projects will be reviewed by leading experts in the relevant fields.

I almost feel badly for my classmates at New Hope Town High who will be stuck in Mr. Morris's bio class and Ms. Arthur's modern history. Almost, but not really. No one there really cares about science the way I do. Sure, there are some keeners—Jeanne and Diane to name a few— who were okay to study with, but really all they cared about was getting good grades. And the teachers are the same. Well, one or two love to teach—Mr. B., the calc teacher, for example—but most of them just mail it in. All in all, high school has been a sub-par experience for me so far, but that is about to change.

Other parts of the handbook describe life at the Academy: the private bedrooms and public study spaces, the cafeteria, the school store, and something called Friday night socials. I can't imagine living away from home with so many strangers. I also can't help but wonder if there might be one boy there who I know. It's possible. If he did well enough on his exam, then their reasoning about compassion would have to apply to him too—and that means I might see him again. Soon. I frown at myself in the mirror. I try to be objective. Maybe the bruise isn't as bad as it seems.

***

"Tic, do you need help up there?" Mom calls from the bottom of the stairs, "Are you packed?"

"Yeah," I answer, mentally reviewing the minimal contents of my backpack. NESA has uniforms, sort of, so I don't need to pack clothes. Clothes are colour-coded by year, so first years wear black, second years wear charcoal grey, third years wear heather grey, and fourth-year students wear white. I was able to pick out a selection of sweats, jeans, T-shirts, and tanks in my size that will be waiting for me when I arrive. It is cool to think that the clothes we will be wearing didn't just used to be some random stranger's but were actually worn by other students before us, students who might have graduated already and are doing great research. They will also give us state-of-the-art tablets, which is a relief because my tablet is cheap and old, and I never did find my phone in the woods. The school store has stuff like shampoo and toothpaste. All I have packed is a hairbrush and my pajamas. I take one last look around my room and make an instant decision to take *Walden* with me as well. I pick it up and give it a quick flip-through. Mr. Kisway had encouraged me to write my thoughts in the margins and to underline passages that I liked. Sometimes, not often enough, he and I would look at them together and chat. I stop on a random page and read what I have underlined;

"I learned this, at least, by my experiment: that if one advances confidently in the direction of his dreams, and endeavors to live the life which he has imagined, he will meet with a success unexpected in common hours."

I'm thinking about this when Mom calls up the stairs again, a slight edge to her voice. Wonder if she is nervous about my future too?

"Well, come on then, food's getting cold."

Even though Mom has made my favourite veggie lasagna, I only nibble at it. I feel guilty because we try to save money by mostly only eating what we can grow as well as dairy and eggs from Uncle Al. The flour to make this pasta is a celebratory splurge, but I am just too nervous to appreciate it. I notice Mom is also picking at it, but Uncle Al isn't having any trouble. He has heaped his plate high with lasagna and salad and is chowing at a steady pace. This will be the last time the three of us are together for a while. In an hour the driver will be here to bring me and one other student travelling from nearby Arquette up to NESA.

"So, Tic, are you excited?" Uncle Al asks as his fork scrapes his plate, gathering up the last remnants of tomato sauce.

"Yeah . . ." I hesitate and then confess, "Sort of. I guess I am kind of nervous too. I never thought leaving would be so hard."

"Me too," Mom says softly, looking down at her plate. I think of her here all alone and I am jolted by a panicky feeling in my chest.

"Maybe I shouldn't go," I say.

"Of course you have to go, Tic," Mom says firmly, having resurrected her game face. "Imagine if you can help to fix all this—the storms, the heat—for everyone?"

"But what if I can't?"

Mom puts her fork down and pushes her plate away. "Tic, I know we don't talk much about your dad...it's hard for me. We loved each other so much that when he died, I felt like a part of me died too. I don't know what I would have done if I hadn't already been six months pregnant with you, but I was." She's looking somewhere beyond me now, remembering. "He was a great scientist, one of the best. He was passionate about the environment, about his work. He would get so excited by some new thought he had, some discovery he had made, and he would come home from work and tell me all about it. I tried to follow along, but for the most part it was beyond me. I would just smile and nod, loving his enthusiasm." She stops talking and we are all quiet for a moment.

"I'm sure he would have been proud of you for going and trying," Uncle Al says, looking me right in the eye. "Don't ever think you can't do this. A great man once said, *Only those who dare to fail greatly can ever achieve success.*"

"Who said that?" Mom asks.

"John F. Kennedy."

"Who's that?" I ask.

"A former United States president. Don't they teach you history at school?"

"Not much, I guess. What happened to him then?"

"He was assassinated," Uncle Al answers.

"Was it the by the Faithful Few?" I ask.

"No," Mom answers. "The Faithful Few killed President Schwartz. I remember exactly where I was when I heard about it."

"Me too," Uncle Al says. "President Kennedy was way before that, even before I was born, so I guess that's what you would consider ancient history."

"Being president sounds almost as dangerous as being a scientist," I say jokingly, and I immediately regret it. Mom looks upset.

"The Heretic Wars have been over for two decades. Being a scientist isn't dangerous anymore," Uncle Al says, trying to make Mom feel better.

"Unless you take unnecessary risks," Mom mutters. Our little goodbye party gets hushed and somber, claustrophobic and crowded with dead men.

"Well," I say, glancing uneasily at the clock, "maybe we should go wait on the front porch?"

"Let's do presents first," Mom says, surprising me. Smiling, she and Uncle Al each produce small boxes wrapped in coloured paper. I unwrap the gift from Uncle Al first. Inside the box is an engraved pocketknife. We all stare at the smooth oblong of dark, gleaming wood carved with my initials. It fits perfectly in the palm of my hand.

"Not exactly high tech." He sounds embarrassed. "Maybe it's not the right thing for a girl going off to school but—"

"I love it," I say, folding my fingers around it. "I've always wanted one." And it's true. Ever since I can remember, Uncle Al had his pocketknife with him. He would pull it out and use it for everything: thrusting it in the ground to check for moisture, removing a stubborn pebble from an animal's hoof, and even, after making a big show of rubbing it clean with his shirttail, slicing apples for me to snack on. I flip a release on one end with my thumb and squeeze the polished wood sides together firmly, and a shiny blade jumps out.

"Be careful with it, Tic. It's plenty sharp." With my left hand I awkwardly try to fold the blade back in. Silently, Uncle Al lends me a hand, closing it and flipping the latch back on.

"It's a great gift, Al. It's beautiful and, if nothing else, it will remind Tic of you," says Mom.

I tuck it in my pocket and hug Uncle Al as hard as I can with one arm still in a sling. He leans over and rests his sandpaper chin on my head and strokes my back in his calm, sure way. When I let go of him, his hand goes to the corner of his eye, erasing his tear. I look over at Mom, and she holds out her gift to me. I carefully unwrap the picture frame that is

47

usually on Mom's bedside table. It's the last picture we have of my dad. He's standing with his arm protectively around Mom's shoulder. I am technically in the picture too since she was pregnant then. It's the only picture of the three of us together, but to be honest, I have never found my place in it entirely satisfying.

"Are you sure about me taking this?" I ask, not because I don't want to take it but because we have so few pictures of him.

"Of course I'm sure," Mom says. "I still have the big one." We both look up at the 8 x 10 photo from their wedding day that sits on our mantle. It was taken four years before the second one. In the one I hold, Dad's hair has been cut short and Mom's has grown longer. She still looks young and fresh, but he looks, I don't know, tired, maybe? Older? Something in his posture or in the way he is smiling with his mouth but not his eyes makes me wonder. I never knew him, so who am I to say, but he looks different. He looks worn.

Mom reaches over and strokes my hair. "I love you," she says.

Before I can respond there is a knock on the door

***

Question 7:

World population has been decreasing for the last several decades due to _____.

a) Natural disasters
b) Decreased reproduction rates
c) Famine and war
d) a & c
e) All of the above

Answer 7:

e) All of the above

Hurricanes, fires, and floods are responsible both for immediate deaths and deaths related to subsequent lack of access to heat, food and medical care. Reproduction rates have decreased worldwide partially related to poverty, malnutrition and illness but largely because of cultural shifts in values and norms. There is a recognition that every human life puts a strain on the climate. Famine is caused by fires, drought as well as sea level rise and increase salinity of once arable land.

***

A man in a black suit introduces himself as James and asks if I am ready. *Am I?* I hesitate. I take a long look around our cottage, the only place I have ever lived, seeing everything and nothing at the same time. I'm about to say no when I look at Mom. Her arms are folded across her chest defensively, and now that the moment is here I can't speak. We stare into one another's faces, and I sense that despite her confidence over lunch that this is the right thing to do she can't release me. It has to be me. It has to be my decision.

"Yes, I'm ready."

"I'll meet you out front in a minute," Mom says as she turns away and takes the framed photo over to my backpack.

"Go on, Tic," Uncle Al says and starts clearing plates. I know he is hanging back to make sure Mom is okay. I know he will always look out for her, and I feel so incredibly grateful.

James holds the door for me as we step out onto the front porch. A few feet away, a shiny car with dark, tinted windows awaits us. The back door of the car flies open and a head of red pixie hair framing sparkling green eyes and a face full of freckles looks up at us. A hand waves frenetically in greeting.

"Hey," calls the girl. "Great place you've got here!" she says as she clambers out of the car. "Can I check it out, or are we leaving straight away?" She's already moving towards us but stops just before she reaches the front porch and squats down to examine the bright-orange blossoms of our climbing squash plants. "I love this! What is it?" she asks, leaning her whole face in to smell the flower. I am so transfixed by her energy that I don't see Ruthie coming until it's too late. Ruthie has her front paws up on the girl's shoulders and pushes her backwards onto the ground. She licks her face in long, sloppy strokes, tail wagging wildly.

"Ruthie, stop! Stop it!" I call as I hurry down the steps towards them.

"Alexandra, are you okay?" asks James.

"Ummph, ya," she says, giggling and scratching Ruthie behind both ears.

I grab Ruthie by the collar and try to pull her off with my left hand but am not able to. During all the commotion, Mom and Uncle Al have come out onto the porch.

"Down, dog," Uncle Al commands. Even though she is my dog, Ruthie obeys Uncle Al instantly, lying as flat and still as she can in the dirt, her tail twitching, and her eyes still focused adoringly on Alexandra.

"Sorry about that," I say, extending my good hand to help her up. She grasps it and comes up smiling. Mom brushes dirt from Alexandra's shoulders, fussing, being Mom.
"Mrs. Brewer, this is Alexandra Cameron." says James.

"Nice to meet you, Alexandra. This is Al Savory, our neighbour," Mom says, and Uncle Al nods a silent greeting. "I hope Ruthie didn't hurt you."

"Nah, I'm fine."

"We really should get going if we are going to make it to NESA on time," James says, standing by the open car door.

"Yessir," Alexandra replies crisply, winking at me. "Nice to meet you, Mrs. Brewer, neighbour Al."
"Nice to meet you too, Alexandra," Uncle Al says.

"Like I told James already," she says, rolling her eyes in mock frustration, "everyone calls me Phish. I'll explain in the car, and you can tell me what happened to your arm and face." She goes over to Ruthie who is still lying down and gets down on her knees to plant a big kiss on top of the dog's head. "Take good care, you sweet beast."

James sighs, and Phish gets up and heads to the back seat.

I look from Mom to Uncle Al and back again. Mom gives me a last hug as Ruthie, unable to stay down any longer, walks in circles around our legs. I get in the car, still looking at them as James closes the door. They stand side by side waving as he starts the car and we pull away.

***

I am telling Phish about my collarbone fracture, trying to downplay the stupidity of going out in a three in the first place as we head out of New Hope Town. I am relieved when the billboard for R.W. Salvage—"Everything you need, and more!"—gives me an opportunity to change the conversation. "Tallest man-made structure in No Hope Town," I say pointing it out to her. "We are such a hick town, huh?"

"No Hope Town, huh?" she says grinning at the town's nickname, "Cute. But at least you have an R-dubs here. That's something anyway."

"Yeah," I say. I watch the hodgepodge of buildings that make up my hometown disappear behind me. The schools, town hall, and a handful of homes represent the only new builds. All are dark-grey, reinforced cement cubes on stilts that look stark and out of place. Most of the houses look pretty much like they did decades ago, with the exception of having been raised up six feet onto cement pylons. They are different colours, shapes, and sizes. Individual and mismatched, tended and repaired, and sometimes left gaping, blank, and ruined when people decided to move on. No one would make a significant investment in a small town that sits so close to the Edge like this. I wonder when I will see it again. "So, what's the story with your nickname, Fish? Are you a swimmer or…"

"Nah, not that kind of fish. Phish with a *P-H* as in 'getting people's usernames and passwords by setting up fake websites and tricking them.'"

I have an idea of what she means and this sounds way more interesting than swimming. "And?" I say.

"Last year I finally got sick of Brittany and her pals making fun of me for being a computer geek, which I totally am, but still. You must have a "Brittany" at your school, right? A girl who flings her long hair around and acts like she's the queen of the school?"

I nod, picturing Lindsay O'Malley who used to be nice until two years ago when she made it her mission to be a royal.

"I mean, I don't really care what anyone says about me, but when they trashed my locker and ruined my favourite jacket I decided to get even. I sent them a link to a WebStar look-alike page that I made and got them to re-enter their IDs and passwords, which I then used on the real WebStar page. One click and all their bitchy messages about everyone at school went from private to public. They took tons of crap and had no idea how it had happened. A few days later I got a new jacket, and then I left them a message to make sure they wouldn't bother me again."

"What was the message?" I ask. I can't believe how smart and brave and kick-ass she is.

"It said, 'Don't mess with the Phish.'" She is grinning from ear to ear, but I feel like I missed something.

"But . . ."

"My new jacket had a smiling, pink shark on the back, and I sewed the word Phish on the front left pocket. I wish I had a pic of Brittany's face when I asked her if she liked my new jacket. It was the definition of done." After we both stop laughing she says, "So what are you really good at?"

"What do you mean?" I ask. I like her a lot already, but she does seem to go off on tangents that I can't always follow.

"Well, I don't know that much about environmental science, but I'm really good at computers. I mean, I'm not bragging, but they did mention it in my acceptance letter. I just figured everyone who gets into NESA has some special skill, right? So what's yours?"

I have never thought about it like that, and the question catches me off guard. "I don't know. I guess I know a fair bit about nature, living in the country and whatnot, and to be honest, I studied my butt off for the exam forever, but the only thing it mentioned in the letter was about compassion."

She looks at me with one eyebrow arched high.

I shrug. "Yeah, I'm not sure what that has to do with anything either."

***

Since the Change, roads buckle and crack or gigantic sinkholes appear all the time, but crews are usually on them pretty quickly. We only had to slow or stop three times for their work on the way to NESA. There has been almost no traffic until now, and the five-hour drive has flown by.

Phish told me stories about her whole family: her father who owns a repair shop and is a genius with his hands and her mother who works at one of the refugee camps just outside of Arquette. Incredibly, Phish has three siblings. I don't know anyone who has that many. She must be used to people being shocked because she offers an apologetic explanation without me even asking. She is the oldest, and it isn't that unusual that her parents decided to have a second child. What is surprising is that her mother was pregnant with twins and decided to go through with it. Her brothers, David and Jack, are thirteen and wild. She also has an adopted sister, Anna, eleven, who her mother brought home with her from the refugee camp one day. Her family is huge and sounds like so much fun: busy and loud and different from my quiet, dull home life.

Phish also asked me a million questions about Mom and Uncle Al, about living in "the country," as she calls it. I tell her about Mom canning and pickling absolutely every fresh fruit and vegetable we can't eat right away and about Uncle

Al winning state prizes for his cows. She asks if I am ever afraid of living so close to the Edge, and I tell her the truth: of course I am.

We're almost there. The sun is hanging low in the sky to the west of us, and for the past hour the road has been skirting the base of ever taller, ever larger mountains. There are lots of trees and granite cliffs but hardly any signs of civilization. James turns off the main road and the car slowly climbs a winding, narrow road up and up and up through a forest of evergreen trees.

In front of us is a line of cars similar to our own. James tells us we are almost at the Academy, and we are quiet for the first time. When we get to the top of the mountain, the trees end abruptly and there is a large, flat plate of rock as big as three football fields. Dozens of solar trees are laid out in a grid. Their shiny thirty foot tall metal trunks each support twenty one solar panels arranged in a natural spiral. Presently the panels are all rotated to the west to catch the rays of the setting sun. The solar trees are beautiful in their own strange, man-made way and useful for converting energy from the sun to electricity for the school, but they are impotent compared to the real thing. Real trees are continuously pulling carbon dioxide out of the atmosphere, something the solar trees could never do. At home I liked to picture the invisible floating carbon dioxide molecules I breathed out, being sucked into tree leaves, and used to build solid plant material, new branches, and new leaves, which themselves will pull even more carbon dioxide from the air in an endless cycle.

Twenty black, shiny cars are already parked in two neat rows across the northern edge of the rock. James pulls in to a spot at the end of one row. More cars follow and pull in to a new row spots. The rough, grey granite stretches from the line of cars to a big, black box of a building that dominates the whole southern edge of the field. It looks solid and precise and utilitarian. As plain as it is, I am still a bit in awe. It's one thing seeing a picture of it on my small tablet screen and another thing to be in its stark, almost monolithic, presence. "End of the line, girls," James says.

***

Question 8:

What percentage of the world's electricity comes from renewable resources?

a) 25%
b) 50%
c) 70%
d) 80%
e) 100%

Answer 8:

e) 100%

One hundred percent of electricity is supplied by renewable resources, including, but not limited to, solar, wind, hydro, and underwater turbines.

***

We watch for a moment as our fellow students make their way individually or in pairs across this levelled mountaintop to the front door. I am searching for his wavy, blond hair.

"Let's go," says Phish, bouncing on her toes and tugging my arm.

Closer up now I see that the walls are all glass, coated in a dark film that makes the windows function as solar panels. I'm guessing that covering the whole building in the stuff was pretty expensive, but given how isolated the Academy is, and how much power it probably uses for some 240 students and staff, it makes sense to capture as much solar as possible. There are also giant wind turbines spinning briskly as they stand sentry along the eastern edge of the mountaintop. I'm sure at this elevation they are almost always rotating, and there is certainly lots of room up here for more in the future if necessary.

The ten-foot-high double front doors are wide open, and we stop just in front of them. Above, painted in tall, white, swirling letters is the only embellishment on this otherwise austere façade. It's the NESA motto, which I've seen on their website: *Velle Est Posse*.

"You know what that means, don't you?" Phish asks me. I do know that it translates from Latin roughly as "where there's a will there's a way," but I also recognize an already familiar mischievous look on Phish's face. She points at the words as if reading them. "Do Epic Shit!"

Some of our fellow students stare at us as we both walk giggling across the threshold into our new life. Our laughter echoes, bouncing around a gleaming, white marble hallway, mixing with quiet chatter and the echo of sixty pairs of feet gradually making their way to the far end. Progress is slow as people stop alone or in groups to point to the portraits that line the walls and whisper names with reverence: Dr. James Hansen, Dr. Christine Jones, Dr. Richard Mercer. Famous scientists past and present are represented, some stern, some friendly, some looking off into the distance, and some whose eyes seem to follow me as I pass by. I recognize many of them, but not all, and would love to stop and stare too, but Phish is pulling me along.

At the far end of the hall another set of doors stands open, and light pours through. Phish and I enter, following the others through these doors and into a large conference room with six rows of ten chairs that are divided by a centre aisle. Phish lets out a long whistle.

"Fact—I've never seen anything like this before!" Phish says.

"Fact—me neither," I reply.

In front of us is a wall of windows, and it looks like you could step out and leap from one mountaintop to the next, like stones across a giant stream, until you reach the far horizon of the fading blue sky. It is the natural world in all its overwhelming glory.
Students take seats as they come in, and Phish and I do the same. Phish starts talking to the girl on her left, and I use the opportunity to scan the room. I am still looking for Lee, beginning to doubt my memory of what he looks like, a knot in my stomach tensing at the thought that he might not be here after all. I hear the doors shush closed behind us, and

the lights in the room dim, ending my search. The window wall tints dark now, except for a large, white square in the middle. A woman stands, silhouetted by the square of white light behind her, and begins to speak. As she speaks, her words glow into being on the screen.

"Never doubt that a small group of thoughtful, committed citizens can change the world." She speaks with conviction. "Indeed, it's the only thing that ever has." She pauses briefly before continuing. "Margaret Mead said that long before any of us here in the room today were born, and yet its truth becomes more compelling every day. I am Sharon Hunt, Director of North East Science Academy, and it is my pleasure on behalf of all of our staff to welcome you here today.

"I know that many of you have come quite a distance to be here, and for most of you, this will be your first experience of a boarding school. I can reassure you that it is normal to be homesick at first, but soon NESA will come to feel like a second home to you, a second family. I appreciate that in this moment you are excited, nervous, tired, and probably hungry. Am I right?"

There are lots of nods and some murmurs of assent.

"I thought so. We need to cover a few things right away, but I will try to be brief and to the point. First and most important is your personal safety here at NESA. I am sure you are all used to sirens signaling event levels. We use the same system here, with one siren blast indicating minor danger, all the way up to five blasts, which is extreme danger. Your bedrooms are all located in the center concrete core of our building. They are windowless and without Wi-Fi because of the thickness of the walls, but they are also the safest place to be in case of emergency. If there is a level three or lower siren, please get back to your rooms immediately. If there is a level four or five siren, emergency lighting systems will direct you to the nearest safe spot. Again, please follow these warnings immediately. Always stay in your safe spot until given further instructions on the overhead speakers. You will find more safety rules in your orientation folder, and I urge you to review these later today."

A three-dimensional rendering of the Academy pops up on the screen behind her. "Moving on. You will find cafeterias on levels one and three and a gymnasium on level four of North East Academy. The school store and music room are on level two. All of these facilities are available 24-7 for your convenience. There are study areas of all sizes for you to work in. This central meeting room and the rooms on both sides of it are used for guest lectures and Friday night socials. You will find a map similar to this on your personal tablet that will also indicate the location of your bedroom."

Phish nudges me and passes me a pile of computer tablets. Each student is taking one before passing them down the row. I hold the pile with my left hand and manage to slip the top tablet between my sling and chest before I pass the pile to my neighbour on the right.

"Your tablets, once initialized, will also have your personal learning plans loaded on to them. You will see podcasts divided into mandatory, recommended, and optional based on your exam results. These plans will be updated regularly based on your progress. Students usually like having their tablets with them as they move around our school, so please also take a messenger bag as they are passed out, and when you have time—sooner rather than later—put your name on the bag. Okay, if everyone has one now,"—she pauses to make sure we all do—"we will all initiate our tablets together. If you would please press the power button until the tablet turns on, and then follow the instructions on the tablet's screen."

Behind Ms. Hunt, the screen now shows a tablet with an arrow pointing to the power button. Fumbling, I press the tablet against my body while using my left thumb to press the power button. The screen opens to a light-blue page with "North East Science Academy" written across the top and a black rectangle underneath. Below this are instructions to press and hold your right thumb onto the rectangle for a full five seconds while it scans and saves your fingerprint. I struggle to wiggle my right hand clear of the gauzy material of the sling and hold the tablet up to it with my left hand, but no matter how I try, it just isn't happening. Phish sees that I am struggling.

"Can I help?" she asks.

"Please," I say, passing her my tablet.
"Press your left thumb in the box," she says as she holds the tablet up for me.

"But the direction says 'right.'"

She cocks an eyebrow at me as if to say, "Trust me."

I follow her instruction. As I suspected, the tablet feeds back an error message, but somehow Phish is able to respond to it and convince the tablet, typing in words in no language that I have ever seen, that my left thumbprint is acceptable. I type my name in to the next screen while Ms. Hunt continues to speak.

"Your thumbprints are your personal keys to everything here. You will use your thumb to open your tablets and your rooms. They are used to gain access to the gym and to turn on the machines there. They are used at the school store and at the cafeteria to order your food. Our cafeteria, by the way, has lots of healthy and nutritious food available at all times, and we recommend you avail yourself of this service three to five times each day. It has been our experience that many students become so engaged in their studies that they neglect their personal health. For that reason, we do insist that you each spend one hour in twenty-four at the gym, and a minimum of six hours in twenty-four in your bedrooms." There are some scattered coughs and giggles from the students. "Where we will assume you are sleeping." She frowns.

I guess it won't be different here than anywhere else. Hook-ups happen all the time because really since the Change any day could be your last and why wait? Why not enjoy a release that is free and natural? Not that I would know. I guess I must be the only almost sixteen-year-old virgin on the planet. I tune back in to Ms. Hunt.

"Finally, second-, third-, and fourth-year students arrived yesterday, back from their vacations and placements and, in addition to our staff, they will be happy to answer any questions you have as you get settled in here."

The lights come back up, and the window wall turns clear again. The panoramic view of mountaintops and sky is unreal. If someone showed me a picture of this I would have sworn it was Photoshopped. The setting sun has turned the clouds into pink candyfloss and the sky a soft lilac fading to dove grey. Colour is slowly draining from the mountains as green trees fade to black. I have always thought there was a beauty to the ocean, although my mom would disagree, but I am amazed that I have never been up a mountain before. How could I have lived my whole life without seeing this? It's almost too beautiful.

"We have prepared a special welcome banquet for you," Ms. Hunt says and points to her right. The wall slides back smoothly, revealing another large room with tables and chairs in the center and long buffets spread with food around the perimeter. "Please eat, socialize, relax, and enjoy. Welcome, students."

After thunderous applause, everyone starts talking and standing up. Phish throws her messenger bag on and slips her tablet in. I'm having a little trouble with my messenger bag because of my sling, and Phish is trying to help me figure it out.

When I look up for a second he is almost to us. Lee. He is here! Finding his way through the melee, his eyes are fixed on me. Everything and everyone else instantly disappears. I feel nervous-happy-excited.

"Tic? Is that you?" he asks, running a hand through his shoulder-length, blond hair. He is taller and more muscular than I remembered.

I nod, not able to form any words just yet.

"What the hell happened to you?" he asks pointing at my sling.

"Wait, you know someone here already?" Phish asks me. "Is he from New Hope Town too? Are you from New Hope Town?" Phish asks Lee, as I am still speechless.

"No, I'm not from New Hope Town," Lee answers.

"Lee and I met during the exam," I say, finally able to speak as I shift my gaze from Lee to Phish.

"During the exam?" Phish says. "You mean after the exam, or before?"

"No, pretty much during the exam," I say.

"Some girl collapsed in the middle of the exam, hit her head, and was unconscious and bleeding. Tic left her seat to help her," Lee explains.

"Well, you did too," I say.
"Yeah, but only after you did and—"

"Enough already with the modesty, you two. Clearly you are both heroes," she says, laughing.

Lee and I both flush. I fiddle some more with the messenger bag, tucking it under my sling as best I can.

***

Question 9:

How much forest disappears each year?

a) 1,000 hectares
b) 300,000 hectares
c) 4,000,000 hectares
d) 16,000,000 hectares
e) 25,000,000 hectares

Answer 9:

c) 4,000,000 hectares

In the early twenty-first century, 16,000,000 million hectares of forest were disappearing each year due to fires and clear-cutting. Since the Change, rates have been reduced and are now at four million hectares per year. Clear-cutting, the practice of burning vegetation so that crops can be planted, is an international crime. However it continues as a result of subterfuge and bribery.

SEPTEMBER

It's easy to let my mind wander as I run. Lee is on the treadmill next to mine, and he matches my pace as we gaze out the wall of solar windows at the mountaintops stretching away from us. It didn't take as long as I thought it would to get used to waking up in a new bed. It's only been a few weeks, and already this place is starting to feel normal, if not like home. My room is plain—white walls, black floors, a bed, bedside table, and dresser—but it is comfortable and clean. Most mornings I pull on one of several identical pairs of black skinny jeans and a black tank top and put my hair up in a messy bun. I touch my fingers to my lips and then to the picture of Mom, Dad, and me, which sits on my dresser surrounded by some small, pink wildflowers and fragrant pine needles. I refresh these every few days, exploring a bit further each time I hike around in this new forest.

Many of the plants here are familiar species, with minor variations, but I have found a few that I never saw back home, some mountain ferns and flowers that I want to research when I have time. I treasure the peace of this new place, this wondrous mountain, where I sometimes feel like it is just me, the birds, the trees, and the big sky. Sometimes Phish comes with me and although it's not peaceful I enjoy that too. We are both a bit homesick, and it's nice to have someone to share those feelings with.

Everyone here is still getting to know each other, and no one talks about really personal stuff too much. Mostly people talk about whatever they are studying or whatever their passion is, stuff like improved weather prediction models, alternative energy sources with lower carbon footprints, and weather modification. It's actually pretty cool in its own nerdy way. It's nerd-cool or geek-chic or something. I have never been at a place where everyone is so into their studies, and I'm guessing it's the same for most people here. Sometimes conversations about the Change will get so intense that people will stay up until two or three in the morning talking. I try not to stay up that late usually, but there have been a few nights, especially when upper-year students are part of the conversation, that I just lose track of time.

I am a creature of habit, though. I have always had a routine, whether it was for school or work. I have never had much free time to speak of. Most of my life, until now, I woke up to an alarm clock. Even though I don't set my alarm here, I still wake up pretty early. My mind knows that I can sleep as late as I want, but my body hasn't figured it out. Usually by eight thirty I am showered and dressed. I grab a cup of coffee from the caf and head up to a small study room to listen to podcasts. They are completely engrossing, and I can easily—and sometimes do—spend longer than the assigned three hours a day listening. Each one is given by a world expert in his or her field. Some have slide shows or videos you can watch along with them. Each one has a little quiz at the end. After lunch I will research some of the questions I have from my morning podcasts. I am amazed at how much more information we have access to at the Academy compared to what is available to the general public. Secure local, national, and international databases, government-commissioned reports, and high-level scientific research data are all at our fingertips. Then I will look at posts from other students, make comments, and post myself.

When I think about what I would have been doing this year back at New Hope Town High, I am so grateful to Ms. Hunt for giving me a chance. I feel like I have learned more in one month than I could have in a whole year at home. I almost feel hopeful that we really can stop the Change. With all this knowledge it seems like anything is possible.

An itchy bead of sweat trickles down my neck and between my shoulder blades, pulling me back into the here and now. I steal a glance over at Lee, who smiles encouragement back at me. I smile and puff my breath up onto my forehead, making my bangs flutter.

"Five more minutes?" he asks.

"Yup," I say.

On our second day here, Lee messaged me asking if I wanted to work out with him. He said he was familiar with gym equipment and, because my arm was still in the sling, he offered to help me find things that I could do. I thought that maybe it would lead to something else, or I hoped it would anyway. I don't know what exactly I hoped it would lead to, but I thought that on our exam day I sensed something between us. Maybe I was wrong. Maybe it was just the tension of the day. I thought we liked each other. I mean, I know I like him, and he's nice to me, but he's nice to everyone. He's a nice person. So, I am not sure. I am pretty naïve about boys. I never had anything even close to a boyfriend at New Hope Town High. I'd known all those boys since we were little, and I was always considered the "smart one," which somehow disqualified me. That's just how it is in a small school: once you have a reputation, it's pretty hard to shake unless you do something radical.

Sometimes when I am eating with Phish, especially if there's a group of us, he'll join our table, and of course I see him at Friday night socials, but the gym is the only place we spend time alone together. Not that we are alone-alone, there are always a few people in the gym, but—

"Last ninety seconds," he says. "Race?"

"Go," I say, my index finger already on the speed button, pressing it as my legs pump harder and faster, faster, as fast as they can, and there is no possibility of thought now. Then the machine beeps that our run is over and switches into cool-down mode.

I grab my towel off the handle bar and pat my face dry. We each take a long drink of cold water from the fountain and then wipe down our machines. When we are almost at the gym door, Lee stops, so I do too.

"Have you heard of the movie they are showing for Friday night social?"

"*Ender's Game*?"

"Yeah," he says.

"No, but I searched it. It's an old movie about genius kids fighting aliens, I think. It got decent reviews."

"So, are you going?" Lee asks.

"Sure," I say. "I'm not big into aliens or anything, but you never know…it could be good."

"Well, maybe we could grab dinner first and then go together," Lee says, rubbing his hands on his thighs.

"Sure," I say casually because at that moment I am just thinking logically that I will want to eat before the movie, and we are both going, so it makes sense. But then I realize something. He basically just asked me to dinner and a movie. This is possibly, probably, maybe what a date at NESA might be like. Did he ask me on a date? How can someone as supposedly smart as me have missed something so obvious? Or did I? Maybe I am reading too much into it?

We say goodbye, and I head to my room for a shower before meeting Phish for dinner.

I am still thinking about it when I get out of the shower and wander into my bedroom, stopping in front of the picture of Mom and Dad on my dresser. I pick it up with my right hand, examining it closer than usual, looking for more information as I rub my hair dry with the towel in my other hand. I know my parents met at Midhurst College, but I wonder what it was like when they met. I wonder if Mom knew right away that Dad was "the one." Did her stomach do little somersaults and her mouth get dry when she saw him? I am thinking maybe I will ask her for more details when we video chat next. How should I bring the subject up? Will she wonder why I am asking?

My thoughts are jolted by a siren that overwhelms the small space of my bedroom. I startle and jerk, my hands flying reflexively up to my ears.

REEEEE-REEEEE

The tinkling sound that should accompany the breaking glass is lost in the high-pitched wail from the overhead speaker. The siren stops. It is only a two. Breathe. Years of being through alarms haven't made them easier. There is always an initial panic. What is it? Where is it? Am I safe? Is Mom safe? I am safe, I remind myself. I am high up on a mountaintop, not down at the Edge. I am safe in the building too. I am where I am supposed to be already, in my room, in the concrete core of the Academy.

Around my bare feet lie shards of broken glass. I bend down carefully and pick up the broken wood frame that still holds the picture. I flip it over to open it and remove the photo. When I take it out of the frame, I see that there is writing on the back of the picture. In small, green letters it says,

> *Just in case*
> *95-19-4*
> *Leaf*

***

Question 10:

In North America, terrorist groups committed acts of violence after the International Change Agreement was signed because _____.

a) They claimed it impinged on their civil liberties
b) They claimed it was against God's will
c) They claimed scientists were lying
d) They claimed the government was trying to act beyond its scope and authority
e) All of the above

Answer 10:

e) All of the above

Multiple different terrorist groups existed during the Heretic Wars. Although they claimed different key motivating principles, they had a common cause in attempting to stop scientific advances to mitigate the Change. Some of the largest and most persistent groups were the Faithful Few, the True Believers, and the New Republic.

***

The two was a forest fire on a mountain a few miles south of here. The all-clear sounded hours ago, but I still can't sleep. I lie in bed, my eyes closed, my body still, but my mind buzzing. I keep going over and over the message, trying to figure out what it means and coming up with a million guesses but no answers. At three a.m. I finally give up on sleeping. I get up and head to a deserted lounge to

73

look stuff up on my tablet and kill time waiting for a semi-decent hour to call Mom.

>*Just in case*
>*95-19-4*
>*Leaf*

Just in case of what? In case of an accident is all I can think of, but how would he know he was going to be in an accident? Was he psychic? Or paranoid? Or did the "just in case" refer to something else entirely? I have no clue. Moving on. Those numbers could be anything: a password for a file or a computer, or a combination for an old lock, a secret bank account, but I don't know how I can follow up on those possibilities at the moment. What if it's a date? April 19, 1995? It's a place to start anyway.

I start searching, and one link leads to the next. Apparently on that day some psycho named Timothy McVeigh bombed a building in Oklahoma City killing 168 people, including 19 kids, and injuring another 680 people. The same building had been previously targeted by another group called The Covenant, The Sword, and the Arm of the Lord. They were a Christian white supremacist group who had been under siege by the government exactly ten years earlier on April 19, 1985. On April 19, 1995, the government building and several around it were destroyed. The bomb blast measured 3.0 on the Richter scale, the size of a minor earthquake. Horrified but curious, I read more, trying to understand why someone would do that. I learn that it was probably in response to an event on the same date, April 19, two years earlier, in a place called Waco, Texas. In Waco was a compound of religious people called Branch Davidians.

They had been under siege by the government for 51 days leading up to April 19, when finally there was a big fight with shooting and tear gas and a fire. On that day, seventy five Branch Davidians died, including their leader. The Branch Davidians believed in a prophecy of an imminent apocalypse and the second coming of Jesus Christ.

It's all pretty crazy stuff and is starting to make my head hurt, but it also reminds me of the Heretic Wars. We learned about them last year in social studies. The Heretic Wars were also between the government and a group of religious nuts called the Faithful Few. The Few believed the Change was a sign of the apocalypse, and they targeted and killed scientists because they were trying to stop it. I talked to Mom a bit about it when we were studying it since she was actually alive back then. She said that she had seen all the news coverage and once when she was a teenager everyone in her city had had to stay locked indoors for almost three days while the police and army hunted down a bomber. She described how quiet everything seemed then. She tried to explain the feeling to me. She said that being stuck in the house when there is a storm is one thing, it's loud and scary for sure, but in a familiar, impersonal way. Being stuck inside because somewhere a crazy, desperate guy is running around with bombs and being chased by people trying to catch him was frightening in a whole different way.

Mom also said that during that time, and for a while after the Heretic Wars, people who decided to study and work in science fields related to the Change were considered really brave. Aside from my dad being one of those brave scientists, I don't really see how the date he wrote on the back of this photo relates. The Heretic Wars weren't until decades after 1995. I look anyway but can't find anything specific for them on April 19 of other years. But maybe that's what "just in case" refers to. Maybe because he was a scientist he felt he was in danger. I am sure the Wars were over by the time of the accident, but I double-check. The last report of activity for the Faithful Few was over two years before he died.

Finally I can see the sky lightening up, the mountain peaks emerging from shadows, the closest trees becoming distinct, taking on shape and colour. Finally I can call Mom.

She answers my video chat request on the first ping. "Hi, sweetheart. I didn't expect to hear from you so early," she says as her eyes scan my face. "Is everything okay? You look tired. Is your arm sore? I told you that you shouldn't have the sling off yet. "

"Sheesh, Mom, I'm fine, and I told you already the nurse said it was for sure okay that the sling was off." I answer, momentarily irritated by how she worries over me like I'm twelve. I hold my tablet with my left hand and demonstrate moving my right arm around to prove my point. It does ache a tiny bit still, but the nurse said it is good for me to use it and get some mobility back in my shoudler joint.

"Listen, I want to ask you something before you head off to work. Do you have a minute?"

"Of course," she says, sounding relieved by my reassurance.

"So, I was wondering about the message on the back of the photo."

"What photo? The one of the three of us?" She seems genuinely confused.

"Yes," I say as I pull it from my messenger bag and hold the photo up to the camera on the tablet. I flip the photo over so she can see the message.

She doesn't say anything.

"Mom? Can you see the message okay?"

"Yes, I can see the message." She stops, and I wait. Her eyes are scrunched a bit, and she is biting her bottom lip. "I've never seen that before, Tic."

"What? How is that possible?" I ask.

"I guess..." She hesitates. "Let me think."

I am surprised and disappointed that she hasn't seen it before, and now I'm worried that she won't be able to tell me what it means.

"I'm not sure. When I decided to move, I was grief-stricken and hormonal from being pregnant. I wasn't thinking super clearly. I just knew I wanted to start over and I'd had it with big cities. I grew up on a small farm and had this feeling that I wanted to raise my daughter on one. One of your dad's friends, the one who took the picture, came to check in with me a few times after he died, and when I told him what I was thinking, he suggested New Hope Town and helped me find our cottage."

"Cool. Who is he? Have I ever met him?"

"No, after I moved he and I lost touch. His name was Matt. Matt Haley."

"So, what about the photo?"

"Um . . . let me think. I remember, the day I moved in Uncle Al and Aunt Mary came over to meet me, and Aunt Mary brought me one of her amazing apple pies. When they saw that I was pregnant and alone they just sort of jumped in and started taking care of me, because, well, you know them. That's how they are. I still miss Mary after all these years. The cancer took her way too soon."

Is it only my mom who goes off on these tangents? I wonder impatiently.

"So, they helped me unpack and get settled in, and Al found a box I must have filled with stuff from your dad's desk at home. I was pretty upset still, and I told him I didn't care what he did with it all—throw it out or burn it. But he found the photo in that box and framed it and brought it back to me months later when I was over—well, it doesn't matter."

"What do you mean? Over what?"

She pauses and looks away for a moment, then shrugs and faces me. "Being angry at your dad."

"Why were you angry at Dad?" I ask, surprised.

"At the time I felt like he put science before us, before me. He would work late into the night and on weekends, whenever he could. I guess he was a workaholic. But going on that trip and dying on us was the last straw." There's a rawness in her voice as she remembers. She has never told me about these feelings before. She only ever said how happy and in love they were and how great he was. "Oh, I know. I know it was an accident, but I couldn't help feeling like he could have avoided it. The waters were rough and they told me the crew kept telling him to get below deck, but he insisted on taking a few more readings from his equipment. Then...then it was too late."

I don't even know what to think, how to react. For as long as I can remember, my dad has been my idol, a man who gave his life working to stop the Change, and now I hear that Mom didn't exactly feel the same way. Apparently, she resented how much he worked and that he put work before her. Before us. And she's implying that he was careless? It's too much!

"Don't you think you're being harsh?" I ask, not able to hide my anger.

I see tears shining in the corners of her eyes and I want to hug her. "I'm sorry I never told you about any of this before," she says. "At first you were just too young, and I guess when you were old enough I just didn't see the point. Do you know what I mean?"

"Yeah, Mom. I guess."

"I will always wonder what if. What if he hadn't gone? What if he had listened to them and gone below deck? I was trying to protect you from that. I don't know why I'm telling you now except that you caught me off guard."

"It's okay, Mom," I say, feeling too far away and completely ineffective.

She has turned the camera around so all I see for the moment is the kitchen. I suspect she is crying and doesn't want me to see. Her voice comes out strained. "Listen, I really have to get going or I'll be late for work."

I want to ask her more about the message, but it will have to wait.

***

Question 11:

Name ten things that used to be made from petroleum.

Answer 11:

Items that used to be made from petroleum are especially important to recover and reuse. These items include but are not limited to the following:

- Solvents
- Diesel fuel
- Motor oil
- Bearing grease
- Ink

- Floor wax
- Ballpoint pens
- Football cleats
- Upholstery
- Sweaters
- Boats
- Insecticides
- Bicycle tires
- Sports car bodies
- Nail polish
- Fishing lures
- Dresses
- Tires
- Golf bags
- Perfumes
- Cassettes
- Dishwasher parts
- Toolboxes

***

"I thought you said your dad died in an accident?" Phish asks me from across the cafeteria table.

"He did," I say. Lee is sitting next to me, and the photo lies face down in the middle of the table. The caf is quiet. Earlier it was a zoo, with everyone talking about the two last night, but now almost everyone has gone off to study in their favourite spots and the three of us can talk uninterrupted.

"Then why would he write *just in case*? And what does the rest of it mean?" Lee wonders.

"I don't know," I say, feeling frustrated. My lack of sleep is starting to show.

"I'm sure we can figure this out. Why don't we review all the facts?" Phish says, full of confidence and energy.

"It won't take long," I say. "There aren't many."

"Okay, but still. You said this picture was taken two weeks before your dad left for his trip, right?" Phish has flipped it over and my eyes are drawn to Dad's serious face.

"Yeah. Dad had a friend who did photography as a hobby, and he asked him to take their picture."

"So they didn't take pictures a lot with their phones and tablets?"

"No, I guess not. I mean, we don't have many pictures of either of them and only a few of the two of them together."

"So why this picture then?" Lee wonders out loud.
"Mom used to tell me that Dad was nervous about leaving her alone to go on this trip because she was pregnant. She said they debated whether he should even go." Thinking about our talk this morning, I suspect Mom has always told me a more sanitized version of events. I'm thinking the "debate" was probably a fight. "He came up with the idea for the picture as something she would have until he got back."

"Okay, so the friend: do we have a name here by the way, Tic?"

"Uh-huh. A guy named Matt Haley."

"Matt Haley takes a picture of your mom and dad and then gives it to them a few days before your dad leaves."

"I guess so," I say.

"What happened next?" Lee asks.

"My dad went on his research trip to the North Atlantic, and three days later my mom got the call that he had gone overboard in rough weather."

"Wow, that's tough," Lee says.

"I know, right? Pregnant and getting a call like that," Phish adds.

"So, any more details on the accident part?" Lee asks.

"Like what?"

"I'm not sure. Anything. His company must have filed a report," Lee presses.

"The company he worked for, Wincor, went out of business the week after," I explain. "I tried to research them online once a few years back. I was curious about the accident I guess, but also what he was studying and stuff. I couldn't find anything. It was like the company had disappeared."

"Wincor, huh?" Phish mumbles as she pulls out her tablet and starts typing, only semi paying attention to me and Lee.

"There would have been something filed with the national coastguard about it," Lee says, sounding very sure. Suddenly I am hopeful again.

"Do you really think so? Why? How do you know?" I ask quickly.

"Well, that's how it would work with my father's company, I'm pretty sure," Lee says. I feel his leg, which is next to mine under the table, start to bounce.

"Does your father's company also do hydrology research?" I ask Lee.

"No," he says, looking down at the table. "My father owns R.W. Salvage."

Phish looks up from her tablet and she and I are both staring at him now. "Fact!" Phish says, stunned.

"*The* R.W. Salvage? R-dubs? As in, "over five thousand locations nationwide to meet your every need," I say, quoting their ads.

Lee just nods his head and looks up at us nervously from behind a curtain of hair that has fallen over his brow.

"So, you're basically a zillionaire?" Phish asks.

"Yeah," Lee concedes before lifting his chin to stare at me, his blue eyes hard and challenging. "But that doesn't mean I agree with what they do."

Mom and I shop at the R-dubs in New Hope Town for practically everything we can't make ourselves. I am confused at the tension I sense just below the surface until he speaks.

"All the stuff that is sold used to belong to other people, right? People who lost most of everything they owned because of the Change, and then R-dubs finds it and fixes it up and sells it for a profit, and the people who used to own it—"

"Get squat," Phish finishes for him. "I've seen plenty of those people at the refugee camps near Arquette."

"I never thought of it that way," I admit. "But it's not like it's your fault, anyway."

"But I benefit from it. That's why I wanted to go to NESA so bad. I don't want to take over the family business like my parents want. No way! If I had my way, there wouldn't be any more disasters to salvage anything from. Sink the family business!" His voice is deep and passionate.

In the awkward silence that follows this declaration I reach for his hand without thinking. Phish's tablet pings with a new message and she looks down at it.

"Hey, check it out," Phish says, a huge grin splitting her freckles. "Looks like there's a change of plan for this Friday night!" Phish turns her tablet around to show us the message, and even though I haven't read it yet, in that instant, I feel like I swallowed a rock. I'm still not completely sure if Lee meant Friday to be a date, but in my mind, it was going to be one. All I can think is *now what?*

***

Question 12:

The International Change Agreement stipulates that _____.

a) Countries that historically contributed more CO_2 agree to cut their CO2 emissions faster and to a lower rate proportionally than countries who have contributed less CO2 historically
b) All countries will contribute a minimum of five percent of GDP to a general relief fund
c) All countries will expend a minimum of twenty percent GDP on solutions to the Change
d) Countries must abide by all regulations set forth by the ICA committee
e) All of the above

Answer 12:

e) All of the above

Every country initially signed on to the agreement. However, over the ensuing decades, at least ten countries have reneged on their commitments.

***

There are 240 students at the Academy, and this Friday night seats are set up for all of us. The first three rows are saved for the freshmen. I find a seat and wait with the others whose soft whispers form an indistinct hymn.

"Would it be weird if I said I missed teachers? Real face-to-face teachers I mean?" I ask Phish.

"Uh, yeah it would," she answers, and I wish I hadn't said it. The anticipation of hearing and seeing Mr. Sheffield speak live just got to me.

"Why would you even say that? I mean did you have awesome teachers in No Hope High?" she asks in earnest.

"No, definitely not. It's just...I get that having information straight from experts in the field is a million times better and that they need to be at their *real* jobs and not here at school but podcasts are...I don't know, impersonal?"

"Hmmm," Phish says, clearly not agreeing with me.

A wave of quiet rolls from the back to the front of the room as Ms. Hunt and a familiar-looking man enter the hall. The silence sounds like a sharp intake of breath. The man wears dark-rimmed glasses and has thick, black hair and a dark shadow of stubble across his jaw. He radiates a quiet intensity that is magnetic. His accomplishments are legendary at NESA.

"Freshmen," Ms. Hunt begins. "Now that you have had a few weeks here, the real work begins. On Monday you will be assigned and meet with your mentors to begin working on your first project of the year. Tonight it is my privilege to introduce one of our most distinguished alumni. As chair of the National Scientific Council, his advice influences all of the important decisions our government makes around the Change. He is one of the most important scientists in our country today, Mr. Robert Sheffield."

The applause is thunderous, and people stamp their feet and whistle too. He is as close to a superstar or hero as many of us here can imagine. He motions with his hands for us to quiet down.

"Listen, I can't stay long, but I had to come see you all. You may know already, and maybe you are starting to understand better, what a dire situation the world is in. Years ago, the International Organization on Climate Control reported that if people completely stopped emitting carbon dioxide— which was, of course, impossible—it would still take more than one hundred years for the carbon dioxide level to drop to three hundred and fifty parts per million, a level considered safe in terms of climate change. More than one hundred years! Stopping all carbon dioxide emissions will only solve the problem of the Change much too late to be a help to us as a species. All those efforts to cut carbon dioxide emissions are important, but generically, they are focused on destroying the environment more slowly.

"It was bad enough when I graduated NESA a decade ago, but despite our best efforts, things seem to be getting worse. Here at home we have lost Hawaii, Florida, and Rhode

Island completely. Big chunks of Louisiana and California are gone, and Texas, New Mexico, Nevada, and Arizona are uninhabitable. We have millions of climate refugees, and we are lucky compared to most of the world. The intensity and frequency of storms around the world has increased. Drought and famine are killing more people every day, both directly and indirectly, by causing war and facilitating the spread of disease.

"If things continue this way, many millions more will die, and I am afraid civilization as we know it will be lost. You may be our last best hope. I only have a few hours with you this evening. I could lecture, give you more information, but I remember being in your seats not long ago. Having someone talk at you can be boring. Whoever is up there presumes to know what you already know and what you need to know next. You are here because you are original and creative thinkers. I don't know what you need to know, so why don't you tell me. Who's first?"

The questions and ensuing discussions come from the more senior students. They range from specific questions about changing wind patterns around Asia to Dr. Sheffield's opinion on the accuracy of prediction of worldwide famine within the next five years. I watch in awe as he considers each question carefully, often asking for more details before answering clearly and fully. The depth of his knowledge seems vast, if not boundless. It's not often, but when he doesn't know an answer, he admits it, and this shocks and impresses me. I can't think of many adults, especially teachers or people who have authority, who I have come across who admit when they don't know something. It feels like a small weight has been lifted from my shoulders. I guess some part of me always believed that by the time I was grown up I would have to know everything. He is by far the most compelling person I have ever seen.

"How satisfied are you with current models explaining precipitation patterns?" a boy in white, a fourth-year student, asks.

"To be completely honest, I find them only adequate at best. Why do you ask?"

"I think it is important to fully understand why some areas have too much precipitation, while others suffer year after year of drought. If precipitation derives from moisture brought to land from the ocean, how did the moisture used to reach inland so far away from oceans before the Change, and why doesn't it anymore?" The student is speaking quietly but confidently, and he and Sheffield begin to debate one model after another, finding flaws with each. No one else interrupts this conversation, which has begun to feel almost private.

I nudge Phish who is sitting beside me and whisper, "Who is that?"

"Tatum Brown, aka Tate the Great," she answers. "Look him up later." I make a mental note to do just that.

Eventually Tate seems satisfied with their discussion, and Sheffield calls for more questions. Immediately hands fly up and the same thing happens again and again. I notice it's third and fourth years asking questions but no first years do. I guess I am not alone in feeling intimidated by Sheffield's knowledge and power. Finally he says, "I can only take one more question right now, and I would really love for it to come from a first year student. I know you have only been here a few weeks, but maybe because of that you bring a fresh perspective. This place, this amazing institution, and all its resources, are at your disposal now, including me. Someone? Anyone?"

He stops talking and waits, and I am thinking as hard as I can, searching for a question I can ask him because I want to please him, but any scientific question I could ask is bound to seem amateur not only to him but to the upper years. My hand flies up. He smiles and points at me, and I am so nervous I can taste sour at the back of my throat, but it's too late to change my mind. I stand up and ask him something that has always bothered me. "How is it fair that the people who contributed the most to messing everything up end up suffering the least from it?"

His smile is gone, and he is staring hard at me. I stare back. I can't help it. I really want to know.

Ms. Hunt appears at his side her cheeks red and her chin jutting out.

"Tic Brewer, I am sure that is not the type of question Mr. Sheffiled had in mind. Sit down now!" she commands.

I feel Phish's hand tugging on my sleeve but Mr. Sheffield is still staring at me.

"No, Ms. Hunt, that's okay. I wasn't expecting it but, Tic is it? Tic, that is a very important question and I will try to answer it. Developed countries contributed the most carbon dioxide to the atmosphere if one considers not just recent history but going as far back as the industrial revolution. These same developed countries, including ours, have suffered since the Change, but even with the millions in property and people lost it is relatively little compared to how much less developed countries have lost. With the Declaration, developed countries agreed to give more money and resources per capita into the global pot for remediation, but money and resources are a poor substitute for human lives. You asked me Tic, how it's fair? All I can say is it's not fair, but recognizing that, remembering that, is powerfully important. Numbers, especially big numbers, can be both impressive and meaningless. Ten thousand acres of rainforest burned this month, deserts across the globe increased by a factor of one hundred percent this year, one million people were flooded out of their homes..." He takes off his glasses and closes his eyes, massaging his eyelids with his thumb and index finger before replacing his glasses and clearing his throat. "Since I left NESA, I have been all over the world and I have met many powerful people, but I have also met many—so many—powerless people. Remember that they are why you are here."

When he finally leaves, students linger in clumps and knots, energetically discussing the problems and theories that have arisen during the hours that Dr. Sheffield has been with us. I feel overwhelmed by his need and urgency. It has chipped away at my remaining childish confidence that everything will turn out okay somehow in the end. I need to be alone with my thoughts and fears. My feet lead me to the front door of the Academy.

Once outside, I stop on the bottom step and stare up at the night sky. The solar trees' panels are all folded down, leaving an unobstructed view. The stars shimmer with a cold, distant light in the vast pitch. A slight breeze raises goosebumps on my arms. I have gone from wanting to be alone to feeling tiny and lonely in an instant. I am considering going back inside when the door opens and Lee steps out.

"Hey," he says softly.

"Hey," I say back.

"What do you think?" he asks, standing beside me, gazing up at the sky.

"It's a lot," I answer. We are quiet for some time, but it is a comfortable quiet where we can each be in our own thoughts and still be together.

"Should we—"

"Do you want to—"

We both start at the same time and stop, looking at each other now.

"You first," Lee says.

"Do you want to stay out or go in?" I ask.

"What do you want?" Lee tosses it back at me.

"Stay out?" I suggest, feeling a bit awkward, wondering still whether this would have been a date if the Friday night social hadn't been cancelled for Sheffield's visit.

"Sure." It's too dark to see his face clearly, but I think I hear a smile in his voice.

***

Question 13:

Look at the three words below and find a fourth word that is related to all three.

Flower   Friend   Guide

Answer 13:

Girl

Girl Guides was an organization for girls whose mission was to enable girls to become confident, resourceful, courageous and to affect change in the world. The Guides pledge stated "I promise to do my best, to be true to myself, my beliefs and country. I will take action for a better world and respect the guiding law, enable girls to become confident, resourceful, courageous and to affect positive change in the world." They offered a wide range of activities for girls and young women to explore science, art, outdoor challenges, and global awareness. The last reported Girl Guide troop disappeared in Ohio over a decade ago.

***

I haven't been out in the forest here at night, but I have a pretty good sense of direction from my many daytime explorations. As we walk, some part of my brain realizes this might not be the best decision ever, that it feels wrong somehow, heading off into the woods at night, but I am already committed. No way I'm going to suggest we turn back. The path I choose is a familiar one that I found on a hike about two weeks ago, and I have been down here three or four times since. It's narrow and winds through and around trees as it snakes downhill, but we shine light from our tablets and go slowly and carefully. In about twenty minutes we have made our way to one of my favourite spots. It's a small glade, maybe forty feet across, and it is covered in wild mountain flowers and soft moss. Sitting very still here some afternoons, the cries of jays ringing loud, I have seen grouse and rabbits and deer. I have been bringing lettuce from the caf with me lately to see if I can entice any of the animals closer, but so far no luck.

"Cool spot," Lee says approvingly, and I feel happy and proud. We have a little outdoor room to ourselves with trees for walls and the night sky for a roof. A subtle scent of pine needles tickles my nose.

"Thanks."

We pick a spot in the middle and lie down side by side on our backs, staring up at the black canvas poked through with pinpricks of light overhead. "Something about staring up at the night sky like this reminds me of diving," Lee says.

"Diving?" I ask.

"Yeah. For the last few summers I worked for my father's company doing salvage diving. I guess that's what reinforced my ideas about it— about, you know, leaving." I hear that hitch in his voice that happens on the rare occasions he mentions his family. Still, though, it seems like he might open up here in the quiet darkness.

"What was it like?" I ask.

"The world under the water is dark and calm and peaceful, like the night sky, but sadder." He sighs. "It could have been worse. At least I was never on first team. They would go down and scan the salvage area, taking inventory. I had the impression from things I overheard that the first team also did the clean-up if there were any bodies to remove."

I gasp. "That's horrible."

"I think that's why my parents always insisted I be on second team. I guess I know it was better that way."

I close my eyes and try to picture it, the cold, still water with people's lives sunk below. Lee and the other divers with headlamps swimming silently through empty homes and schools while startled fish flee through smashed windows. I try to superimpose it onto the memories of my two trips beyond the Edge.

"The boats have about eighteen berths in a common room that sleep divers and crew, everyone except the captain basically who has his own room. We could carry enough food and supplies for two weeks at a time. Not all of our trips were that long, but some were," Lee says, falling deeper into the telling of his own story, pulling me out of myself. "We worked in pairs, and each morning had a list from the first team's inventory of what to bring up that day. Anything wooden usually came up first, then cloth, then metal, according to their tendency to decay under water. We did all the big stuff first, cars and furniture and appliances. For the big items we used winches, so all you had to do was hook it up and make sure the path up was clear. Mostly everything else we brought up to the surface ourselves, though. We'd hook it onto the boat and they took it from there. We had knapsacks for the small stuff. Once in a while a diver would try to sneak something up for himself, but if you were caught you were automatically fired, so it didn't happen much. I liked a lot of the guys, Harry and big Rob, and Rex, and skinny Sal. They could be rough around the edges, but they were real too, if you know what I mean."

"Sure," I agree, thinking about Uncle Al.

"Sorry, I am babbling on," Lee says, turning on his side to look at me. I turn to face him too.

"No, it's really interesting," I assure him. "When I was twelve, we had a field trip out to see Boston. It's one of those days that will always stay with me. Mom was absolutely beside herself. It's irrational, but given that Dad died at sea, she didn't want to let her only child go out on the ocean. But I can be stubborn too, and there was no way I was going to miss this. There were maybe a hundred kids and teachers, and the sky was a fresh clear blue, and the water had only the faintest ripples. In other words, it was perfectly safe." It feels so easy to talk to him. I feel like he knows me already and I am just filling in the details. "On the way out there I was standing at the railing near the front. It was like the voices of my teachers and classmates had been turned way down and all I could hear was the water slapping the boat and the gulls calling. I was high on the sun and the salty air and the feeling of openness and freedom and I felt amazing and then…"

Lee strokes my arm and I feel our connection grow stronger.

"And then the tops of churches and high-rises started to poke through, and the boat slowed down to navigate through. All the talking and laughing died out, and it was spooky quiet, even the gulls sitting on rooftops just silently watched us as we glided by. We stopped beside the top few stories of the Prudential Building, and the teachers started to talk. It became so much more real and just, you know, incredibly sad." I feel the tears gathering in the corner of my eyes now, the memory of it is so visceral. "And you—you went down under, into those places." I stop not knowing what else to say.

"Yeah. After my first dive I actually didn't think I could do it again. It was horrible. But I guess you can get used to just about anything, right? Mostly it felt like I was visiting a ghost town. Just my imagination, of course, but at fresh sites I always had a sense that the people had just left and would be back soon. I felt like I was peeking in on their private tragedies, their kitchens, their bedrooms. At each place I knew I was in someone's home, and I wondered if they had made it out safe. If all they had lost was their stuff, or…" His voice is soft, almost a whisper, and I have to lean in closer to hear him. He feels the losses, and I don't know that I have ever talked to someone this intimately, ever. He reaches up and wipes away a single tear that has managed to escape from the corner of my eye.

He is staring at me. His face is half in shadow, but I can see his eyes studying me, and I guess I must be staring back at him. I feel lost in his gaze. I should look away. I should close my eyes. I keep staring. Maybe he will kiss me. A small pocket of warm breath is gathering between our faces. He bites his lip and then rolls onto his back away from me. "I have never really talked to anyone about how I felt about it before. It's pretty dark stuff. I hope I didn't bum you out. Let's talk about something else, okay?" His voice sounds tight and controlled. "What's going on about your dad? Did you find out anything else about the accident or the message?"

"A few things," I say. "But none of them make any sense."

"Like what?" he asks,

"Phish looked for anything on Wincor, and even she couldn't turn up much. She said that it seemed like when they went out of business they must have intentionally wiped out their online presence. I don't know if that is common or not so I wanted to follow up on it."

"It does seem weird. Why bother unless you are hiding something?" Lee says what I have been thinking, but I still want to do my research and see if it's a normal thing to do or not. There's no sense in being even more paranoid about stuff than I already am.

"Yeah." I agree. "Also, neither of us could find any type of report filed about the accident with the Coast Guard."

"I really don't understand that," Lee mumbles. "It can't be."
"Maybe he was in international waters or something," I suggest.

"Interesting," Lee says. "But it shouldn't matter."

"The thing is, I am not really sure exactly where he was in the North Atlantic. I think they were supposed to be heading to Greenland. I do know the date of the accident, so the other thing I did was search international weather reports for that day that would have covered a broad area in the North Atlantic."

"And?"

"Nothing remarkable in them. No major storms or anything. I mean, I guess the water could still have been rough, but I was sort of expecting..." I trail off.

"A storm or something?" Lee finishes my thought.

"Yeah," I say. "I mean, you have been on boats a lot, right? What do you think?"

"I dunno, Tic. For salvage we stick pretty close to the shore, so I am not sure my experience is relevant. Still," he says, "the whole thing seems pretty strange."

I am turning everything I know and do not know over and over again in my mind. I am glad that both Phish and Lee are suspicious too, but I also wish they could just tell me not to worry, that this is all normal and that I am overreacting. My thoughts are interrupted by soft snoring, and I look over at Lee. His chest is rhythmically rising and falling. I wonder if he was going to kiss me, and why he didn't, and what it would feel like if he did. I stare at him until my eyelids get heavy and my breathing slows.

***

Question 14:

Look at the three words below and find a fourth word that is related to all three.

Fly   Fighter   Forest

Answer 14:

Fire

The *Lampyridae* were a family of insects in the beetle order *Coleoptera*. They were winged beetles, and commonly called fireflies for their conspicuous use of bioluminescence during twilight. Fireflies produced a "cold light," with no infrared or ultraviolet frequencies. This chemically produced light from the lower abdomen was commonly yellow but could also appear green or red with wavelengths from 510 to 670 nanometers. The *Lampyridae* have been extinct for a quarter century.

***

It's night. Robert Sheffield is walking on a pristine, sandy beach. He doesn't see the enormous wave rolling in. I am watching from a window, safe in a tower at the Academy. I am freaking out. I yell, but he is too far away and he can't hear me. My thoughts are racing, I can't let him die, and then I have an idea. I decide to shine a light to warn him. I look around and find a lantern with a big candle in it. I search desperately for something to light it with. I check out the window again and, incredibly, the wave has grown. It must be one hundred feet high. In the wall of water coming towards him, I see Lee swimming. He's in a wetsuit and has an oxygen tank on his back. He waves at me, looking comfortable and happy in the water. I need to let him know that Sheffield is there. Maybe he can save him. I smell smoke and look back at the lantern. The candle is lit. There's a flame. I reach for it but something is squeezing my arm and...

"Tic! Tic, wake up!" Lee sounds upset. "Do you smell something?"

I open my eyes and don't know where I am for a minute. I must have dozed off, too. It's dark, and Lee is leaning over me, gently shaking my shoulder.

"Tic . . . Tic? I smell smoke."

REEEEE-REEEEEE-REEEEE

At the sound of the siren I sit up so fast my right shoulder slams into Lee's chest before he can move out of the way. Even though it is technically healed, it still hurts like a bitch. I am already on my feet though. There is no time to waste. "It's a forest fire!" I say, and I see tendrils of smoke creeping out from the trees off to my left.

"Which way?" Lee asks.

"I don't know," I say, scanning the glade, a bubble of panic rising up in my chest. "But we have to try to get back to the Academy. We've got to head uphill." I stand up and try to get my bearings, each heartbeat a moment too long to wait. I walk in a circle, forcing myself to go slowly and pay attention. I feel for the slight gradient in the ground beneath us, and when I find it I grab Lee's hand and head up to the forest edge. I find the entrance to the path between two birch trees. "This way," I say.

Once in the woods, I lead and Lee follows a few steps behind on the narrow path. I shine my tablet light on the path at my feet but am barely registering the visual path because of my speed. After walking through the woods around New Hope Town all of my life, my feet just know how to avoid rocks and roots.

I try to ignore the sound of the fire, like a freight train in the distance, and the heat I can feel prickling the back of my neck. Every once in a while I look back to see if I can see any flames, but so far there is only smoke that is getting thicker by the second. The siren blasts again, my unofficial timekeeper, and I think and hope that we are five minutes closer to safety. Lee and I don't talk. Instead, we cough sporadically and keep pressing up hill. I try not to think about what will happen if we don't make it out of here, but my imagination goes to those dark places. I imagine Mom getting another phone call, this one from NESA, saying there has been an accident, and I can't even imagine past the phone call. I can't. I can't let that happen to Mom. *Stop it*, I tell myself. *Focus!* All of my attention must be on this narrow, winding path. I'm navigating uphill as fast as I can in spite of the increasingly thick smoke. The heat is getting more intense, and sweat streams off my forehead and into my eyes. I glance back again over my shoulder, my eyes stinging from sweat and smoke. I can't see more than a few blurry feet behind me now. I can't see Lee.

I am already stumbling back downhill into the smoke. "Lee," I call out, even though my throat is so raw it hurts. "Lee!" I crash towards the heat now, swinging my tablet light in broad arcs, looking for him.

"Tic," he sputters from so close he is almost beneath me. I stop short of stepping on him. He's on his hands and knees. "I tripped. I think I twisted my ankle."

"Get up!" I yell. "There's no time! We have to move!" In the forest behind him I think I can see a faint, yellow glow penetrating the smoke. The crackling sound intensifies. The fire's gaining on us. The siren sounds again. Ten minutes have passed. Lee's face is squinched in pain as he stands up. The path is too narrow to walk side by side, otherwise he could put his arm over my shoulder and I could support at least some of his weight. Instead, I grab his hand and start back uphill. I hear laboured breathing and don't know if it's his or my own. I feel like we have been climbing this stupid mountain forever. We are making slower progress now because Lee is limping. He stops and lets go of my hand.

"Go on without me. I'm slowing you down," Lee says, but even as he says it I am already shaking my head. This is not happening. "I'll be fine. I can follow the path on my own," he insists.

"No way." I try to grab his hand again, but he pulls it free. "Fine, don't hold my hand, but I am not going on without you," I say reflexively.

"But—" he starts, but a siren cuts him off. Fifteen minutes.

I can't help looking over his shoulder where I am sure I can now see licks of flame piercing the smoke wall. I want to run up the hill as fast as I can, faster than I have ever run on the treadmill but against all good sense, my feet remain firmly planted. It's just not in me to leave him here.

"C'mon," I say.

He shrugs, and this time lets me take his hand again and up we go. We climb until I sense the opening of space around us. Trees and bushes thin out as we approach the rocky summit where they have no spot to root. We take the last few steps quickly before we collapse out of the forest and onto the rough-hewn granite on which the Academy stands. We lie on our backs, our chests heaving. There is nothing here the fire can burn, not the rock and not the Academy.

My eyes sting, but I open them briefly as a fuzzy light tracks over us and is gone, and then another does the same. I hear the *whump-whump-whump* sound of electric helicopters. They will be dropping sticky fire-killing chemicals all over the mountain soon. We get up, his arm over my left shoulder, my arm around his waist, and cross over to the front door of the Academy. I press my left thumb to the keypad beside the double doors and one door swings open. I feel exhausted and elated. Victorious. We made it. I look at Lee and see tracks of tears in the grime on his face.

Question 15:

Burning wood releases which important greenhouse gas(es)?

a) Methane
b) Carbon dioxide
c) Nitrogen dioxide
d) Water vapor
e) All of the above

Answer 15:

e) All of the above

When wood burns, it releases not only the CO_2 that it has absorbed during its life but also smaller amounts of much more potent gases like methane and nitrous oxide.

***

It's 10:40 on Monday morning. I know because I keep checking the time every few minutes. It's still too early, but I can't help being anxious. When it is still five minutes too early I see Tate crossing the cafeteria towards me. He's wearing white cargo pants and a plain white T-shirt. Even though we hardly see the fourth-year students (if they bother to come to Friday night socials, they only hang out with one another) I recognize him immediately from the special meeting we had on Friday. I give a little wave and stand up, and then I think I shouldn't have done either and feel awkward but it's too late now.

"Hi," he says.

"Hi," I say.

"Did you want to get something to eat?" he asks, indicating the food and beverage service areas that line the perimeter of the room.

"No," I say, tucking a stray hair behind my ear. "I'm good."

"Okay. I won't either then." He nods at me in agreement, smiling politely.

"No," I say, shaking my head. "You can if you want. I mean, you should. I mean, of course you can...." I am sputtering. So much for making a good first impression. He's going to think he's mentoring a total idiot. But how am I supposed to react to someone who talks to Robert Sheffield as almost an equal?

Tatum Brown's project last year was amazing. No wonder everyone here calls him "Tate the Great." It was called "The White Roof Project." I can't say that I understand the complex mathematical prediction models he used, but I do understand the basics of the project. The colour black traps heat the same way white reflects it. I am at least familiar with the physics of that. So Tate figured out that people have been making roofs and roads black for so long because they don't show as much dirt. But, as the population grew, more roofs were built with black shingles and more roads were paved with black concrete, so more heat was trapped in the cities. He ran predictive models that showed that if all the urban roofs in the tropics and temperate regions were painted white it would save the equivalent of twenty-four billion metric tons of carbon dioxide. How amazing is that? According to what I've read on the message boards, it's already been approved by Robert Sheffield and will be presented to the IOCC later this year. Maybe that explains why he was so comfortable talking to Sheffield when he visited a few weeks ago. It probably wasn't their first conversation.

"Let's sit," Tate says. His smiling brown eyes are warm and welcoming.

I sit and take a deep breath, which starts a coughing fit. The school nurse, Maggie, explained to me that my lungs would recover from the smoke inhalation damage over the next few weeks, but in the meantime my airways are hyperreactive. Tears are streaming out of the corners of both eyes, and I sound like Ruthie barking. If I could even breathe I would be so embarrassed right now.

The next thing I know Tate is behind me, gently but firmly raising both of my arms up over my head, stretching me out. The coughing subsides as I focus on his voice calmly instructing me. "Breathe in"—he pauses—"and out"— another pause—"and in"—a pause—"and out." After another minute he lets go of my wrists and my arms float down to my sides. He takes a seat across from me as if nothing unusual has happened.

"I'm sorry," I say.

"Side effect from the smoke inhalation, right?" he says. "I heard all about it. Everyone is talking about how you and

Lee almost died. Are you sure you feel up to this right now? We can postpone."

"No, I'm okay," I say, wiping my cheeks to dry off any remaining tears.

"Okay. Well, remember it helps to lift your arms up high if you are having trouble breathing. It opens and expands the chest."

I nod and look at him, wondering what he doesn't know.

"I had a foster brother with asthma, so…"

"The nurse said it should be better in a few days or a week," I offer. "Are people really talking about us almost dying? That makes it sound so dramatic."

"Well, it was, no?" He shrugs. "Forest fires aren't that unusual here, but students getting caught out in them sure is."

"How often are there fires?" I ask.

"Oh, a few times a year, probably, though it's definitely getting worse every year. I remember in my second year here there was a four on one of the mountains to the north that lasted two weeks. We could see it from the windows. The air quality was so bad that no one was allowed to go outside. There were constant rumours that we would be evacuated, but in the end they put it out."

I shiver, thinking about the possibility of more and worse fires, remembering the events in a visceral way, so intensely I think I can still smell smoke. My heart starts to pound. I try to shake it off, literally shaking my shoulders before I come back to the moment. Tate has taken hold of one my hands and gives it a gentle squeeze.

"Tic? I asked if you were excited to get to work on your first project?"

"Yes, I am," I say, focusing on his soft, full lips.

"Super. That's great! So you and I should plan to meet every few days." He pulls out his tablet, and I follow his lead. "But in between meetings you can message me anytime, okay?"

But I don't want to bother him. He must be busy with his own projects, working on research that's much more amazing than anything I can do. I am shaking my head. I just can't imagine it.

"Yes, yes. You must. I insist," he says, nodding vigorously and staring at me so that I almost feel embarrassed. I sense only warmth and sincerity and give in to it, and to him. I give his hand a squeeze and smile.

"Okay, I will message you between meetings if I need help, I promise," I say, and we both smile.

"So, tell me, which of the four elements have you decided to ground your first project in?" he asks.

"Water. Definitely water."

"Really? I was sure you were going to pick fire." Tate says running a hand through his sleek black hair.

I shrug, not sure how to respond.

"S'no problem or anything, Tic. Just usually good to pick something you are passionate about, right? So why water then?"

"I live close to the Edge, really close, like one cow pasture away close. So I am pretty passionate about it, especially when it comes to sea level rise."

"Sure, I get it now. I never met anyone who lived that close, but it must be pretty terrifying."

I swallow and nod in agreement.

"Okay so sea level rise gives us lots to work with--thermal expansion, ice melt and run off, groundwater return and more. Have you thought more about what aspect you want to work on? It's okay if you haven't."

"I have, actually. I am thinking about ice melt. I figured it's important because it doesn't only affect sea levels, which is my personal passion, but ice plays a major role in setting the temperature of Earth's atmosphere and oceans and also governing major weather patterns."

"Awesome. You should probably mention some of that in the intro or discussion of your report. It shows you are already thinking beyond the narrow focus to broader implications. They love that shit."

As we start to talk about project ideas, my nervousness finally dissipates, and the next two hours fly by.

***

"What time is it?" Lee asks, rubbing sleep from his eyes.

"Just after three," I tell him.

"Sunday?"

I shake my head. "Monday."

"Monday? Monday. Really?" He thinks about it. He's lying on his side on a bed in the infirmary, and I am sitting on a chair beside him. Nurse Maggie sits at a desk about twenty feet away. She has stopped typing on her tablet and is watching us. Lee starts to sit up and grimaces. I jump up, wanting to help but not sure how or if he needs help, so I end up standing close to him just in case. He manages to swing his legs over the side of the bed. He looks down at his wrapped-up ankle and then up into my face. "Are you okay?" he asks.

I nod, and he smiles briefly before his lips tighten again.

"Shit. My ankle is really throbbing," he says.

"Should I ask the nurse for more painkillers?"

"No, I'll be okay. I just can't remember exactly—wait, the nurse?" He stops and looks around.

Nurse Maggie smiles and nods at him. I was here for most of the weekend, first as a patient and then as a visitor, sitting beside Lee's bed while he slept. Maggie and I had a chance to talk a bit during that time. She reminds me of the nurses at Maplewood, where my mom works, or some of them anyways, the good ones. She is soft-spoken and has a way of listening that makes it easy to talk to her. I am grateful she is giving us a few minutes to catch up.

"Yeah, they kept you here," I explain. "I was here too for the first twenty four hours. Smoke inhalation treatment, observation, and stuff." I remember drifting in and out, having nightmares about the fire, and waking up and seeing Lee in the bed next to mine. I am pretty sure Maggie gave me some medication to calm me and help me sleep. I remember how thick my head felt.

"Are you sure you're okay?" Lee asks, searching my eyes for reassurance.

"Yes, I'm fine. You had some burns on your back," I tell him. Yesterday I watched Maggie put fresh dressings on them. They were red and raw, but she was sure they would heal up in a few weeks' time. I also was surprised to see that he has a tattoo on his chest. Centered over his breastbone is a map of the continents as they looked before the Change, surrounded by a three-inch circle with lines radiating out from it. I am dying to ask him about it, but now is definitely not the time. "They are first-degree burns because you were behind me, so you were closer to the..." The word *fire* is stuck in my mouth, and I swallow it down. "Doesn't it hurt?" I ask.

"No," he says, shaking his head. "I guess the painkillers are pretty strong. And my ankle?"

"Just a bad sprain," I assure him.

He motions for me to come even closer. I am already standing between his legs and I lean in so that our foreheads are touching. His hands are heavy on my shoulders and I wonder how much effort it is for him to sit up? Is he dizzy? In pain?
"You saved me out there," he murmurs, his voice low and throaty. I roll my eyes up to meet his, but he is looking down, his thick gold blond lashes almost brushing his cheeks. I feel a heat rising up from my core.

"No," I start to object, but the words die on my lips. He is stroking the side of my neck with his hands, and my skin tingles, little sparks shooting off in every direction from his touch. My breath catches in my chest and I dare not move.

"Thanks," he whispers and then kisses me soft and slow.

Maggie's chair loudly scrapes the floor as she stands up, and we pull apart. "Okay, you two, visiting hours are over," she says in a friendly voice.

***

Question 16:

How much atmospheric pollutant is put out by a 1.5-acre forest fire?

a) The equivalent of 4 gasoline-powered cars every second
b) The equivalent of 40 gasoline-powered cars every second
c) The equivalent of 400 gasoline-powered cars every second
d) The equivalent of 4,000 gasoline-powered cars every second
e) The equivalent of 40,000 gasoline-powered cars every second

Answer 16:

d) The equivalent of 4,000 gasoline powered cars every second

According to some scientists, a 1.5-acre fire puts out more and more damaging atmospheric pollutants every single second than four thousand cars using gasoline.

***

"How's your tea?" I ask Tate.

He nods and smiles as he brings his mug down onto the table. "Excellent, and yours?"

"I'm waiting for it to cool down a little, but even the smell makes me happy," I say taking a sniff of the fresh lemon scent.

We sit in silence for a bit, but it feels comfortable and okay, even though I only met him for the first time four days ago. We have been messaging a lot about my project.

"I'm glad you chose water as your element. Did you know it symbolizes life in my culture?"

I shake my head. "What culture?" I ask and then put my hand up to my mouth too late to take the words, back but thankfully he doesn't look offended.

"Mohegan culture. Don't worry huh? It's okay. You probably never met any indigenous people in New Hope Town, right?"

"No, I never did. It makes sense that it symbolizes life though, after all it's where life on earth started and I can't think of anything that can live long without it."

"Yeah, it also symbolizes purity and fertility."

"Lee! What are you doing in the caf?" I ask, shocked to see him approaching us.

"Nurse discharged me, so I came looking for you and," he looks over at Tate and--maybe the way they are looking at one another means something to people with testosterone, but it's just uncomfortable for me. Tate stands up and puts a hand out.

"Tate Brown."

"Lee Wright."

"Hey we can meet later, Tic, if you want to uh…" Tate says. He looks from me to Lee and back at me again.

"Well I don't know," I hesitate, and now they are both looking at me. "It's just that Tate is mentoring me on my project and I did have a few questions but—" I try to explain to Lee who cuts me off.

"I should go lie down anyway," he says as he turns and walks away.

I bury my face in my mug, using the pretext of sipping to settle myself.

"Sorry if he seemed rude or…I'm sure he is just tired," I try to explain.

"Yeah I'm sure that's it." Tate says, and it's hard for me to tell from his tone if he believes it.

"Should we talk about the project?" he suggests.

"Yes, please," I say

"Excellent. So, from our messages what are you thinking? Icebergs? Ice shelves? Glaciers?" Tate asks.

"Well, ideally I would love to look at models for melt rates for all of them, but I don't know if that's within scope of this project. If I want to narrow it down I would rule out icebergs. Not that they aren't important in contributing to atmospheric and water temperature, but they are not as central to my primary question." I pause and am reassured by his nodding, so I press on. "Between glaciers and ice shelves it's a bit harder, and I am hoping maybe to be able to look at both. Glacier melt affects sea-level rise as fresh water runs off melting glaciers into oceans but..."

"Only on glaciers that are near the oceans right? That's true. Twenty, fifty, a hundred years ago there were a lot more glaciers on land, in mountains and shit, but since the Change, fewer and fewer." Tate says.

"Yup. So ice shelves are probably the most important. That's where glacial ice meets ocean and..."

I'm interrupted by a message ping from my tablet. My first thought is Lee, and I glance down. I freeze. It's not from Lee. It's a message from Ms. Hunt and the subject line reads: *Report to my office*

***

I take in the smooth shiny surfaces, the glass desk with a red chair behind it, and two black chairs in front. It's super clean but plain. Ms. Hunt's office doesn't have anything that looks personal in it, and even though her assistant told me I could sit while I waited for her it doesn't feel right. I have no idea why I am here and neither her summons nor her assistant have given me any clue--but I can't say I have a good feeling about it. My post podcast quiz results all seem to have been good enough to allow me to continue on to the next lesson. I try thinking about other areas of performance that they are monitoring, like posts and comments on others posts, but I don't know exactly what they are looking for and I can't think of anything out of the ordinary. Maybe I am not in trouble.

"You're here," Ms. Hunt says as the door slides open and she walks in. Suddenly the room feels smaller. She walks past me and around her desk, pulls out the chair, and sits. Unlike her assistant she makes no indication that I should sit so I don't.

"How are you feeling? Any trouble with your breathing?" she asks.

"Uh no," I say and then clear my throat, "I'm not having any trouble."

"I've spoken to the nurse. She gave me the full report. You and Lee were very lucky. You know that, right?"

I nod and wait. She looks pissed. She steeples her fingers together, elbows resting on the desk, index fingers tapping as she looks at me. I am reminded of exam day when Lee and I appeared in front of her and the others to explain ourselves.

"I wonder if it was a mistake, admitting you here, Tic."
Shit! Shit! Shit!

"Obviously, you know I was not pleased about the question you asked Mr. Sheffield," she says looking at me expectantly.

"Um yeah, I could tell. I'm not sure why though? I mean he seemed okay with it," I say.

"Yes, well, I did consult with him after and he truly wasn't offended, but we often have important guest speakers here, Tic. We host national and international heads of state and some of them, people from developed countries, people who help fund NESA and the amazing opportunity that you and your classmates have; some of them might have been offended."

I am truly confused. It was just a question.

"Your question may have been interpreted to be calling out more developed countries, saying that they have acted unjustly. In any case, no harm was done, this time."

She stares at me, and I know I am being judged. I hate the feeling.

"That is not why I have called you here though. There is no rule against asking questions however inappropriate or immature they may be. There is a rule, though, about not being out of sight of NESA at night. Friday night both you and Lee broke that rule, and as a result you both almost died. I know that it was made very clear to students on multiple occasions that breaking rules is grounds for expulsion at the discretion of the director," she says.

"I'm so sorry. I guess I forgot that rule, but please, please, please know that it was my fault. I was the one who suggested we go for a walk that night. It's not Lee's fault." I beg.

"I will talk to Lee when he is feeling better, but right now this is about you, Tic, about your future here at NESA."

I take a big breath in and out through my nose and try to think of what to say to defend myself so that I can stay here, but I draw a blank. I know that she is right. As soon as she said it I did remember reading that rule in the student handbook. I just never thought about what the implications of breaking it could be.

"I have reviewed your work so far and see no issues on that account. I do, however, have concerns based on several occurrences now about your judgment and maturity. I have made a decision."

I look at her impassive expression and try to prepare myself for whatever she may say.

"Consider yourself on probation. You may stay at NESA, for now."

***

Question 17:

Which of the following contributes to sea levels rising when it melts?

a) Icebergs
b) Glaciers
c) Permafrost
d) a & c
e) All of the above

Answer 17:

b) Glaciers

Only melting glaciers contribute to sea-level rise. Because icebergs are already in the water when they melt, they do not increase sea level. Although melting permafrost is devastating for flora and fauna, it does not directly contribute to sea level rise.

OCTOBER

"How's everyone doing?" I ask.

"Oh about the same," Mom says. It's my favorite answer. "Uncle Al's had a good apple season, so I have been making sauce almost every night. Ruthie is spending more time with him while I'm at work. Work is...work. Leslie is retiring next month. Do you remember her? She's one of the nurses on the second floor. Oh, and before I forget, Mr. Kisway sends his regards. He says he has picked out a special new book for you and hopes you will come visit him when you're home."

It amazes me that even through the small screen of my tablet she has the ability to instantly make me feel guilty. She told me during one of our video chats weeks ago that he had been ill, and I hadn't thought about him once between then and now.

"How's he doing anyway?" I ask.

"So much better now. The antibiotics have kicked in, and his cough has really settled down."

"That's great." I nod and am genuinely relieved to hear it. "So have you thought any more about the message? Have you come up with anything else?"

Mom's only response is a sigh of exasperation, Understandable, I guess, as I have asked the same thing more or less for the past three weeks. I tuck my legs up under me, settling in on the couch in the far corner of the large, open lounge area before continuing.

"It's just, I had another thought about it. You said that Uncle Al found the photo in a box of Dad's stuff, right? So what if there is something else in the box that explains the message?" I am reaching, I know, but I am running out of things to ask her. She has already told me repeatedly that she doesn't know any other helpful details.

"What?" She looks seriously annoyed with me.

"Well, it's just that I was wondering if--do you still have the box?"

She's shaking her head before I even finish speaking.

"Well, maybe Uncle Al has it?" I suggest.

"I really doubt it, Tic. Why would he have kept it all this time when I told him I didn't want it?" She sounds irritated, and hearing her say she didn't want it puts me on edge too. Did she ever stop to think for a minute that I might have wanted my dad's stuff? Mom and I have a tendency to feed off each other's moods, which is great when we are in a good mood but not so great when it gets like this. Is it like this for all mothers and daughters or just for us?

I respond in the most neutral voice I can muster. "Maybe he put it somewhere and forgot it."

"It's possible." She frowns, reluctantly conceding. "You know, he keeps tons of old stuff in the loft up in his barn, so I guess it could be there."

I remember playing hide-and-seek up in the loft when I was little. It's huge and crowded with old farming stuff: tools and boxes and crates. I used to love exploring in those boxes for hidden treasures. My favourite was a gorgeous old wedding dress I found and played dress up in. Was my dad's old stuff really up there? Had I been so close to it all those years and never knew? I am already wondering what kind of stuff might be in the box: personal stuff, or scientific stuff to do with his work, or both?

"You could have a look up in Uncle Al's loft and see, right? Imagine if it is still there after all this time," I say.

"You need to stop this, young lady!" she says, and I snap back to reality. I know from experience that when she starts calling me "young lady" I am getting on her last nerve. "It's been almost a month since you found it. You don't know what the message means, and I certainly don't know what it means, and, what's more, I don't see why it matters! Why can't you just leave this alone and move on?"

"I don't know! I don't know why, okay?" I say, pissed off with her for not just saying yes, for making this so hard. "Maybe it's because I grew up with no father and I always felt that something was missing." Oh crap! Mom's face has slid down into a place of deep, still sorrow. "I mean, you were amazing, Mom. You did everything. Everything." I am suddenly on the verge of tears. "Maybe it's because I am away from home, away from you," I confess.

"Oh, honey," Mom says.

"I miss you, Mom," I whisper. She and I have always been there for each other, just the two of us against the world. Now we have been apart for two months. It feels like forever.

"I miss you too," she says, flashing a brave smile. "How is Phish doing? Are you two still spending a lot of time together?" And that is so like Mom. Normalize, distract, and redirect to a happier, lighter topic. While I have been throwing a pity party, she has put her game face back on.

"She's good," I say. "I hang out with her almost every day." I think about all of the reasons I am lucky to have her for a friend, not the least of which being that she is almost as interested as I am in decoding Dad's message. "In fact, she finally dug up something on Wincor yesterday. They were bought out by a huge company called Alpha-Omega that owns all different kinds of other companies. I haven't had a chance to—" I stop. "Mom? What is it?"

"Nothing, Tic. It's nothing," she says, musing out loud. "I think Alpha-Omega is an insurance company."

"You've heard of them," I say, surprised. "Why do you think it's an insurance company?"

She sighs, and I think maybe she isn't going to answer any more questions, but then she does. "After your father died, I started getting money from them every three months. There was a note with the first payment. I forget exactly what it said, but it made me think it was his life insurance policy paying out."

"Then how come we never have any money?"

"So, here's the thing, Tic. When the first envelope came in the mail I was still really angry, and it seemed like the money was somehow supposed to replace what I had lost, and that was so impossible and ridiculous that I actually threw it in the trash."

"Fact?"

"Yes," she says, "but then you were born, and we didn't really have much money, and I was worried about how I would take care of you—financially, I mean. Every time an envelope came with more money in it I saved it for you, for your future. I was thinking—hoping—it would add up to enough to send you to a good university. It's only been a few months since we found out you were accepted to NESA. I haven't had time to think of what else you might need the money for. But anyway, it's there for you."

I can't believe what I am hearing. I can't believe that all this time when we couldn't afford anything new, or anything nice, there was money untouched. And I can't believe Mom worked so hard at Maplewood all these years when she didn't have to. But, really, when I think about it, I can totally believe it. It is such a Mom thing to do: selfless, generous, loving.

"Oh, Mom," is all I can say, and I wipe a tear from my cheek.

"If you ever need it, my love, it's there for you. Let's plan to video chat again next week, okay? Same day and time?"

"Okay. And Mom?" I say. I want to say so much but all I can manage is the usual three words: "I love you."

We say goodbye, and I know I should find a private study area to do some work on my project. I should, but I don't. Instead, I start to research Alpha-Omega. If they own a lot of companies like Phish says, then maybe they own an insurance company too. I quickly scan through the first information that comes up. Alpha-Omega are the first and last letters of the Greek alphabet, as well as a title for God in the book of Revelations, which prophesied an apocalyptic end of times. The Faithful Few were big believers in that crap. The things people did in the name of religion gives me a chill. I change the search to "Alpha-Omega Corp." I don't get very far before I feel someone sit down next to me on the couch.

"Hi," Tate says. "Am I interrupting?"

"No, of course not," I say, closing the tab on Alpha-Omega for now.

"I was looking at some of the charts you sent me and..."

"I screwed them up, didn't I?" I open my project folder and pull up the mathematical predictive charts. I am not a math or stats genius of any kind, but I pride myself on being thorough in using the simple tools I have mastered. I spent hours poring over these before sending them, and I know I made a mistake somewhere because the results just don't make sense. For the life of me I can't figure out where I went wrong. "I mean, the quasi-retrospective predictive model I found for ice melt and the scientific reports are so out of sync. And then when I tried to extrapolate the predictive model based on current data into the future, well, there's just no way my answer is right."

"Okay, so let's back up a minute. Can you explain your thought process to me?"

I take a deep breath and try to slow down. I have gotten more comfortable with Tate over these past few weeks. I even recognize the single furrowed vertical line just slightly to the left and above his nose is a wrinkle he gets when he is thinking hard. "I was thinking that scientists say fifteen or twenty years ago would have not only measured glacier melt but also developed predictive models of what we could expect in the future."

"Of course."

"So, I decided to look those up and see if they got it right, since what was their future is now our past or present. NESA database access is so awesome that I was able to find lots of accurate information, but when I plotted it out, they were off on their predictions. Way off."

"So, either they got the math wrong or there were other external, unanticipated factors affecting glacier melt," Tate continues.

I nod.

"Well, I can think of some plausible theories that explain the accelerating loss of ice."

"Because the dark water absorbs more heat than the reflective, white ice, so as the ice melts, the water around it heats up even more and melts more ice in a vicious circle." I suggest.

"Definitely true. Maybe even more importantly, as seawater warms, its ability to take in CO_2 from the atmosphere diminishes because the solubility of CO_2 in seawater decreases as temperature increases. This leads to more CO_2 in the atmosphere, more heat trapping, and accelerated melting of ice. I'm not sure if they would have been aware of this at that time and accounted for it in their model or not."

"Okay, so there are lots of possible reasons they got it wrong, that's a relief. So next I tried using their predictive model, which we both agree shows a much slower rate of melt in the last twenty years then what we have actually measured to predict our future. If you use that model going forward, it looks like the glaciers should still be around for another four or five decades given margins of error. And that should be plenty of time for almost everyone to adjust to the serious rise in sea level that will happen if or when the last one finally melts. I mean, look how fast and far we have come already, right?"

"Sure, and I agree with where you are headed so far. It doesn't make sense to use the old predictive model, which clearly got it wrong."

Tate says, "Yeah that's what I was thinking too. So, I decided to plot the melt rates for all the larger glaciers for the last two decades and used some calculus to extrapolate to see what that predicted. I figured even if we don't understand all the reasons glaciers are melting at any given rate we still have to trust the actual data on the melt rates. At least I don't see why we shouldn't, do you?" He leans in close so we can look at the graph together. This is where I am sure I must have done something stupidly and obviously wrong. "According to this, it would mean that all the ice in the oceans, all of it, will be melted in the next five years!" I say.

"Let's look at it together. Maybe we'll come up with something different. If not, I've got a couple of experts in mind that we can send it to for input."

"Okay," I agree, feeling reassured. We start at the beginning, pointing at different charts and formulas, and quietly discuss questions and possibilities.

"Hey." Lee's voice is close and loud, and I am so startled that I jump back a bit on the couch, away from Tate and away from Lee, who is towering over us.

"Jeez, you gave me a scare," I say, laughing off my moment of panic, and I slap at his leg.

"Did I?" he asks and is staring at me like there is some deeper meaning to this question that I am too dumb to get.

***

Question 18:

What kind of transportation can be powered by electricity?

a) Cars/trucks
b) Boats
c) Trains
d) Helicopters/airplanes
e) All of the above

Answer 18:

e) All of the above

Airplanes were the last mode of transportation to use fossil fuels. This came to a rapid end when the solar-electric airplane was invented in 2016.

***

I am sitting in one of the common areas, and I know I should be listening to my podcasts for the day or working on my project or both, but I can't stop obsessing about Lee. It's just weird. I mean first he kissed me in the infirmary and I thought things were going to get going between the two of us, and we did have a couple of make-out sessions in his room, but it never seemed to go anywhere beyond that. And now we seem to be spending less time together than before. True, we had to put our workouts on hold for a bit until Nurse Maggie cleared us both to start back up slowly. But once she did we hardly ever worked out together anyway. It was always one excuse after another, or that's what it feels like to me. And then there are at least two times in the caf

132

when I know he saw me but chose to sit somewhere else. The less time we spend together, the more time I spend thinking about him.

"Tic? Tic! Hello, earth to Tic!" Phish's voice penetrates my bubble, and the look on her freckled face is slightly irritated. She plops down on the couch beside me

"Sorry, I'm such a space cadet this morning."

She looks at me critically for a moment, and I wonder if I should talk to her about Lee, but I am a bit embarrassed to. Most kids our age (a) have had sex, and (b) are not into anything beyond hooking up and here I am being a dork about some kissing.

"You okay?" she asks.

"Yeah. I'm just not sleeping well lately," I say, which is the truth.

"Oh. You should see if they have valerian root tea here. That's what my Mom used to use when she couldn't sleep. Anyhow, I found out a bit more info about the photo."

Now she has my full attention, and she can tell. She sits back for a minute and makes me wait. "What?" I ask.

"Well," she says. "It's not big or anything but…"

She is totally teasing me now, which maybe I deserve for zoning out before. I put my palms together in a silent plea to her. She relents and starts spilling.

"Well, since your mom didn't seem to have much more personal detail to add I thought maybe I would try to find out more about the other person who for sure knew something about the photo: the photographer. I mean, it's kind of grasping at straws, but you never know. I guess I was even thinking that you might contact him."

"I never thought of that," I admit. It seems strange that I would call a guy out of the blue who knew my dad all those years ago, but maybe." So what did you find out?"

"I started by searching Matt Haley, photography, and the year your dad died. Lots of results came up. I followed those that seemed most likely to be him until I was as sure as I could be that I had the right guy. I messaged you some of the links, but here's the deal. He was a professional photographer who mostly did photojournalism. Even though he took your family photo, he wasn't a guy who usually took portraits and stuff, but it makes sense if he was a friend of your dad's. He travelled a lot. I'm not sure where his home base was. He has photos from within the same few weeks of all different parts of the country. He went wherever there were storms, fires, and floods. He took lots of after shots of places and layered them with older photos so you could see all of the changes in one glance. Some of his shots are aerial too, so he must have had access to emergency or news station 'copters. Here, look."

She passes me her tablet, and I flip through ten, fifteen, twenty images. I can see what she means. I stop and study one of a little girl holding a teddy bear and sitting next to an old woman with a blanket wrapped around her. They are on a roof. The little girl is reaching her bare toes towards the water that is just at the edge of the roof. The girl is looking over at the woman who is looking at the photographer. The expression on her face is as hard as stone, a mask of brittle strength keeping sorrow from drowning her. "Wow." I say.

"I know, right?" Phish agrees, looking at the photo with me.

You can see towns and cities flooded all the time on news videos, but they flash over them so fast before switching back to a talking head who describes what we are too scared to see, spewing the cold, hard numbers from a perfectly made-up face. This is different. The destruction he captures is perfectly frozen in time and feels personal. Even with something like a forest fire, he captures trees burning from the ground, not just some aerial view of mile after mile of forest. I have to force myself to stop looking at them.

"So what else did you find out?" I ask, passing the tablet back to Phish. "Is he still around?" I ask cautiously, suddenly aware that if this is his line of work, he could easily have been killed in any number of disasters.

"Well, I'm not sure exactly. My guess is he's still alive but..."

"But what?"

"But I'm not sure you will be able to get in touch with him if you want to."
"Why not?" I say, trying to be patient. I'm not sure why she is being evasive.
"Because he's probably in prison," Phish says.

"What?" I say, totally caught off guard.

"Well, his last photos were from shortly before your dad died. After that I couldn't find a single photo credited to him, but I found this." She flips her tablet around so I can read the news article for myself.

Matt Haley, convicted earlier this month in a closed trial on charges of breaking and entry, arson, and terrorism for his destruction of an office building in York County was sentenced to life in prison. In passing sentence, Justice Judge Daniel Stanton said the unusual gravity of terrorism offences means he had to send a strong enough message to deter others considering carrying out similar crimes. He said there was little evidence presented that mitigates the presumptive sentence of life in prison.

"I am satisfied that life imprisonment is the appropriate sentence," the judge added.

Although Mr. Haley had pleaded not guilty to the charges he is widely believed to be the first member of the eco-terrorist organization Greenleaf to be caught and convicted. Although less active since the signing of the International Change Agreement, Greenleaf, and similar organizations, are believed to be responsible for millions of dollars of property damage during the Heretic Wars.

Mr. Haley's lawyer says they will begin the appeals process.

I read it again and still feel confused. Was my father friends with a terrorist? Not that I ever knew my father, but, I don't know, it just doesn't seem possible. Did my father know? Was he involved?

***

Question 19:

When is the last time that carbon dioxide levels were less than 350 ppm, a level considered safe in terms of global warming?

a) 2025
b) 2013
c) 2000
d) 1989
e) 1969

Answer 19:

d) 1989

In 1989 the carbon dioxide level surpassed 350 ppm, and in 2013 it surpassed 400 ppm. The year 2025 marked the first time that carbon dioxide levels in the amtosphere stabilized.

***

This Friday night's social is a dance, and it should be interesting. So far we have had game nights and movie nights and a talent show, which was surprisingly decent, and, of course, Sheffield, but this is the first dance. I've never been to one, but I guess I'm not the only first year who never went to a dance in their old high school. At least I don't have to worry about what to wear. Everyone here has the same clothes, more or less, tees and tanks, jeans and sweats in whatever color your year wears. Some girls wear make-up and do stuff with their hair, but lots don't.

By nine o'clock the hall is full. Tables are set up along one wall with water and juice, and chairs line two more walls. At the front is another table with speakers and lights and a microphone and lots of wires and cables snaking around it. It seems like almost everyone showed up, and the upper years all seem pretty pumped. Their energy is contagious, and the room is heating up even before the party starts. There's a loud thumping on the mic and a screech of feedback as Mr. Miller, the head of the gym, holds the mic up and bangs it with the flat of one hand. Everyone stops talking, more or less, and turns to face him.

"Welcome to the first dance of the year. Most of you know how this rolls out, but for our first years' benefit, and for anyone else who may have forgotten over the summer, let's review. Dancing is great exercise--"

"Boooooooo!" comes from behind me. "--and great fun." The crowd of students hollers and pumps their fists in the air.

"We want you to get physical, get wild, but not too wild. No pushing, no bumping, no thumping and no slamming. Also remember that unlike your bedrooms where you *sleep* unmonitored here there are others watching, including staff."

A groan goes up from the room. It's been pretty obvious that people are hooking up in their rooms and now it's crystal that staff know. Interesting.

"I also want to thank Amber for spinning the tunes tonight," he says, pointing to a tiny girl in white with big glasses who is almost invisible behind all the equipment on the table. People cheer, and someone yells, "Yo yo Amber," and the room is practically vibrating with anticipation.

"Alright," Mr. Miller says before passing the mic to Amber, "have fun, kids."

"Lights," Amber says, and the room goes pitch black. There is a second of silence only before a pulsing rhythm floods the room and colored lights start flashing. Almost everyone is on the dance floor instantly, but I notice I am not the only first year who has migrated back to a wall to observe.

It occurs to me that on some level this is fucked. Are we literally dancing as the world is burning? I get that it's possibly, probably better for our brains if we take a break once in a while and have fun so we can come back to face the challenge of the Change fresh, but seriously, dancing? And then Phish is in my face jumping straight up and down like a crazy person, yelling something I can't hear over the music. She grabs my hand and pulls me onto the dance floor.

Surrounded by bodies all gyrating to the music I start to move too, and before I know it I have stopped thinking. I'm not in my head at all. I'm moving in sync with the crowd, smiling at everyone, with everyone. And it feels great. I lose track of Phish. I lose track of time, and I am just about dying for a water break. I notice some of the guys have taken their shirts off, and I'm not the only one slick with sweat.
The lights and the music change, a song comes on that's soft and slow, and the multi-colored lights change to all white,

like tiny stars sweeping the ceiling, the walls, and the dancers. All around me people are paired up, boys and girls, boys and boys, girls and girls, all drawn together like magnets. I see Phish in the arms of a girl with a blond ponytail and heather grey shirt. I start to make my way to the closest wall, and then there is a hand on my shoulder.

"Wanna?" Tate asks me.

How can I refuse? At first I feel awkward. I wonder if it's because I haven't been physically close with a guy except for the few times with Lee. Or is it because I know Tate as my mentor and as comfortable as I am now talking to him he still feels so above me in some ways. His shirt is off and with his arms circled around my hips I can feel the sweat from his chest sticking to my shirt. But he smells like a forest, and I start to relax and listen to the music.

> "he says that he wants love
> but he don't,
> and she says that they'll break up,
> but they won't,
> ahhh ahhh ahhh ahhh ahhh
> ahhh ahhh ahhh ahhh ahhh"

I scan the couples close to us on the dance floor, curious to see if any are taking advantage of the low lighting, and I'm not disappointed. Just behind Tate and to the right I see a guy's hands kneading the back of a girl with the tiniest white shorts I can imagine. His face is buried in her neck, and I am about to look away for privacy's sake when he looks up. Lee is staring right back at me. I bury my head in Tate's chest and feel so ashamed I can hardly breathe.

Then Tate's arms go slack and Lee is there with the girl draped on him.

"Switch," I think I hear him say.

"No thanks. You don't wanna switch do you, Vanessa?" Tate says.

She is grinning and stroking Lee's chest, but he shrugs her off and squares up so that he is facing Tate, just inches apart.

"Back off," Tate says.

"Make me," Lee growls and shoves Tate back a few steps. Others around us have stopped dancing and are watching intently. As confused as I am by all of this I have a moment of utter clarity in which I think about the staff in the room. Lee and I are both on probation still and whatever issues these two are having I can't risk getting in trouble here. With no clue what to say or do I step into the space between them fast, while there is still space between them.

"Lee, let's get out of here, okay?" and it's amazing that my voice sounds way more smooth and sure then I feel.

***

Question 20:

Water treatment plants use solar energy to process all water, including waste water, by removing _____.

a) Biologic contaminants
b) Minerals, like salt
c) Non-biologic contaminants
d) a & c
e) All of the above

 Answer 20:

e) All of the above.

Using highly concentrated photoelectric cells, solar energy is able to remove all contaminants and desalinate water, making it safe for everyday use. This has greatly increased availability of potable water for populations living close to water sources, including oceans.

***

We are standing in the hall outside his room. Twice someone else in his hall comes in or goes out of their room, and when they do, Lee and I stop arguing and stare sullenly at the floor, the walls, or each other until the hall is deserted again.

"What is wrong with you?" I ask.

"I don't know, Tic. What do you think is wrong with me?" he challenges.

I feel like answering with an insult, but I bite my lip and ball my hands into fists instead. "Just tell me Lee," I demand.

"Nothing! Nothing is wrong with me. You on the other hand. Lately, you are always Tate this, and Tate that, and Tate said."

"Well, he is my mentor," I spit out. Only now it's starting to dawn on me that he is jealous. We never really talked about our relationship, per se, and I am not naïve enough to think that every time a guy and girl fool around that makes them a couple.

"Yeah, I know. Tate the Great is your mentor. Big deal!" he says loudly.

Wow, I think. *He really is jealous.* I am still processing my new discovery and only dare a quick glance at him. His eyes are shiny, and his cheeks are flushed. I try to squeeze my own face tight so I don't smile, but I don't think it is working.

I reach for his hand and before he can pull away I press his thumb to the pad. As the door slides open I manage to compose myself a little. He is still waiting for me to respond to his comments about Tate. Instead, I lead him into the room and close the door behind us.

"Sit," I say, pointing to the bed.

He is pouting, and a wave of his blond hair falls over his right eye. He is so handsome, even in his anger—especially in his anger. "What?" he says sullenly, sitting on the edge of the bed.
I answer by straddling his lap, my hands on his muscular shoulders. I bring my face in very close to his. "You," I whisper, and I kiss him on his forehead. "Me," I whisper,

and I plant a soft kiss on his nose. "Us," I say, as my lips press against his.

I feel giddy with the idea that he would be jealous of Tate and me. His hands are in my hair, and he is kissing me back. I feel tender and powerful and exhilarated, and I am kissing him harder. I press forward, and he leans back and back until suddenly he stops hard as the back of his head meets the wall.

"Ow!"

"Are you all right?" I ask, pulling away.

He sits up and starts to push me off his lap. I get the idea and roll myself onto the bed beside him. He gently pushes me down, his chest on my chest. He leans up on his elbows and smiles down at me. "I'm more than all right," he answers in a husky voice.

I giggle as his body presses into the length of mine.

***

Hours later I wake to the heavy feel of Lee's arm across my chest and the warmth of his body curled against mine. Skin to skin, we shift without losing contact.

"Hey, sleepyhead," he says.

"How long have you been up?" I ask, lifting his arm so I can roll over and face him.

"Not long," he says.

"Hmm," I sigh. "Last night was—"

"Sweet." He smiles and brushes some hair out of my face.

I feel relaxed, happy, and also a little shy. I wonder if he can tell that it was my first time. "Can I ask you something?" I whisper.

He answers by kissing me, and I can't resist kissing him back. After a few minutes we come up for air.

I ask, "Have you had a lot of...." I don't want to say *sex* because that's only part of what I mean. "Relationships?"

I am still lying down, but he sits up and looks around the room, fixing his gaze on the blank wall opposite the bed. He shakes his head. I am honestly shocked. He is so sweet, and good-looking, and—let's face it—rich. I thought he would have had a few at least.

"How come?" I blurt out and instantly regret it. "Sorry," I say. "Just ignore me. I have never had anything, any relationship, even close to this and I clearly don't know what I'm doing." I reach over and rub his shoulder, waiting for him to respond.

After a moment he turns and looks at me, forcing a small smile. "Maybe we should shower?" he suggests.

"Sure. Do you want to go first or second?" I ask.

"How about together? Saves water, right?"

"True. Reduce is even better than reuse," I agree.

Just like the bed, the shower is really only proportioned for one, but we make it work for two. I offer to wash Lee's back. The burns have healed but are still visible as deep-purple splotches in several spots. He turns around and tries to draw me into his arms, but I push him back against the shower wall, gently pinning him there with my left hand as my soapy right index finger traces his tattoo. Neither of us speaks. When I am finished, I cover it with my hand and look up at him. He is looking away over my head, his expression distant and unfamiliar.

"What's the tattoo?"

"A permanent reminder of my dysfunctional family," Lee says.

"Oh?" I am dying hear more, but Lee has other ideas.

"My turn to wash you now," he says firmly, removing both my hands and kissing me lightly on the forehead.

***

Question 21:

Look at the three words below and find a fourth word that is related to all three.

Nuclear   Feud   Ties

Answer 21:

Family

***

I wake up with a jolt from a really deep sleep, the kind where you don't even dream because you're so far gone. The kind where your alarm clock could be going off for five seconds or five hours and it doesn't wake you. But an alarm clock has got nothing on the blaring siren that comes through the speaker. It's dark, and I snap up to a sitting position, my muscles twitching with the adrenaline surge.

"What? What?" I say, feeling disoriented. The door is in the wrong place. Oh. Lee's room. The siren has just stopped, but I don't know if I woke up with the first one, and anyway I was too startled to count. How many? As the ringing fades from my ears, I try to remember. Two? Three?

"Shh," Lee says calmly, sliding his hand up under my tank top and rubbing my back. "S'okay."

I take a deep breath and lie back down beside him. His arm wraps around my shoulder and I rest my hand on his bare chest.

"How many?" I ask.

"Four."

My heart rate picks up again. Four! Four is serious. We haven't had a four since we have been here. "Are you sure?" I ask.

"Yeah, pretty sure. We'll know in another five," he says.

"Hey," he says, reaching over and lightly running his finger down the side of my neck to my collarbone, "there are worse things than being stuck here together."

I push his hand away before it can travel any further. I roll away from him and reach for the light on the bedside table. I turn it on and start fussing with my hair, taking out my ponytail and combing it with my fingers so that it hides my face until I can settle down a bit.

"How come you're so chill?" I ask, embarrassed that I am so freaked out.

"I dunno. I guess it's conditioning." He rubs his sleepy eyes with his fists. "Our house is up on a mountain and is pretty much a fortress. My old private school too. I have never really had too much to worry about when it comes to alarms. I have always been about as safe as a person could be. Well, until last month, anyhow."

I remember him describing his house to me: his mansion, guest houses, tennis courts, and swimming pools. I think of my little cottage, so fragile in comparison, and I shudder.
"Are you okay?" he asks. "You know there's nothing to be afraid of, right? We are totally safe here."

"Sure. I know," I say, shivering anyway. "Do you think it's another fire?"

"Possibly, but odds would favour a hurricane," he says.

In New Hope Town almost every siren meant a hurricane with or without storm surges. Fires were rare and small, tornados and earthquakes even less common. The last four was this past winter. I was also stuck in a school then: my old school. It also wasn't a terrible place to be stuck. It was a designated evacuation shelter for our town so it had tons of spare food and water, and gym mats for sleeping on. There were also lots of opportunities for distraction. I hung out with Jeanne and Diane. Diane had a deck of cards and taught us a game called Prezi, which we played for hours on end. I was also able to touch base with Mom by phone intermittently, so I knew that she was at Maplewood. It's at the far west end of town and two stories tall, so it was definitely a safer place to be than our cottage. The only real worry was the cottage itself and, of course, Ruthie.

I look over at the clock and see that it's just after eight in the morning. If it's a hurricane, if it hit New Hope Town, if Mom is working her usual shift, then she should be at Maplewood already. That is too many "ifs" for me not to worry.

Lee starts to rub my shoulders, and I want to relax, but the siren goes off again. His hand pauses on my skin and I count to four. Damn! I was still hoping he might have been wrong. He goes back to massaging my shoulders, but my muscles remain tense. As much as the thought of a fire freaks me out after our experience last month, I am wishing that it's the cause of the alarm. A fire would be way better than a hurricane because it is much, much more likely to be local. After the siren's echo stops, I roll over to face Lee.

"I need a distraction. I need to get out of my own head. I can't stop trying to picture New Hope Town. I can't stop worrying. Talk to me," I beg.

"About?"

"Tell me about your tattoo," I say.

"Really? Can't we talk about something else?" he pleads.

I shake my head vigorously. I figure now that we have been intimate physically, I should pretty much have the right to know anything and everything about him. I'm not sure if it really works that way, but it should. "I want to know everything about you. Start talking," I command.

He looks so miserable that I am having second thoughts, but before I can voice them, he makes the decision to start talking. "It's a combination of the Earth and the sun. I think my uncle Chris came up with it, but I'm not sure. Everyone in my family has it. The night I got it is probably one of my earliest memories. It was the night of my sister Eva's second birthday, so I was four and a few months."

"Wait a sec. You got a tattoo when you were four? Fact?" I ask, really surprised. I mean, who gives a four-year-old a tattoo?

"Yes. I told you my family is screwed up, okay?"

I nod.

"Should I go on?" he asks.

I nod again. "Please," I say.

"I had already been asleep a for a while when my father woke me. He had a flashlight in one hand and coaxed me onto his hip so he could carry me with his other arm. I asked him where we were going, and he said it was a surprise. I remember thinking that I liked surprises, but couldn't it wait until the morning?" Lee's hand strokes my arm as he speaks and he is lost in the memory.

I imagine a little tow-headed boy in train pajamas resting his head on his father's chest as the moon peaks in the window. "Uncle Chris joined us in the hall, and we went to my sister's room. My uncle went over to her bed, and then he boomed, "Where is she?" My eyes flew open, and it seemed like at the same time a floor lamp beside a rocking chair in the corner of the room came on.

"My mother was sitting there with Eva asleep in her lap. She spoke softly to not wake my sister, and she didn't sound angry, which made me feel a bit better. She said, "You're not taking her."

"Uncle Chris walked towards her slowly and was talking calmly too. 'C'mon sis, you know it's for the best, and she won't feel a thing, I promise.' He was very close to her then. 'Neither of them will.' She took her eyes off him to look over at me then and he lunged and grabbed for Eva. She must have been a little surprised, but she held on to Eva tight, and then it got bad."

Lee stops talking and looks at me. He stares into my eyes for a long moment and I hold his gaze, trying to let him know without words how much I feel for him. He closes his eyes and then continues quietly. "Uncle Chris was pulling so hard on Eva that Mom had to stand up to hang on. Eva had woken up and was screaming and holding on tight to Mom's neck. Then he hit her. Mom. Hard. She stumbled back and lost her hold on Eva. In a second he had Eva. Her arms and legs were all still stretching towards Mom, and Mom was still on her feet, trying to close the distance between them. Chris managed to hold on to Eva with one hand, despite her squirming, and with the other he shoved Mom back. She slammed into the wall behind her. Her head made a thudding sound, and then she slid to the floor. For a moment we all froze." He swallows, and his eyes glisten.

I take his hand.

"She coughed and spit and then begged my father to stop him. I wriggled out of my father's arms and went to her. One of her eyes was swollen shut, and she had blood dripping from the corner of her mouth. I didn't want to look at her face. It scared me. I looked at my father instead. At first he didn't say anything; he just shook his head. He walked over to us and held his hand out for me to take. 'C'mon little man, Mother needs her sleep now, see. Let's let her rest.' She did look sleepy, and I didn't know what else to do, so I took his hand."

"Shit," I whisper. Never in a million years did I expect to be hearing this.

"Yeah," he says. "I was looking back at her the whole time we were walking away, and then she moved a bit, reaching out one hand to us, so I stopped. She licked her lips and whimpered, 'Please.' This time Uncle Chris answered. He said 'You'll thank me when the time comes and they are saved.' My father picked me up and we left. That's it. They must have drugged us because the next thing I remember is waking up in my bed with a big bandage on my chest. Later that day a doctor came to the house, took the bandage off, and cleaned the skin with alcohol that felt hot and cold at the same time. I didn't see my mother again for ten days. She was resting in her room. When she came out, her face was normal, but she was just very quiet pretty much from then on. I mean, she functioned, she was polite and stuff, but she was changed. I don't know how to explain it exactly. It was like she was going through the motions of being a person, of being a mother, but there was no feeling behind any of it."

"I'm so sorry," is all I can think to say. The tattoo reminds me of something. Something I don't know exactly. I try to think where I could have seen it, but if it's his family crest or whatever, I don't see how I could have seen it before. Still, I must have seen something similar but I just can't place it.

***

Question 22:

Hurricane deaths are a result of storm surges, which can reach _____.

a) Higher than 35 feet
b) Higher than 50 feet
c) Further than 100 miles inland
d) a & c
e) All of the above

Answer 22:

d) a & c

Storm surges can reach thirty five feet high and one hundred feet inland and are responsible for ninety percent of deaths associated with hurricanes.

***

Inside the school building they blast the sirens every five minutes only for the first thirty minutes but then, because there is no way that everyone would not have heard them, they switch to every thirty minutes. It makes it impossible to fall asleep, for me anyway.

Much later, when we are both dressed, and sitting on the bed talking about our projects, the all-clear sounds. I jump to my feet and grab my tablet. As awesome as it is to be safe at NESA, it is also unbearable because of the concrete walls around our rooms. We have not had access to the outside world via our tablets for almost twelve hours. Outside Lee's door we hear the commotion grow in intensity. Lee is on his feet too, grabbing his bag.

Students are pouring out of their rooms into the hall. I've never seen NESA in such a state of turmoil. People are rushing in every direction, looking for friends, jostling one another, and calling out questions to anyone who will listen. Words like "storm," and "four," and "hurricane" hurl through the hall, ricocheting off walls and crashing into people. Lee grabs my hand, and we navigate the crowd until we are in a big lounge area where there is reception. I don't bother looking for a seat but drop to sit on the floor, my back against a wall.

I am staring at the screen of my tablet holding my breath, willing Mom to answer my call. I wait and count and wait and lose track. I end the call and immediately redial. More ringing. More waiting. I can't stand it. I end the call again. I squeeze my eyes shut tight. *She's okay*, I keep telling myself. *She's okay*. She has to be okay. She is at Maplewood. Maybe she doesn't have her mobile with her. I can call Maplewood. I try to remember their number but can't. I open a tab, search it, and call. More ringing. No answer. I wait. Probably everyone there is so busy taking care of the clients they don't have time to answer. I let it ring. Someone will answer. Someone has to.

Lee is sitting on the floor beside me. He nudges me and passes his tablet to me. Reluctantly, I tear my eyes from my own screen to see what's on his. It's a newsfeed. It says that hurricane wind speeds reached 145 miles per hour. The storm reached land just south of York and headed north for several hundred miles until finally losing speed and heading out to sea just north of New Bath. The radar showed it had passed over a large area of the northeast seaboard. Swirling red, yellow, and green pixilated colours move up the map, sweeping over lots of small towns on the Edge, including New Hope Town. The bright, shiny colours give no indication of the massive destruction this level-four hurricane must have caused.

I pass it back to him and try Uncle Al's number. I'm not surprised when there is no answer. He usually leaves his phone in the house, says he will just forget where he put it if he carries it all over the place, and mostly it's off unless he wants to call someone, which is almost never. His barn is super-safe anyway and he's probably holed up in there with the cows. I wonder about Ruthie. Is she under the kitchen table? Is she over at the barn? I hope she got herself somewhere safe and wasn't out wandering.

My tablet pings with a message, and my heart races. But it's not Mom. It's Phish wanting to know where I am. "Where are we?" I look up from the screen at the lounge littered with students, some talking, most absorbed in their tablets.

"Three north lounge," Lee says.

I type it in and go back to reading the newsfeed. Correspondents are reporting from big and even medium-sized cities and towns, showing flooded streets and ruined homes, and estimating death tolls. There are no official counts yet, but this doesn't stop them from trying to outdo one another with their reports. Some are saying hundreds of deaths; others are saying many more. It will take weeks to clean up and at least that long until the officials will come out with a final statement on the cost of this one, in terms of damage and loss of life.

"Hey!" Phish calls out as she walks up to us and sits down.

"How you doing? Have either of you guys reached home yet?"

Lee and I both shake our heads. "You?" I ask.

She nods. "Yes. It sounds like there was some minor damage, but because Arquette is nestled between mountains, they help to protect the city from the worst of it. Plus it's all new build, so all is okay there. My family's okay."

I look down at my tablet, which is still ringing Maplewood with no answer, and try to think of what else I can do.

"Are you hungry?" Phish asks. Each room has an emergency food supply, enough for three days of food per person. Lee and I shared a nutrition bar in his room a few hours ago, but we were being careful knowing that the food had to work for two people instead of one. We didn't how long we would be in lockdown.

"Yeah, starving!" Lee says, and he and Phish stand up. "C'mon, Tic, we'll help you figure this out, but let's get some food too," he says softly, reaching down to help me to my feet.

The cafeteria is packed, but we order food and manage to find three seats together. Phish starts mechanically putting French fries in her mouth, one after another, with her left hand while she types on her tablet with her right. Lee is plowing through a double-cheese soy burger and scrolling through screens on his tablet. I am too nauseous to eat, too worried. I try Mom's mobile again but still no answer.

"Government sites are useless for real-time info," Phish moans in exasperation. "They take too freaking long to update things. I could hack into something better, but I think I'll try some bloggers first."

Phish continues to tap and swipe on her tablet, making noncommittal grunting noises in response to her finds. After a few minutes she stops, French fry poised half way to her mouth and stares at a page for a minute before looking up at me.

"Found one. Here's a blogger named S.S. Minnow. Have a look."

I take her tablet and read the blog post:

Just a quick post to let you know that, thankfully, I have come through another four unharmed. I ventured out just now in my trusty kayak, "Kate." Near me, the water is only about knee-deep and full of the usual bric-a-brac: bikes, lawn chairs, clothes not brought in from the line. I sense, as I have before, the strange silence that follows storms, the absence of bird chatter that goes unnoticed until it is gone, and its loss is startling and strange. It will return, I know, and much as I try to appreciate it when it does, I am certain that in the near future it will have disappeared into the background once more.

There were few other hardy souls out this morning, but I did meet a family of three from New Hope Town who had spent the night in their canoe. They were cold, tired, and hungry and accepted my offer to join me for a meal at my home. While their little one slept on my cot, I fried them up some of Frieda and Bertha's eggs. Over coffee, they told me that they weren't going back to New Hope Town. As far as they could tell, almost everything was either destroyed, under water, or both. I gave them some apples and pointed them southwest, where they will find land and help.

When I was out earlier, I saw that a big, old maple has come down on my neighbour's roof, and now I shall fulfill my promise to him to don work gloves and help him to saw off its branches.

I break down. I picture buildings I have known all my life being ripped apart by wind and water, and once I start crying it is hard to stop.

***

Question 23:

How many people have died in hurricanes in the last 250 years?

a) 1.9 million
b) 4 million
c) 62 million
d) 200 million
e) 1 billion

Answer 23:

b) 4 million

Four million people have died in hurricanes in the last 250 years. Droughts, though not nearly as dramatic to watch or experience, have been responsible for many more deaths as they increase the risk of fires and famine.

***

"How are you doing, Tic?" Ms. Hunt asks me after she shows me to a chair in her office. Her voice is calm and steady. She remains standing, leaning against her spotless, glass desk. Her eyes slide off my face, landing just above my left shoulder.

I shrug. What can I say? I'm shitty. I still haven't been able to make contact with Mom—or Uncle Al, for that matter. I am imagining the worst, have been since the minute the alarm sounded yesterday morning. But there's another part of me that keeps insisting this can't really be happening. I am sure that Mom is fine and that I will look back on this whole thing like a bad dream. I feel like my skin is peeled off and everything is touching my nerves. I haven't slept in twenty-four hours and, aside from a few cups of coffee, I can't remember if I have eaten anything.

"I have some news," she starts, and I startle, suddenly more alert despite my fatigue. "We found your mother. She's alive but—"

I jump up, but my knees give and I sink to the floor. I have no idea what she says next or if she is even speaking. There's only white noise between my ears. I don't have a single thought. Intermittently my chest heaves violently in a hiccup.

Slowly I become aware of Ms. Hunt on the floor next to me. She passes me a box of tissues and pats my knee. "Do you want some water?" she offers.

I nod, not trusting myself to speak yet. She stands and goes to a cabinet. I watch her open it and pour ice water from a sweating, silver pitcher into a large glass. I hear the ringing tinkle of the ice like a bell. She hands it to me and the cold glass makes my hand burn. I drink a sip and then a longer one. "Thanks," I say. I am so relieved. I feel like a weight has lifted from my chest and I can breathe again.

"Where is she? Why hasn't she answered my calls?"

"She's in a refugee hospital in a camp in Arquette," Ms. Hunt says. "She was injured, and they had to do surgery."

I nod, listening carefully now.

"They said the surgery went well, but she hasn't woken up from it yet. Her condition is serious, and they are watching her closely. We haven't found out anything about your neighbor Al Savory at this point."

I wait, but there is no more information coming. "I need to go to her," I say.

"Well, there's a lot to consider, Tic. You are currently the school's responsibility and—"

"There's nothing to consider," I say loudly, as I push myself up off the floor. Physically I am still a bit wobbly, so I put a hand on her desk to steady myself. But my voice is firm as I talk over her. "It's always been the two of us against the world. Mom needs me. I need her. I need to go!" I feel like a caged animal ready to bolt. I will run to Mom if I have to.

"Okay, Tic," Ms. Hunt says with the quiet authority of someone used to being obeyed. She pulls a small, white cloth from her pocket and rubs the spot on her desk where my hand left a smudge. "I thought you might feel this way. I have a possible plan. Sit down and let me explain it to you."

***

Lee and Phish are waiting for me outside the office. I give them the good news that Mom is alive and fill them in on the few details that I have. They lead me to the cafeteria and load up their trays with foods they know I love like baked macaroni and cheese, potato chips, and chocolate pudding. I realize they think I have not been eating enough this past little while, and I appreciate their concern for me.

I am not hungry, but I make an effort to eat for their sakes. It doesn't take long before other students are coming up to the table and asking for updates, or having already heard, they come over to wish me luck. Phish handles the bulk of these frequent and brief conversations for me. I'm uncomfortable being the center of attention, even at the best of times, and this is anything but. Pretty much all I can think of is how many hours, how many minutes until I am at Mom's side. I do the numbers in my head, using best- and worst-case scenarios.

"I just heard." Tate's voice and the touch of his hand on my shoulder bring me back to the present. I look at his soft, sympathetic eyes and make an effort to smile just a tiny bit. "Can I sit?" he asks.

Phish reads my face and answers for me before I can even open my mouth. "Of course," she says, pulling back the chair to her left.

He sits beside her and across from Lee and me. Lee is obviously uncomfortable but keeps his mouth shut.

"So you know that Tic is leaving early tomorrow morning?" Phish asks.

"I didn't realize you were going so soon," he says to me.

"A driver will take me to the hospital in the camp at Arquette so I can be with my mom," I tell him.

"My parents have agreed to chaperone her, which is really no problem," Phish explains. "My mom works at the refugee camp anyway, and I'm sure my sibs will be excited to meet her."

"Tic, are you sure about this?" Tate asks, sounding worried.

"Yes," I say.

"You don't think it's a good idea?" Lee asks gruffly.

"Well, I understand the impulse, of course, but, yes, I guess I am nervous about it."

"Why? It's perfectly safe," Phish says defensively. "My family will take good care of her."

"I'm sure they will. It's not that."
"Then what is it?" I ask.

"Every year, a few students leave NESA to be with their families after an event has impacted them. The intention is always to come back once things are settled, but sadly some of them never do."

The three of us sit in stunned silence. None of us has considered this possibility before. I mean, it makes perfect sense that I am not the first student in the history of NESA who has been in this type of situation, but I just hadn't thought about it at all until now. A cynical part of me wonders if that is why Ms. Hunt is being so helpful? Maybe she sees this as the perfect opportunity to get rid of me.

"Fact," Phish says under her breath like it's a swear word. Lee puts his left hand over my right one and holds on. I don't, won't, can't think about what comes after I see her, whether there might be a reason for me not to come back.

"She's my mom. I have to go."

***

Question 24:

How long did the Heretic Wars last?

a) Six months
b) Two years
c) Eight years
d) Fifteen years
e) Twenty five years

Answer 24:

d) Fifteen years

The Heretic Wars started with the car bombing of Dr. Michael Hull and ended fifteen years later with the explosion of the Denver Research Institute, the last known act of terrorism by the anti-Change forces.

***

After another sleepless night, I was anxious to be on my way. When the hired car and driver arrived early this morning it was still dark out, but I was ready. I took a few extra clothes in my backpack and some snacks from the cafeteria for later. I guess a small part of me wonders if Tate is right and I won't be going back to NESA, so I decided to take the photo and Uncle Al's knife at the last minute and I put them in my messenger bag with my tablet.

Phish and Lee were both there to see me off. Phish told me to give both her mom and my mom hugs from her, and she hugged me. We both started to cry just a little. While I was still wiping my tears Lee wrapped his arms around me and kissed me so hard that now, hours later, my lips still feel bruised. He stopped kissing me long enough to whisper in my ear. "Please don't go," he pleaded.
"I'll come back," I whispered, not knowing if it was true. My hands wrapped around the back of his neck and I pulled him in for one more kiss. And then I let go of him. I got in the back seat of the car, and the driver gently closed my door for me and came around to his side. He got in and started the electric engine, and we left North East Science Academy. The motion of the car lulled me to sleep, and my body finally gave in to its accumulated fatigue.

***

I open my eyes now and turn my head slowly from side to side. My neck is sore and there is some dry spittle in the corner of my mouth. Self-consciously, I wipe it away and look at the driver's face in the rear-view mirror. He's a bald, middle-aged man with ear hair, and he looks over at me and smiles warmly. I smile back at him out of polite habit and then remember: Mom is in the hospital. Her condition is serious. I look out the window for a clue to our location. It's light out now, but the sky is filling in with horsetail clouds and I can't see the sun. Trees and rolling hills are low compared to the mountains around NESA, and I wonder how close we are to Arquette.

"Um, sorry, but I forgot your name," I say.

"Billy Williams, at your service," he says, pretending to take off an imaginary cap. "You can call me Billy. Here's my card." He shoves the card towards me. "If you ever need me, just call. I'm a professional driver. I've taken lots of important people around." I take the card and put it in my messenger bag.

"Billy, how long until we are there?" I ask.

"Well, I'd say it's another hour to Arquette if we don't hit too many road repairs. To get to the west camp where the hospital is, add another fifteen or twenty minutes," he says.

"Thanks," I say. I dig in my bag and pull out my tablet. I figure I will distract myself for the remaining hour doing more research on Matt Haley. I wonder how much Mom knows about him really, and how much she will tell me when she wakes up. I thought we didn't have any secrets between us, but I'm less sure of that all the time. Take the Alpha-Omega business: when was she going to tell me about that?

I find bits and pieces about Matt by following links, mostly news blogs. As far as I can tell, he broke into a building and was found in an abandoned office suite by a security guard. He may or may not have taken pictures of some documents and then torched the place before the guard shot him in the leg as he was escaping. Matt had never been arrested until this incident, but when they fingerprinted him, they found he matched with prints left at other crime scenes. The cases were all related to an underground vigilante movement called Greenleaf. Something about what I am reading isn't fitting together quite right, but I can't put my finger on it.

I look up Greenleaf next. They were a small, secret organization that formed around the beginning of the Heretic Wars, or maybe even before that. They didn't think the government was doing enough about the Faithful Few, so they took matters into their own hands. They mostly killed individuals who were suspected of being members of the Few. Once in a while they blew up buildings or set stuff on fire. I don't know what to think. On the one hand they were breaking the law and should have let the government handle things, but it's kind of cool that they were so passionate about protecting scientists. They were hardly ever arrested, and when they were, there was never enough evidence to convict them. Everyone denied being members of it, but clearly there were members, so of course some people were lying. Matt Haley denied being a member, but what if he was? He broke in to a building, took pictures, and set stuff on fire. It could be consistent with Greenleaf, I guess, depending on what the place was he broke into.

I go back to the newsfeeds and links, looking specifically for the name of the building. When I find it, my mouth goes dry. I pull myself together and double-check what I am seeing. Then I message Phish. Matt Haley broke into my dad's old work, the office that belonged to Wincor. I wonder what he was looking for and if he found it? I also ask Phish if she has had any luck locating Uncle Al. I have continued to try his phone periodically ever since the storm, but haven't had any result, so I asked her to use her "computer skills" to see what she could find out. I have been more focused on my mom, but it's not like I've forgotten that he is missing in action.

I look up from my tablet. There is a valley below us, and row after row of grey, concrete two-storey buildings set in a neat grid. I sit up straight.

"Yup, that's it all right," Billy says. "You can tell a new-build town from a mile away. Roads are straight, houses are straight, looks like ticky-tacky. Now that's a really old song." He starts humming it.

Soon I'll see Mom.

***

Question 25:

How many climate refugees are there estimated to be worldwide?

a) 1,000,000
b) 17,000,000
c) 163,000,000
d) 200,000,000
e) 500,000,000

Answer 25:

d) 200,000,000

Estimates put climate refugees at 200 million worldwide, although this is likely an underestimate as, for a multiplicity of reasons, it can be very difficult to collect accurate data.

***

"Here's the camp," Billy says in a hushed voice.

It's afternoon. The clouds have accumulated and are washing everything in a grimy, filtered light. We turn left onto a concrete road. It's less of a road really than the only space on a vast field of pavement that is wide enough for our car to drive on. To our left are rows of shipping containers up on blocks. To our right are huge canvas tents, and through their open flaps I see they are filled with chairs and tables. All around us, between the shipping containers, in the tents, and on the road, are people. So many people that our progress is slowed to a snail's pace.

"I could honk but--" Billy trails off, but I understand his hesitation. Almost everyone has tattered clothes and a haunted look in their eyes. Well, not some of the kids, who are running around inventing games and making new friends. Still, the feeling of despair is pervasive, and honking seems inappropriate.

We reach the hospital, the only permanent structure in the camp. We pull to a stop, and a large woman with curly, red hair and a bright-yellow sundress comes over to the car. I recognize Phish's mother from our video chat last evening. I step out of the car, and she folds me into her.

"You must be Mrs. Cameron," Billy says.

"Yes," she answers over my head. She half releases me, one arm remaining protectively around my shoulder, and she reaches out to shake Billy's hand. "Thanks for bringing her." she says.

"Yeah, thanks for bringing me," I echo.

"No problem. Remember, call me anytime you need a ride now," Billy says. "And good luck, kid." He salutes us and gets in his car, slowly easing his way back down the road.
Mrs. Cameron looks me over and says, "C'mon, let's go see your mom."

The hospital is just as crowded as the camp outside. People are waiting in long lines by desks and others sit in chairs or on the floor. Some are filling out forms, and others are eating. Some even seem to be asleep despite the noise. There are no signs that I can see, and I would be lost in here if not for Mrs. Cameron, who clearly knows where she is going and politely but firmly moves around and past the chaos. She leads me down one corridor and up another. We walk through a large room with row after row of beds. There is moaning and crying and a stench that is not masked despite enough bleach to make my nostrils burn and my throat itch. I can't help but look at the faces of the people in the beds even though I am afraid I will see a familiar one. Mrs. Cameron presses on, and I have to hurry to keep up with her. We have left the ward room and are in a quieter hallway when Mrs. Cameron stops and looks back at me.

"You okay?" she asks.

"Yes," I say. "How do you know the way?"

"I work at the food tent here in the west camp. I came early today, before my shift started, to find your mother. I figured you would be anxious to get right to her."

"Thanks," I say. "And thanks for agreeing to chaperone me."

"Of course," she says. We walk down the hall and turn left. She stops at the second door on the right. "The nurse this morning told me she hadn't woken up yet but that she can still hear when people talk to her. Why don't you go in? I'll see if I can find a doctor or a nurse to come give you an update."

I am suddenly nervous, afraid to go in and see her. *Whatever I see*, I tell myself, *at least she is alive*. I take a deep breath and push open the door.

There are four beds. I see Mom in the one by the window on the right. I take in the sight of her head wrapped in bandages, the dark bruises under both eyes, her skin both pale and puffy. I go to her side and lift her cool, limp hand in both of mine, watching her chest rise and fall under the blankets in a slow, steady rhythm.

"Mom," I whisper, "I'm here. I'm here now, Mom."

I search her face for any flicker of a response. Nothing. I fight back tears and swallow the grief that sticks in my throat. She looks like she's sleeping. I have a strong instinct to yell and to shake her until she wakes up, but I fight it. I guess a part of me believed that when I got here and she heard my voice, she would wake up, just like a fairy tale. I feel more desperately sad and angry and scared than ever.

"Mom, you have to get better. I know you can do this. You have to do this," I say. "I love you. I love you so much!"

Behind me someone clears their throat. I hold tight to Mom's hand and tear my gaze away from her. There stands a man in blue hospital scrubs with a stethoscope around his neck. He is very still, his hands clasped in front of him, looking at me. Mrs. Cameron is beside him.

"Tic, this is Dr. Peltier. Dr. Peltier, this is Tic Brewer, Sarah's daughter," she says.

"I'm glad you could make it here, Tic. I would like to give you a full report on your mother's condition and answer any questions you have, if you are okay with that."

"Yes," I say, returning his steady gaze.

"She came in with a group evacuated from Maplewood Nursing Home. She was unresponsive upon admission, but one of the clients from Maplewood admitted here at the same time was able to give us an account of what happened to her."

"Who was it?" I ask. "I used to work there in the summers and on weekends, so I know a lot of the clients."

"Um, let me think. I can picture him. Old, obviously, and frail. He came in with galloping pneumonia. Name was Kisman, Kissey."
"Kisway!" I say.

Dr. Peltier nods.

"Is he here?"

Dr. Peltier presses his lips together tightly. "I'm afraid he passed last night."

"Oh," I say and feel a sudden stab of sorrow in my chest.

After an uncomfortable few moments Dr. Peltier continues. "Before he died, he was able to tell us that your mother and the other staff were evacuating clients up to the roof where they hoped to be rescued by helicopter. Your mother was helping another staff member carry a client in a wheelchair up the stairs. Your mother was pushing or lifting from below when the staff member above lost her grip. The wheelchair and client came crashing down half a flight of stairs on top of your mother. She hit her head and cracked some ribs but was able to get up again and make it to the roof on her own. A few hours later—"

A voice interrupts him from the loudspeakers. "Attention: Code Blue, Ward D2. Repeat: Code Blue, Ward D2." Dr. Peltier listens intently and with a curt apology takes off running from the room.

***

Question 26:

Reproductive rates have decreased since the Change because of _____.

a) A widespread availability of contraception
b) A shift in cultural norms around family size and its impact on the environment
c) Food scarcity
d) Uncertainty about the future
e) All of the above

Answer 26:

e) All of the above

As a measure to help control rising population contraception was made free and available worldwide at the beginning of the 21st century. Cultural norms also began to shift around the same time. Poor nutrition due to food scarcity decreased fertility rates and increased miscarriage rates. Many people are hesitant to bring new life into such dangerous times as now exist for humanity.

***

For the rest of the day I sit in a plastic chair at Mom's bedside, holding her hand and telling her that I love her. There is no change or response. Mrs. Cameron went to work in the food tent and told me she will come back at the end of her shift. There have been two more Code Blues since Dr. Peltier ran out. Mom's nurse explained to me that a Code Blue is when someone in the hospital dies and doctors try to resuscitate them. She said it works sometimes but even with the best medical science, many times people are just too sick and it doesn't work. Dr. Peltier came back and filled in the rest of the details about Mom's head bleed and the surgery they did yesterday to evacuate the blood that was causing pressure on her brain.

Minutes turn into hours. My stomach gurgles, reminding me that I haven't eaten yet today. I take an apple from my backpack and rub it with my shirt until it gleams. Then I take the pocketknife from my messenger bag and cut myself thin slices. The apple is gone before I know it, so I take a second from my bag and eat that one too.

At five o'clock the nurse comes in to check Mom's blood pressure and heart rate. While she is doing this Mrs. Cameron arrives and puts a hand on my shoulder. "Visiting hours are over in five minutes."

"But I have to stay with her," I say, clasping Mom's hand.

"We'll come back first thing tomorrow, Tic, okay?" Mrs. Cameron says. "Besides, you look like you could use some rest."

"But I want to stay with Mom," I say, feeling like a whiny toddler.

"I'm sorry, but there's just no way. It's against hospital policy," the nurse says, folding her arms across her chest.

"I told Ms. Hunt that I would be responsible for you, and I can't keep my word if you are here."

I rub my eyes. As stubborn as I am, I see that I have met my match in these two. I can't think of anything to say to convince them to let me stay.

Outside the hospital it's starting to get dark. People are still milling about, but now they are half-covered in lengthening shadows and it's a little spooky. We stop outside one of the big tents.

"Wait here," Mrs. Cameron instructs. "My friend Linda said she would give us a lift home. She volunteers in here. I'll run in and get her."

Mrs. Cameron leaves and I wait, looking through the open tent flap. Inside are rows of lights suspended from wires that run the length of the tent between aisles of plywood walls. Curious, I step inside. The plywood boards are covered with photos of faces in every stage of being broken. Written on each photo is a number and the word *found*, followed by a place. I begin to slowly and methodically read down one column and up the next, studying the faces of the dead. I stop at a photo that looks like my old high school principal, Mr. Shea. One of his eyes is swollen shut and the skin on that cheek is blue and caved in. It is hard to tell if it's him. I check the card next to it. The location found is New Hope Town. I taste bile in the back of my throat.

"Tic, Tic!" Mrs. Cameron says loudly to get my attention. I blink and see she is beside me with another woman, her friend Linda, I guess. "You should have waited outside," Mrs. Cameron says.

"What is this place?" I ask.

"It's a place for people to come and look for friends and family who died in the four," Linda states matter-of-factly.

"And if they find them here, then what?" I ask.

"Then we ask them to give us as much information about the person as possible for our records. As long as we have a full name, we take the picture down. It gets transferred to a list of names of deceased that's updated daily in tent sixteen," she explains.

"Wow," I say, shocked at having numbers turn into faces turn into names. "And you work here?"

She nods.

"Doesn't it bother you, all these dead people?"

Linda grimaces and shrugs. "They're dead, whether we put their pictures up here or not. At least this way—for those who find their loved ones—there is some closure. As horrible as it is, it's usually not a total shock to them, and for the vast majority, it's better than not knowing."

I am still a bit skeptical, even though it makes sense.

"For those who don't want to know, who aren't ready to know, well, it's not like we force anyone to come in here to look. It's their choice," Linda says.

                                    ***

I don't know if it's because I am tired or if all new-build towns are like this but the buildings in Arquette seem to blur together. Each is a grey replica of the next: a two-storey concrete box on stilts with metal steps leading up to a metal balcony and a second set of steps spiraling up to a door on the floor above. We stop and get out at a building that looks exactly like its neighbour's on either side. The first flight of stairs leads to the balcony and a door marked "Repair Shop." A "Closed" sign hangs in the window. I follow Mrs. Cameron up the spiral stairs to the second-storey door of their two-room apartment.

When we enter, the room feels like it is overflowing with people. Phish's twin brothers and her sister are sprawled in chairs and on the floor and in the midst of an argument about what each hates most about school. I recognize them immediately from Phish's description. Her brothers are thirteen, long and lanky, all elbows, knees, and ribs, with short, auburn hair and faces slathered in freckles. Her eleven-year-old sister is the beauty of the family, and has chestnut hair in long curls all the way down her back and skin like milk.

Phish's father is at the stove. He is tall and thin, and his neck and face are covered in a damp mix of sweat and soup steam, which he wipes periodically on his shirt sleeve as he tends to a big pot on the burner. No one stops what they are doing until Phish's mother whistles loudly and everyone turns to stare at us.

"We have a visitor. A friend of Alex's from the Academy. This is--"

"Tic," the twins say.

***

Question 27:

How much water disappears every year from the continents because of impermeable surfaces?

a) 700,000,000 cubic metres
b) 10,000,000 metres
c) 100,000 cubic metres
d) 7,000,000 cubic metres
e) None

Answer 27:

a) 700,000,000 cubic metres

Continents lose 700,000,000 cubic metres every year because of impermeable surfaces causing ocean levels to rise.

***

After we eat the soup, a tomato broth with dumplings that is spicy and filling, I power on my tablet and call Phish.

"Hi."

"What was that?" she asks.

"What?"

"*That*," she says, as if I am being obtuse. "There was a horizontal, pixelated line that flashed across the screen for a second when we connected."

"I don't know what you are talking about," I say.

"Okay, whatever, never mind," she says. "How are you doing?" Her brothers have popped up behind me, one on each side, and are now making funny faces at her over my shoulders. "Hey you clowns," Phish says. "Great to see you, now get lost."

They pretend to push each other out of the way without really doing any such thing, but then they leave to start clearing the table.

"Hi, Anna," Phish calls out. "I know you're there."

I turn the tablet around so they can see each other, and Anna waves and smiles.

"Hi, honey," her father calls out.

"Hi, Dad. Hey, Tic, you should give Lee a call, okay? He looks like a lost dog here without you, just moping around and following me everywhere, asking if I have heard from you."

"Um, yeah. I'll call him," I say.

"Why don't you go on into the bedroom for some privacy?" Mrs. Cameron suggests, and I do.

"So?" Phish asks.

"She hasn't woken up yet," I say.

"But she's stable?"

I nod.

"Do you want to talk about it?" Phish asks.

"Not now, I guess. It's kind of overwhelming. Maybe later."

"Sure," she says.

"Did you have any luck getting through to Uncle Al today?" I ask her.

"No, I couldn't reach him. I did hack into the Arquette camp registration site, though. I couldn't find his name there, which is odd because that is where most evacuees from New Hope Town have ended up."

"Oh," I say. I reach a hand down into my messenger bag and feel the smooth wood of the pocketknife he gave me. Memories of him, the way he would sigh at the end of a meal, his smell of soap and sun come flooding in. "Do you think--"

"I checked the list of those confirmed dead too, and he's not on it."

"Thanks," I say. I think about the boards in the tent and wonder if I have the strength to check them. It makes me nauseous thinking about it. Instead, I suggest, "Maybe I could go check his farm. He might still be there."

"Doubt it," she says quickly, and then, "I'm sure everyone's been evacuated. Sorry to be all negative on you, but the images I have seen of New Hope Town show that it is pretty much under water. There are roofs and shit are poking out, but I doubt any people are still there."

"Yeah, well the town is in a bit of a valley and Uncle Al's barn is high up on a hill, and it's built super strong. It doesn't usually even take any damage from a storm, so--" I stare at her, silently daring her to contradict me.

"Yeah, it could be okay," Phish says, backing down.

"Listen, I'm pretty done right now," I say, sitting down on her parents' bed. "And Phish, thanks."

"Sure, I understand."

***

It's a new day, and Mom lies unmoving in her hospital bed. I got the quick update from Dr. Peltier when I arrived this morning: "Nothing new, but keep talking to her. She can hear you." And so I try. It's hard to maintain though, hour after hour. It's hard to think of anything new to say, and I keep repeating myself.

I take a break and turn my back on her to stare out the window for a bit. I watch as parents half-heartedly drag their kids away from giant puddles. It rained last night, and undulations in the concrete field have created two shallow but wide man-made lakes. In one, a little girl with flying blond hair and bright-red rain boots is jumping up and down, making sprays of water shoot off in all directions. The other kids in the puddles are wearing anything their parents could find or nothing at all on their feet. They don't seem to care. The bright sun is painting rainbows on the wet pavement around them, and towering above the scene the panels on the solar trees have rotated east to catch the rays.

Behind me I can hear her breathing. It's the only sound she makes. The three other patients in the room are all equally silent. They haven't had any visitors, and I wonder where their families are. But I don't want to think too much about that.

I loved playing in puddles when I was little. Who doesn't? I would have killed to have ones this big to jump in. Around our house the rain sunk into the ground pretty quickly. I was always prepared though. I knew where every dip and rut was. After a storm I would typically get one good play in before the water levels dropped to the point where it wasn't worth putting my boots on. I wonder what happens to this stagnant water since it can't ever soak down into the earth. Does it all evaporate? Earlier I could see some wispy tendrils of mist rising up from the hot blacktop, which puts reminds me of Tate's white roof project. If this whole field was white instead of black, how much cooler would it be? It still wouldn't solve the problem of trapped water, though. It gets me thinking about Tate and how great he has been as my mentor these past few weeks. I am starting to understand his concern about me not returning to NESA. I can't imagine what will happen next, but whatever it is, I know I need to be with Mom.

I'm startled from my thoughts as my tablet pings with an incoming call.

"Hi," I say, studying Lee's face. I don't know why I am surprised it hasn't changed a bit when I have only been gone just over twenty-four hours. It feels like longer.

"Hi," he says. "Phish gave me the update on your Mom last night. Anything new since?"

I shake my head.

"How are you doing?"

"Oh, you know." I shrug. "I'm glad I can be here with her, but I am super worried. I just wish she would wake up."

"Sure."

Neither of us says anything, and it feels way more awkward to just be looking at each other's faces on the screen and not talking than it ever did in person. I let my gaze slide away from his over to the window. The little girl with the red boots has been pushed down by another kid and is now sitting in the puddle trying to decide if she should cry. I turn the camera on my tablet so he can see what I am seeing. I watch him take in the scene as the little girl pouts but then stands up and stomps and jumps. Her expression says that she is determined to make the biggest splash she can. "It was really depressing when I got here yesterday, but maybe I am getting used to it. It doesn't seem quite as bad this morning."

"Looks like a lot of blacktop," Lee says.

"Fact," I say. "A whole field of it."

"More money in Uncle Chris's pockets," he says with a hardness in his tone.

"What?"
"One of my uncle's companies is People's Pavers. You must have seen their trucks fixing roads right?"
"Sure," I say. "Lots. I guess since the Change roads pretty much constantly need fixing somewhere."

"Fact. Yet more people in my family are making profit from the Change. You think we're rich? We are poor compared to my uncle. People's Pavers is one of his most profitable companies, but Alpha-Omega owns dozens of companies, big and small."

I can't quite process what he just said. "Wait, what?" I say, thinking maybe I didn't hear him right.

"Tic," From behind me a hoarse but familiar voice says my name.

"Mom?"

***

Question 28:

A single hurricane can stir up millions of miles of air and can dump _____ gallons of rain in a single day.

a) 500,000
b) 1 million
c) 2.4 million
d) 2.4 billion
e) 2.4 trillion

Answer 28:

c) 2.4 trillion

A hurricane can dump as much as 2.4 trillion gallons of rain in a single day.

***

"I'm here Mom, I'm here." I grab her hand and lean over her so she can see my face from her pillow. Her eyes are blinking, tearing, squeezing shut and trying to open.

"Tic? Tic, where am I?" Her voice is hoarse and panicky. "What happened?" The look in her eyes is wild with fear.

As far as I am concerned a child should never see their parent terrified. It is horrible. Seeing her confused and frightened crumbles a small piece of my soul away. I speak to her in a soft, soothing voice. "It's okay, Mom," I tell her. "You are in a hospital, and everything is okay."
Her eyes dart all over but then settle on my face. "You're okay?" she asks, as if I was the one who had been in the four instead of her.

"Yes, I am fine." I am squeezing one of her hands with both of mine and she reaches up with the free hand to touch the bandages around her head.

"My head hurts so much," she says, and I know it must be true because Mom never complains.

"Do you want me to get the doctor?"

"Soon," she says. "First, tell me what happened."

I give her the basics as I understand them, and she closes her eyes while she listens. I am worried she is going to go unresponsive again, but then she speaks.

"What about the cottage?" she asks.

"I don't know for sure, but--" I hesitate, not wanting to upset her. She senses something and opens her eyes, mutely interrogating me. "I'm guessing it's under water. What I heard is that all of New Hope Town is under water."

"No! It can't be!" she says struggling, to sit up, but she is too weak and can't manage it. "All the money from Alpha-Omega is there."

"Wait, what?" I ask. "You mean to say they were sending you actual money? Like paper or something, not e-cash? Who does that?"

She is sobbing now. Since she had mentioned it on our last call, the thought of the money had crossed my mind. I had just assumed that she meant e-cash. That's really all anyone uses now. It's weird that anyone, especially a big company, would still send money in the mail. Money is so old fashioned that I have only seen it a few times in real life.

"It's in a watertight lockbox, Tic. Maybe it's not too late." She hurries to get the words out as she lifts her right hand off the bed, reaching for something. "The box is on the top shelf in the kitchen behind the pickled beets. The key is in my jewelry box." I would never in a million years have gone near the pickled beets, as Mom well knows. "You have to go look for it, Tic, please." Mom is starting to look frantic again, an agitation in her eyes and in the corners of her mouth. "Please," she begs. "Promise me you will at least go look. Promise!" And then her eyes roll back in her head and her whole body starts to shake. She is convulsing so hard I am worried she will fall off the bed.

I throw myself on top of her, trying to pin her down. "Help!" I yell. "Help! Help! Help!"

I ride out her bucking and thrashing, my eyes squeezed shut, all my focus on my body on top of her body. And I keep yelling. I only stop when a pair of hands grabs my shoulders and pulls me off. Two nurses are holding her down now while a third draws medication up into a syringe. The doctor who pulls me off is barking orders. Almost as soon as the needle goes in, she stops seizing. I watch as the doctor pries her mouth open and shoves a tube down her throat.

"Bag her," he commands, and a nurse starts squeezing a balloon attached to the tube. "Everyone ready? Good, let's roll!" He points to the door and they pull and push the bed on wheels towards it.

I am standing still, and I think they have forgotten about me until the doctor turns to me on his way out.

"We have to take her back to the OR and then she'll be in the ICU. Go get some rest, and we'll call you when you can see her again. It'll be a while." And then they are all gone. The space where she was, where her bed was, is blank.

I stumble through hospital corridors without paying attention until eventually, somehow, I am outside. People of the camp continue about their business, but I feel as if I am watching them on a screen with the sound turned off. Mrs. Cameron and I rode bikes here this morning. We parked them in the bike rack beside the hospital. I walk over and find Phish's purple bike. I unlock it and walk it to where the camp meets the road.

"Promise," Mom had said.

I mount the bike and ride east.

***

Question 29:

What percentage of our country's annual sales of non-consumable goods are made from recycled materials?

a) 15%
b) 33%
c) 50%
d) 70%
e) 100%

Answer 29:

d) 70%

Currently seventy percent of goods sold are refurbished, reused, or made out of recycled materials. The goal is to increase this to as close to one hundred percent as possible.

***

I bike along the main road, heading east for several hours. It's cool and clear, and there are hardly any buildings or other travelers. Or maybe there are. I'm not really paying attention. All I can do is push down on the pedals again and again, wondering, *is she in the operating room now? What about now? Now?* I need to keep peddling to get as close as I can before nightfall. I need, I need…I need to take a break for a few minutes.

I grab a piece of shade under a tree near the road and drink half of the warm water from a bottle that was in the bottle cage on Phish's bike. I pull out my tablet, suddenly worried that maybe I missed a call from the hospital. Maybe there was an update on Mom.

No. No missed calls, but two messages from Phish. The first one is several hours old and says, *Lee told me the good news about your Mom waking up!!!* ☺. The second message is from Phish about twenty minutes ago and just says, *Call me ASAP.*

I don't call her. Instead I make sure the volume is all the way up, in case the hospital does call, and then I put the tablet back in my bag. I simply can't waste precious daylight talking to Phish. I apologize to her in my head as I remount the bike and continue peddling east.

Luckily there is still some daylight left when I finally stop. The air smells of wet decay, creeping fungus, and salt. Two hundred yards before the water line the road itself is still clear, but to each side of it are mounds of debris. I straddle the bike and look around. A tire, a car door, and a toilet lie heaped together. Sticks poke out at odd angles, and clothes hang limply like flags of lost countries. Another pile consists of a mattress, its springs sprung, draped over a fridge, and a grimy blue, plastic playhouse large enough for a toddler or a small dog. Soon enough all this junk will be reclaimed: a small amount by individual scavengers, but most by large companies contracted by the government who will come with dump trucks to haul it away for refurb. After that a fence will go up. This is the new Edge.

Just off the road to my left is a trailer. An old, red pickup truck and a new, white van are parked on the dirt beside it. The door is half-open, and I can hear two men talking inside. I wonder if I should go in, introduce myself, explain what I want to do, and ask for help. I am not sure how receptive they would be to my plan, though, so I keep listening.

"Things quieting down here then, Joe?" one man asks.

"Yup. The first day was plenty busy. Boats bringing people in and buses and ambulances carting them off. I didn't catch two winks the first day, Frank. Then, too, all sorts of folks comin' in here and asking questions, wanting to borrow a boat to go out and have a look, for something or someone. They need to be convinced to let the rescue team go about their work and just wait. They just get in the way and then need to be rescued themselves."

I hear the word *boat,* and I think *Jackpot!* Silence is interrupted by slurping. Then I hear rustling movements inside.

"I should head off and bring what supplies I brought to the search team out there. Do you want to come with?"

"Yup. Let's take the biggest boat out back. It should fit everything okay."

I crouch behind the nearest pile of junk and watch as two men in plaid shirts come out of the trailer. They open the rear doors of the van and carry an assortment of bags and boxes from the van to a boat, which must be tied behind the trailer. When they are finished, one comes back to lock the van while the other pulls the boat's engine to life.

I wait until the sound of the engine has vanished in the distance, and then I wait a little longer trying to decide. Based on what I overheard, I am glad I decided not to barge right in and ask for help as there is clearly no way they would have let me take a boat out. I do desperately need a boat, though, if I am going to get to where our house is: east of here and probably under water.

I could try picking my way along the new Edge, looking for an abandoned craft, but what are the chances I would find one? Also, who knows how long that would take? I want to get back to the hospital as soon as I can. I am definitely leaning towards "borrowing" a boat, but that means I had better get going soon, before they get back and before it gets dark out. I have never taken something that didn't belong to me before. I feel guilty that I don't feel the least bit guilty doing it. Does that make me a bad person? I could leave a note in the trailer, but then they might send a search crew out for me, and that could prove inconvenient if they find me before I find the house.

I head for the trailer, hoping to find anything there that might be a help to me. Hey, if I am already "borrowing" a boat I might as well see if there is anything else I need, right? The door of the trailer is still half-open, and it squeaks on rusty hinges as I go in. The smell of coffee is inviting. I see a brown coffee mug with a rainbow on it and a white mug with a cartoon mouse on it standing side by side on a table littered with charts and maps. The cups have been drained, so I put them aside and examine the maps on the table more closely. They show the Eastern Edge in different levels of detail. Some look pretty old, but thankfully many have dates on them. I find one that has New Hope Town on it dated just a few months before the storm. Using this as a guide I am able to find other maps that I feel represent the same general area but no longer show any evidence of New Hope Town. These are dated and timestamped for the last few days. Judging by the timestamps it looks like they are updated every twelve hours.

I take two maps from the mess on the table: one showing New Hope Town before the four and one from twenty-four hours ago. There's one from twelve hours ago, but if there are differences I can't see them, and I figure the most recent one is the most likely to be needed and missed. I fold them and put them in my bag. I feel a gnawing in my stomach and, looking around the tight quarters, I see a pot on the stove. I grab a spoon from the sink and help myself to cold vegetable soup. When the pot is almost empty I tip it up to my lips and drink the dregs before replacing it on the stove. I take two apples and a canteen of water from a small fridge. I put one apple in each of my hoodie's pockets, and I jam the canteen into my messenger bag. I can zip it closed, but it's tight. I look around at the piles of electronic equipment, all switches and knobs and numbers. A large screen is half-hidden behind a makeshift clothesline with three men's wool socks dangling from it. Messages are flashing on it. Time to take off.

Behind the trailer along the water's edge is a row of metal stakes sunk deep into the mucky earth. Each stake has several small crafts tied to it, rowboats and canoes mostly and a few kayaks. I untie one of several identical navy-blue fiberglass canoes. Tucked under the seat is a paddle, a life jacket, and a long coil of rope. I drag the canoe into the brackish water and get in, setting a course parallel to the shoreline. The water is calm here. There are no waves to speak of and as I paddle over this flooded land, I am making good progress. I wonder if the men will notice the missing canoe. If it's dark when they get back, they probably won't bother counting boats. They would have no reason to. At least that's what I tell myself.

Twenty minutes later the last bit of daylight is gone, and I stop and pull up onto the saturated shore under a copse of tall trees to wait out the night. I tie up to an overhanging branch, and I climb a small embankment and walk a few yards farther inland. The ground is soft and damp, and I stop under a big tree.

I consider my options: I can sleep in the tree or on the ground. First of all I would have to climb the tree in the dark since I don't see how I could hold my tablet with its flashlight and climb at the same time. I have read about people sleeping in trees, and they often tie a rope around themselves so if they roll over in the middle of the night and fall out, the rope catches them. They would still fall part way, which I guess is better than falling all the way, but it sounds unpleasant. The damp ground is looking more attractive all the time. I go back to the canoe and get the life vest. It makes a nice waterproof cushion to sit on as I lean back against the tree.

Question 30:

Pine beetles _____.

a) Kill pine trees by the millions
b) Are only killed by cold
c) Have contributed to the Change
d) Are benefiting from the Change
e) All of the above

Answer 30:

e) All of the above

Pine beetles represent the largest forest insect blight in North America and have significantly affected the capability of northern forests to remove CO_2 from the atmosphere. Where they used to only do damage for a small part of each year and then die with the colder weather now, with warmer temperatures, they are active year round.

***

I have camped before with Uncle Al, but I have never spent the night outdoors alone so far from any other people. The glowing light from my tablet's screen only makes the darkness around me feel thicker and more closed in. In an instant I am a bit less lonely as Phish's worried face fills the screen.

"What the blank's going on? Are you okay?"

"I'm okay, okay?" I say.

"You're sure?" she asks.

"Yeah, I'm sure. It's just what happened was--"

"STOP!"

I am so startled that I stop talking and my jaw hangs open. I snap it shut. What has gotten into Phish?

"I'm going to send you a message. Now. Read it," Phish orders and then abruptly ends our video chat.

Immediately there is a new message from her in my inbox. I open it and find nothing but a link. I follow it to another link and another. Finally, the trail ends and I am on an ancient e-mail server. There's a single button on it labelled CREATE ACCOUNT. This is bizarre, but aside from calling her back, I don't see what else there is to do, so I create an account. I message her NESA account from my newly created "prehistoric account:"

???
Xo, Tic

Phish's response is immediate:

You have a stalker.
Xo, Phish

I respond:

Explain.

I wait a bit longer, and finally Phish messages me back:

Remember yesterday when we video-chatted and there was a flash of a line right at the start of the call? You didn't see it, or register seeing, it I guess, but I was sure I saw it. And I saw it again when we just chatted. I did some research as to why that would happen. It could be a technical glitch, but it had never happened to me before, so I did some more digging. It could also happen if someone is recording or tapping your calls, in other words spying on you. I traced the record of our call back into the server and sure enough I could see that a third party had been online with us. I checked records of my other calls, and that never happened before. I didn't check records of your other calls yet because I would have to go into your account to do it and didn't know if you wanted me to or not. Do you?

So then I was starting to get all paranoid and wondering if whoever is listening in is also reading your written messages. (Is it paranoia if someone really is stalking you?) But I would also have to go into your account to check on this, and believe me, I was tempted. Do you want me to?

In the meantime, I figured the safer thing was to assume that your messages are being read too, so I had you create an account on an outside server. I can't guarantee this is safe, but I feel better about it. I think it is safe enough, for now anyway.

So, aside from the questions above about entering your account, here are two that are burning a hole in my brain right now:

1) Do you have any idea who is stalking you and why?
2) Where are you?

Love, Phish

I have to read it a few times. I just can't believe that someone would be spying on me. It seems pretty unrealistic. I consider the possibility that Phish has gone bonkers, but that seems unlikely too. I look out into the darkness and wonder if someone is watching me even now. I shiver and then type my response.

This is pretty crazy. You know that, right? Why would anyone spy on me? I have no deep, dark secrets, I swear! Yes, you have my permission to go into my account and snoop.

As to where I am—I am not sure exactly, but I can tell you that I am fine and that I will be back in Arquette tomorrow. Please tell your mother that I'm really sorry and I will explain later.

Love, Tic

P.S. Maybe you should fill Lee in on all of this.

I send and wait. I listen to all the noises of the night. The gentle lapping of the water against the side of my canoe, the leathery flap of bat wings, and the low bass croaking of frogs contribute to a chorus that might have been soothing if I hadn't caught Phish's paranoia.

OK. In the meantime, I will do some more research on the Haley case and see if I can figure out where he is serving his sentence and if it is possible to be in touch with him. I am dying to know what he was doing there. Do you think it is related to your dad?

***

Surprisingly, I fell asleep pretty fast, but I wake to the sensation of being lightly tickled on my cheek. I brush at the spot. I feel something hard and mobile and alive on my face and go from half-asleep to hyper-awake. I am not a wimp about insects usually, but I do *not* like them crawling on me in my sleep. I wipe at my cheek again until I manage to fling it off. Eyes open now, I look down and see almost every inch of my pants and sweatshirt are covered in a black, shiny, shifting mass of beetles. I jump up and brush them off with panicked swipes. The mindless creatures fall off me and lose interest. They are attacking the birch tree en masse. They swarm it, single-minded in their voraciousness, eating its skin and boring into its woody flesh.

I grab the life vest and shake the beetles off of it. The canoe is right where I left it. I untie it and paddle out a few strokes before stopping to study the trees. In the grey dawn light I see that very few of the trees have green leaves or needles on them. On some the foliage has turned a burnt-orange colour, and others are bleached a pallid grey. If they weren't so damp from the storm, they would be a fire hazard. These trees could have been pulling carbon dioxide from the atmosphere. What a waste. Stupid fucking insects!

I eat one apple, saving the other for later, while I look at the maps I borrowed from the trailer. When I am as sure as I am going to be about directions I start paddling east. The sky is overcast, and a warm wind is blowing in fits and starts as if it can't quite decide what to do. The water is choppy, and I'm going slower than I had hoped. It doesn't help that

I'm hungry, thirsty, and anxious. I hope I can find New Hope Town. Even with the maps, everything looks so similar and so different that I can easily imagine getting lost. The sky is worrying me too. If it starts to rain and really blow, then what? I'm tired, and I've worked up a sweat when I see a familiar landmark. The billboard stands like a beacon, still well above the waterline, pointing the way to R.W. Salvage: "Everything you need, and more!"

I think of Lee. Before you know it his family's boats will be here scavenging, their divers pillaging New Hope Town, swimming through my old school, through our cottage. Just thinking about it, I feel violated. But at least I know the way home from here from a hundred shopping trips with Mom. I should know the way home from here. That is when it really hits me. Now that I finally know exactly where I am I know what it's supposed to look like. I should be able to see the town, the homes, the cluster of buildings around the main square, the high school off in the distance. Instead, all I see as my canoe lifts up and down on the wavelets are dark islands poking through. I paddle up to the nearest one. The roof of this home is only half there, the other half caved in under a tree that carelessly pokes from the attic, it's shattered trunk stabbing upwards. Seeing it with my own eyes makes it real: New Hope Town is truly gone. Blinking furiously, I turn from the sign and pour my anger into every stroke, beating the water with my paddle as I flee the stupid, overbearing sign.

***

Question 31:

How are people killed in hurricanes?

a) Drowning from storm surges and flooding
b) Trauma from flying debris
c) Electrocution from downed powerlines
d) Gas or electrical fires
e) All of the above

Answer 31:

e) All of the above

Additionally, many people die of starvation and illness in the days and weeks following a storm.

***

It is harder than usual to find my way home, with the roads and most of the familiar buildings underwater. Random junk floats and bobs on the surface, and I push it aside with my paddle. Wooden spoons and plastic toys have lost their way, lost their meaning. It's hard to imagine that just last week these exact items were being held and used, some of them by people I know and not by strangers. I can't help but wonder what happened to them: Ms. Kindle, the lunch lady at school; Bernadette, the charge nurse at Maplewood; Diane and Jeanne; Nick, our high school QB; and Mr. B. and all of my other teachers. Who made it out okay? How many didn't?

I have to focus hard to keep heading east, and I look at treetops and rooftops for some guidance. Finally I see the band of treetops in the distance that are all that is left of the "dark woods," where I broke my collarbone just a few months ago. As I get closer I see that from the top branches of my maple tree a few withered leaves hang on desperately despite the fact that they are doomed to fall. The roof of our cottage is intact, poking out above the water. I'm home.

I push the top pane of the attic window down and carefully shimmy and slide my way in. I land on my desk. I have the rope for the canoe in one hand and I tie it to the curtain rod. Water blankets my bedroom floor. My desk chair has fallen over, and the sides of my quilt are darkened where they rest in the water, but otherwise my room looks unchanged. I wish everything was unchanged. I wish I could go back in time and be waking up here with Mom downstairs cooking breakfast and telling me to hurry up. It's still so hard to believe that New Hope Town is gone and Mom is in the camp hospital. I slosh around my room, touching things, trying to convince myself that this is real. I open the dresser drawers and my old sweaters and socks are in their same tidy piles. The stuffed tiger I loved as a little girl sits on my pillow mocking me with his orange glass eyes and sewed-on smile.

I put my bag on my desk. I take off my sweatshirt, track pants, and wet socks and shoes. In just my T-shirt and underwear, goosebumps prickling my arms, I slowly descend the attic stairs until I am standing in cold water up to my shoulders. I stop and give myself a three-second count and duck under. I come up again a second later hair plastered to my head. I take a deep breath and dive under, swimming down the staircase to the main floor.

The only light comes down the stairs behind me and is hardly enough to see by. I shouldn't need it though. I spent my whole life until recently in this room. I swim through it and that in itself is surreal. I'm glad it's dark down here. I wouldn't want to see any more than what I already can. I want to see less. The rickety kitchen table is upended, as is the blue chair, and I am tempted to set them upright again. But to what purpose? Our few belongings are scattered all over as if someone picked up our little house and shook it like a child's toy, a snow globe, and grew bored and set it down. I swim over to the kitchen shelves and, even though so many other things have fallen off, the beets still sit solidly, exactly where they always have. I move them aside and find the lockbox right where Mom said it would be. I swim back up to my bedroom with my treasure.

On the steps I stand half-in and half-out of the water, and as I look at the lockbox I realize that I will need the key. That means another trip downstairs, which I am not excited about. It's cold and dark and it creeps me out, but I don't have a choice. I leave the box on my dresser and go back down the stairs. I take another big breath and swim to the only other room on the main floor, Mom's bedroom. With no light at all from the attic stairs creeping in here, it is much darker than the main room. I swim over to her bedside table, fumble open the drawer, and take Mom's jewelry box. I got what I came for and am more than ready to get out of here. There is a pressure in my chest as I swim one last time through the main room wishing I could salvage more, but where would I start? Where would I stop?

Upstairs I change into dry clothes from my dresser and sit on my bed holding Mom's jewelry box. I stare at the swirling engraved letters of her name on the lid. I went through a phase where I liked to play dress-up, and Mom indulged me, to a point. Her jewelry was always strictly off limits. Mom used to say that this was her "bank," which is kind of ironic now that I know it held the key to her other bank on the bed with me too. I lose some time thinking about her, wondering how she is, how the surgery went.

Eventually I shake myself out of it and come back to my room, with the jewelry box in my hands. Mom never wears any jewelry except her wedding ring. She used to have two other rings, a string of pearls, and a pair of sapphire earrings. Over the years when money was tight, she sold them all, one at a time. For a few years now there has been only a necklace with a gold pendant left in the "bank." Mom says it isn't worth much and that it's got more sentimental value than anything, and that's why she hasn't bothered to sell it.

I open the box. It is empty except for the pendant necklace and the key for the lockbox. I pick up the pendant, which I haven't seen in years, and idly play with the chain while I stare at the key. I'm stalling. On one hand I am excited to open the lockbox to see if it is dry inside. It must be. I can already imagine how thrilled Mom will be if it is. I am also beyond curious to know how much money we are talking about. On the other hand if it's soaked, if it's ruined and I have to tell Mom, she will be devastated. I look down at the pendant and am so shocked I drop it on the bed like a hot ember. I pick it up again gingerly and bring it close to see every detail that I can.

The design carved on it is a sun with squiggly lines in the middle that look vaguely like continents. It is the sun and the earth combined. It is Lee's tattoo. This is so beyond! I thought Lee said this tattoo was some family thing that his uncle made up. Why does my mom have it on a necklace? Is she—are we—related to Lee? Shit! Have I been sleeping with a long-lost cousin or something? She told me that all of her family died in a storm in New York while she was away at university. I grab my tablet to call Lee when I remember about the stupid spying business. Maybe I will message him from my prehistoric email account instead.

As soon as I open the account I see there's a new message from Phish marked urgent, so I figure I better look at that first.

ALL of your video chats were tapped. ALL of your written messages through NESA were also being copied by a third party. Also, your tablet's search history was totally readable. Sorry. These messages are safe so far I think, but it will be harder for me to tell if they become compromised because they are on an outside server, not the NESA system. Anyone who reads the message with the link I sent you and follows it will figure out what we are up to. I think the safest bet is for me to create a new student at NESA and then you can reset your tablet as the new student. That way I have a better chance of seeing if anything through NESA is compromised. All you need is a new thumbprint (lucky for you, you have two) and a new student name. Since I am doing the programming, I will choose a new name for you. I choose--Joni Taylor.

Give me until 2pm today and then use a small, pointy object (paper clip, hairpin) to push the tiny reset button in (it's next to the power button but smaller). When you power on, it will ask you to swipe your thumb (use your right one this time!) and type your new name.

P.S. You should still use your Tic account some, too. It would be totally suspicious if all of a sudden Tic Brewer didn't exist. Or I hope it would anyway since I have no clue where you are and what you are up to.

P.P.S. I still haven't found out any more about Uncle Al.

***

Question 32:

Packs of wild dogs _____.

a) Have been found close to every major city
b) Are known to attack, kill, and eat humans
c) Are believed to have been pets
d) a & c
e) All of the above

<u>Answer 32:</u>

e) All of the above

As pet owners have become unable to sustain their own basic needs, have become climate refugees, or have died, their pets have become feral. For this reason, owning pets—although not illegal—is regarded as irresponsible.

***

Crap! I was still holding on to a lot of hope that Phish would track down Uncle Al. It starts me worrying about him all over again. I think about the board of faces and suddenly I am tearing up. I don't want to give up hope. This is where my whole life was and now it lies around me in ruins, my little bedroom, my things, like a slap in the face, they are so meaningless compared to Mom, Uncle Al, and Ruthie. I can't give up yet. Maybe…Why not? I am so close I should be able to row over to his place in no time. It's not likely he's there, but you never know. He hasn't turned up anywhere else, so it's worth looking. I could also check up in his loft for my dad's box. If it is there this might be my last chance to get it. I am getting hungry and briefly consider going back for the beets, but then again they're pickled beets. I think I would rather starve.

I'll open the box later. I put the key to the lockbox on the chain of the necklace with the pendant, and fasten it around my neck. Lockbox in hand I climb out the window and into the canoe. The treetops of the "dark woods" separating our properties are above water, and I decide it will be easier and quicker to go around them instead of trying to navigate through. As I round the edge of the woods on the far side I feel vindicated. Just like I told Phish, Uncle Al's barn is still there. The water comes up the hill to within a few feet of the ramp, but the barn itself sits high and dry on six-foot concrete pylons. I am so excited to see it I do a fist pump and the canoe rocks.

With new energy I pull deep and long with my paddle, left, left, right, right, getting closer with each pull. Is there something off about the barn? It takes me another two strokes to figure it out: there is smoke snaking out of the ventilation ducts. I don't understand, but I am propelled by anxiety, and I don't even feel the last few strokes that bring me forcefully up against the hill. I pull the canoe out of the water and sprint.

The barn door is barred from the outside, but my collarbone has healed and I have no trouble now using both hands to lift the beam off its U-hook and pull the door open. I take a step back and then a cautious, curious step forward. Even though I am still outside on the ramp I can feel the heat radiating from the interior, and some coils of smoke sail out the top of the open door. How is there a fire inside? Is it related to the four? That was over three days ago. How—

My thoughts are interrupted by the vision of a large body emerging from the smoky barn door. "Ruthie!" I cry. She crashes into me and I sit down. "Good dog," I say again and again, running my hands through her fur, petting and scratching her. She enjoys it for a moment and then turns and heads back up the ramp. "No Ruthie," I say grabbing her collar to pull her away. "No. Not safe."

But she is so much dog that she is the one pulling me as I hang onto her collar. I let go and she heads straight through the door. I follow her in. It's wicked hot and the unmistakable voice of a fire is crackling up in the loft above us. Luckily most of the smoke is heading up and out of the ventilation ducts that are spaced every three feet along the walls where they meet the roof. Where is this dumb beast going and how am I going to get her to leave with me? I am sure I can't last very long in here.

I grab her again and only manage to slow down her progress. She continues moving forward until she comes to a full stop at one of the posts that runs the length of the barn to hold up the loft. What? Why? And then I see why.

"No!" I let go of Ruthie's collar and crouch down close. "Uncle Al," I gasp. He's lying on his side, eyes closed, not moving. I shake him and yell, "Wake up! Wake up!"

He moans and opens one eye a crack. When he sees my face up close to his he opens his eye wider. "Tic," he says and starts to cough. He turns his head and I see his other eye is swollen shut. He tries to move, to sit up I think, but is pulled back down to the lying position. His arms are pulled behind his back. Why?

I crawl around behind him. His hands are tied to the post. I try to pull at the knots, but they won't give. I try harder, but it seems hopeless. The ropes are tied too tight. I am not going to be able to untie him. I can't leave him here, though. I can't! I won't!

I reach into my bag and feel for the pocketknife. My fingers find it and pull it out. I squeeze and the blade flips open. It's as sharp as the day Uncle Al gave it to me. In a minute I have sawed through the rope and he is free.

"C'mon," I say. "Let's get out of here."

I help him to stand up. He grimaces and grabs onto the post as his right leg almost gives. There is a big, dark blotch on his thigh that doesn't look good, but we both know we have to get out of here, now. He leans a hand on my shoulder and, using me as a crutch, we follow Ruthie out of the barn.

Outside, we sit down beside the canoe, close to the water's edge, gulping in the fresh air.

"Are you okay?" I ask.

"I am now," he says, rubbing his wrists where the rope dug into his skin. "What are you doing here, Tic? Where's your mother?"

"I'll explain later. What happened in there?"

"I was waiting things out in the barn because I didn't want to leave the cows. I had more than enough supplies for them and me, for a few more days, anyway. I just didn't want to leave them, you know?"

I can absolutely believe that. Uncle Al loves his cows and would do just about anything for them. "But the fire? The rope? I don't understand," I say.

He starts to answer and then starts coughing and can't stop. He wraps his right arm around his left ribs to try and hold his chest still as tears stream out of his good eye. When he finally stops he says, "It's because of your father, Tic."

***

Question 33:

Describe as many uses as you can for a sweatshirt.

Answer 33:

Answers may include but are not limited to the following: a bag, a pillow, a flag, a head covering, a towel for dusting/cleaning or drying, cut into strips to make ties, or braid strips to make a rope

"What!" I say. "What does my dad have to do with this?" I look behind us at the barn. The wood of the roof is finally starting to catch and flames are licking up and out the top.

"They were looking for his stuff," Uncle Al says.

"Who was looking for it? Wait, was it there? Did they get it?" My thoughts are so mixed together I am having a hard time getting the words out coherently. All the while I keep looking back at the burning barn.

"Two guys. I don't know who they were. Ruthie and I were catching up on paperwork in that old stall that I converted to my office, when she started growling. I got up and as soon as I opened the door to the drive bay, I heard them too. They were heading right for the loft ladder, their city shoes clacking on my old timber boards like tap dancin'. I asked if I could help them and they sure seemed surprised to see me there. I didn't know if they were a rescue squad or thieves, but before I could ask anything else, they came at me.

"Ruthie went for the shorter one's leg. The taller one pulled a knife. When he came at me, I blocked his first swipe." He says this proudly, and even though he is old, I think he really is tough. "I missed blocking his second one. I almost blocked him though, almost." He looks at his leg. There's blood all around a big gash in his jeans over his right thigh. It's so horrible I don't want to look, but I can't seem to look away. "After that I sort of collapsed. He kicked me a few times and then I must have lost consciousness for a minute.

When I came to, they were tying me to the post. I don't know what happened to Ruthie. I couldn't see her."

Ruthie is lying beside me, and I pat her head and scratch her neck. I will have to check her over and see if she is hurt, but for now I am all ears as Uncle Al continues.

"They went up to the loft, and I'm guessing they poured gasoline all over. Then they set it on fire and came down the ladder. When they walked passed me I heard the shorter fellow say something about how Jim Brewer's stuff could burn with all the other crap, and then they left."

"So, my dad's stuff was up there," I say, swallowing. Disappointment sits like a stone in my stomach.

He shakes his head. "Nah, I kept your dad's stuff in the bottom drawer of my desk. I was thinking you might want it some—Hey, what's a matter?"

I don't answer him. Instead I jump up and start racing back towards the heat and the smoke in the barn. I hear Uncle Al calling after me to stop, but I don't listen. I have to try. Because someone bothered to set the barn on fire and almost kill Uncle Al to destroy it. Because it might explain the message on the back of the photo. Because he was my dad and this was his.

The smoke is starting to accumulate now inside the barn. There's too much of it to flow out of the vents and I can hardly see. The heat is smothering. A section of the loft has collapsed and the fire is feeding on the dry timber of the stalls on the main floor. I feel my way along the wall until I reach the door to Uncle Al's office.

Once inside, I close the door. Thankfully, Uncle Al put in a window when he turned this into his office. It is closed and dirty, but it means that I have some light in here. There's a wall of filing cabinets, a chair, and a big, old oak desk with three drawers. I open the largest drawer on the bottom and pull out a flask, a scarf, and a framed photo. I hold the photo near the window and in the fuzzy light see Aunt Mary holding a bouquet and smiling at the camera. I put it on his desk and pull out the last thing in the drawer, a box marked "BREWER" on the lid. I don't have time to look through it now, but I open it just for a second to put the picture of Aunt Mary in.

A roar fills my ears and the floorboards beneath me vibrate. I peek out the office door and am staring at a bonfire that's fallen from above just a few feet from me. I grab the box off the desk and take a single step outside the office door. If I stick close to the wall I can skirt around the flames. But I am frozen on the threshold. The damn heat feels like it's cooking my face, and I have a brief flashback to the burns on Lee's back. I step back. There has to be another way. Think. Think. The flames are hypnotic. I can't look away. I can't think. I can't breathe. I feel so tired. I want to sit down. No, this can't be how it ends! I hug the box close to my chest and wheel back into Uncle Al's office, closing the door behind me. And then it is so obvious.

I put the box on his desk and use both hands to slide the window open. Even though I am on the main floor of the barn, it sits on six-foot pylons, so it will be a bit of a drop, but nothing I can't handle. As gently as I can I drop the box out the window. I slip one leg over the windowsill and, sitting astride it, slip the other over so I am sitting on the ledge. I bring my right arm across my body and grab the ledge a foot past my left hand. I turn myself to face the building and let my legs hang. I lower myself until I am dangling from my fingertips and then I let go.

***

Question 34:

How many species of plants, insects, birds, and mammals become extinct every day?

a) 2
b) 50
c) 200
d) 500
e) 1,000

Answer 34:

d) 500

An estimated 500 species become extinct every day. This does not include microbes and fungi, which are also losing diversity at an alarming rate.

***

I land on my hands and knees, grab the box, and am up and moving. I turn the corner around to the front of the barn and pull up short, shocked. Uncle Al is crawling, dragging his right leg, towards the entrance of the barn. Before I can say anything, he collapses face-down in the dirt. As I rush to him I see a dark-red trail streaking the dirt behind him.

"Uncle Al," I cry, "I'm here! I'm out." I sit down beside him and see shimmering beads of sweat on his ash-white face. He is breathing but unconscious. I look down at his leg and gasp at the blood oozing out. I need to stop the flow now.

I take off my hoodie and wrap it around his thigh, above the gash. I tie a knot, pulling it as tight as I can. The oozing slows but doesn't stop. I think I need to get it tighter. I run down to my canoe and grab the paddle. It's a bit big and unwieldy, but I am able to tie the knot around it and twist. As I am tightening it, Uncle Al rouses briefly. He is mumbling and I am shushing him, trying to soothe, trying to focus. His eyes find mine for a minute, and he seems surprised. His face relaxes as he lapses back into unconsciousness. Finally, the bleeding stops.

I think briefly about trying to get him in the canoe and rowing him to shore, but I am worried I won't be able to lift him in or wake him enough to get him in. Plus I would still have to find my way back to a piece of shore where there is a road or people nearby, and I am not sure I can do that. Not quickly, anyway. The maps in my bag would help, but I am really worried about him, about how much blood he has lost, about losing him. I pull out my tablet to call for help, figuring I can always try plan B if I don't get a quick response.

As I am about to power it on I stop. Like a punch in the gut, I remember. Someone was recording all of my video chats.

It seemed crazy paranoid. Except now as I look up at the barn fully engulfed in flames and Uncle Al dying next to me, it seems very, very real. Mom and I had talked about Dad's stuff being in the barn's loft. Not only that, but the timing suggests that whoever was spying knew I was in Arquette and that I was looking for Uncle Al. They must have decided to act before I had a chance to come explore. I look at my dad's box on the ground beside us. Whatever is in there, someone was hoping to destroy it and was willing to kill in the process. They, whoever "they" are, now believe Dad's stuff is burned and Uncle Al is dead.

I hope that Phish was able to do her magic. I have to call for help no matter what, but I would rather "they" didn't know I was ever here. I pull out my pocketknife and gently use the tip of the blade to exert pressure on the reset button. The screen goes blank for a few anxious moments and then the NESA logo appears. Under the logo is a box and the instructions to place my thumb on it for five seconds. I use my right thumb. After five seconds I am asked to type in my name. I type "Joni Taylor," which feels pretty weird, but whatever. It works! I say a silent thank you to Phish.

I call the emergency rescue line, and after two pings a middle-aged man with black-framed glasses and a bright-red sweater fills the screen. I explain the situation and where we are. He confirms that rescue ships are in the area and can be here in twenty minutes. I turn the camera so he can see Uncle Al, the tourniquet, and the wound. He has me count his heartbeats, which are faint and fast at one hundred and thirty. I don't want to leave Uncle Al's side, but I do for just a moment to run down to the canoe and get Mom's lockbox. I hear the faint hum of the boat in the distance. I have a brief moment of panic, irrationally worried that the spies have come back, until I see the white flag with the red cross on it. I breathe a sigh of relief.

The medics get Uncle Al on a stretcher and carry him on board first. I trail behind carrying my dad's box and the lockbox. I keep looking back at the barn feeling like I am forgetting something.

"Ruthie!" I shout. I drop both boxes, turn and run away from the rescue boat, back towards the barn. "Ruthie! Ruthie!" It doesn't make sense. She should have been right beside us this whole time. It's not like there is anywhere for her to go here. This is just a little mound of land sitting above water with a barn on it. Could she be hiding under the barn?

One of the rescue works grabs me by the arm and pulls me back as I try to get closer. "Stop," he says.

I try to shake his hand off my arm. "My dog," I gasp by way of explanation. Surely this man will understand I need to find Ruthie and he'll let go of me. He doesn't, though.

"You can call her, but you are going to have to move back. Way back. That barn is going to collapse and it's not safe to be this close."

"But—" I look at him now, pleading with my eyes.

"I'm sorry. I really am, kid, but if your dog's in there, she isn't coming out."

"You don't understand," I say struggling against him, trying to pull my arm free.

"Ruthie went back in there to save me. I have to get her out…"

I am cut off by a loud boom as something inside the barn crashes. Even as I turn to see the sparks flying high into the air the rescue worker is pulling me further away from the barn.

"No!" I cry as I stop struggling and give into his will. I know he is right, even though I don't want to believe it and I can't breathe. He lets go of his grip on my arm, and I don't move. Something has just left me, just washed right out of me. I don't know what it is, but I feel empty and tired.

"We need to get your uncle to a hospital," the rescue worker says gently. He puts an arm around my shoulder and walks with me down to the boat.

***

From the boat I watch the barn become smaller and smaller until finally it disappears from sight. I will never see it again. I will never see Ruthie again. Images of her float into and out of focus--her big head on my lap as I sit reading on the porch, her shaking off after we washed her, spraying water everywhere, even her knocking Phish down.

We are transferred to an ambulance heading back to the hospital in Arquette. Since the surgery was yesterday I hope that Mom will be awake when we get there. I can't wait to show her the lockbox, which is on the floor between my feet. I haven't opened it, but by now I guess I have more or less decided to wait until I am with Mom. I feel like maybe she should be the one who opens it. Whatever is in there, dry or not, we will face it together. The second box, Dad's box, is in my lap. I am both desperate and afraid to open it, wondering what it could contain that has led to such violence and destruction. But I don't open it either. Not yet. Not in the back of this ambulance with the EMT watching me.

Uncle Al hasn't woken up yet, but they have assured me his vital signs are stable. They insisted I use an oxygen mask and started an intravenous line, but I refused any painkillers or sedatives. I tell myself that it is because I need to be alert in case Uncle Al wakes. I need to be alert for when we get there and I see Mom. But the truth is that I don't want to be separate from any part of my pain right now. Even the pain of losing Ruthie is still a way of holding on to her.

I should video chat with Phish and Lee, but I don't know if I am up for it, and I figure I will wait until I look a little less "medical." At least I can safely send a message. I copy both of them on it.

Heading back to Arquette now. It's been quite the day.

I tell them everything that happened from when my mom woke up to the present. I leave out Mom's pendant as I am pretty sure Lee wouldn't have told Phish about his tattoo, but I will definitely ask him about it later. I finish by promising them I will video chat once I have seen Mom.

It's almost dark when we arrive at the hospital. The EMTs bustle efficiently around us, handing our IV bags over to orderlies, turning off and removing our oxygen masks, and giving reports to two nurses who hover close by. Uncle Al has woken up and Mrs. Cameron is waiting for me. When she has finished hugging me I introduce them.

Uncle Al gets sent off for X-rays of his ribs, which are probably broken, and his leg, which probably isn't. A doctor comes in and asks me a ton of questions before she pokes and prods me. She checks my oxygen levels, listens to my lungs, and checks a small burn on my left arm. When she cleans the burn it hurts like a thousand bee stings all in the same spot. Only slightly less painful is the injection of antibiotics she gives me in my right bicep. While the nurse bandages my burn the doctor speaks quietly with Mrs. Cameron, giving her instructions on my medical care, I guess. Finally they are finished with me.

"Can we go see Mom now?" I ask.

"Well--" Mrs. Cameron says, looking uncertain.

"I know it's after visiting hours, but I'm sure they could make an exception. Even just for a few minutes." I pick up the lockbox. "This is why I went. She was so worried it was lost in the four. She made me promise." I stop talking.
Mrs. Cameron is looking at me and slowly shaking her head from side to side. There's this expression on her face that I don't want to have to interpret.

"But she made me promise," I beg. "She made me promise."

"I'm sorry," is all she says.

I look into her eyes and know what I don't want to know.

***

Question 35:

Look at the three words below and find a fourth word that is related to all three.

Home sea bed

Answer 35:

Sick

***

Mom is dead. I can barely think. I just feel numb, like somehow my body has continued on without me. I am floating somewhere above all of this, looking down. I am in Phish's parents' bed. The lights are off, and the shades are drawn. The noise of people in the other room seeps under the door, but it is just that, meaningless noise. I can't sleep, but I can't seem to wake up either. People come in and check up on me: Phish's mom, Uncle Al, a social worker. They ask me questions. If I can process the question enough to respond, it's usually with a shake or nod of my heavy head. I know they all want to help and they all mean well. I know it, but I don't care.

Why did I waste my whole life think about my dad? Trying to be like him? Chasing after him? He left before I was even born. Mom was the one who was always there for me. Who did everything for me. Who gave everything for me. I should have done, given, loved her more.

I have barely eaten, but I am not hungry at all. They bring me meals, but everything tastes like glue and ends up just sitting in my mouth. I chew and chew but can barely swallow. A few bites is all I can manage. It's exhausting. Phish's mom helps me change my clothes, brushes my hair, and gives my face a wash. I don't resist, I'm just not any help. I am like a rag doll. I feel bad about it, bad that I'm so useless and that she has to take care of me.

I haven't cried yet. Not even when they first told me. Nothing, not a single tear. I think that's horrible. It makes me feel horrible about myself. What's wrong with me? My mother is dead and I can't cry. But I can't make myself cry. I don't know. I don't know. I don't know. How exactly is my life supposed to go on now?

A shaft of light momentarily penetrates the dark womb I have created for myself as the door opens and closes. I shut my eyes tight against it. A whisper of soft footsteps approaches. I feel the bed shift slightly as whoever it is sits down beside me. A hand gently strokes my hair. The tenderness is too much. I pull away and turn over on my side to face the wall. I don't know who's here this time or what they want. I only know I want them to go away and leave me alone. Instead, I feel the bed shift even more. The visitor has crawled into bed with me and has wrapped herself around me, pointing her bony knees into my thighs, her chest to my back and her skinny arm thrown around me. She doesn't say anything. She just holds me and I fall asleep.

When I wake up, it's dark and quiet. I feel like I am awake for the first time in days. I feel like I am here, and I can feel her breathing beside me, and I can breathe. I feel at least semi-normal. My eyes are open and have adjusted to the dark. I roll over and see Anna.

"Hi," I say.

"Hi," she says back.

I don't know what to say next.

"I'm glad you slept," she says.

"Yeah, me too," I say, my voice sticky with disuse. "I feel a bit better."

"Good," she says, smiling and rubbing sleep from her eyes. We stare at each other silently and then I kiss her on the forehead.

"Let's go back to sleep, K?"

"K," she says softly, already halfway there.

***

I wake up in a pool of sunlight. The curtains have been shoved wide open and Phish's little sister is sitting cross-legged on the end of the bed studying me.

"You're up," she says.

"Looks like," I say. I sit up, stretch my arms high over my head, and bend my ear to my left shoulder and then my right. I take a big breath in and sigh it out. I look at Anna. Her face is full of anticipation and I follow her gaze. That's when I see that she has Mom's lockbox and the box marked "BREWER" on the bed in front of her.

"What's in the boxes? Can I see?" she asks.

"Oh," I say.

The boxes. Mom. Ruthie. The barn fire. Uncle Al. The stalker. Shit. Shit. SHIT. Look around. Take a breath. Get a grip.

"So?" Anna asks. "Can I?"

"Okay."

She comes closer and I put them on the bed between us. "Which first?" I ask her.

"Hmm." She taps her index finger on her chin a few times, contemplating the decision. "That one," she says, pointing to the lockbox.

"Sure," I say. I take off Mom's pendant and give her the key off of its chain.

I watch as she inserts the key and the box opens effortlessly. She holds it up and looks in. She looks disappointed and my heart sinks. She pulls out a roll of paper held by a hairband and examines it briefly before handing it to me. "It's money, right?" she asks.

I nod, holding it in on the flat of my palm. "It's dry," I say, hoping that if Mom is anywhere she can hear me.

"Is it yours?" she asks while she looks in the box again as if she is hoping or expecting there is something else there.

"Yes," I say, sadness creeping in again. "I guess so." I can't tell how much it is and I really have no interest in it.

"Now that one," Anna says, pointing at the box marked "BREWER."

I put the roll of money down on the bed beside me. "Okay," I say and take the lid off the box. We both lean in to see and our foreheads rest against each other.

"Is that your mom?" Anna asks in a hushed voice, equal parts fear and wonder.

"No," I say, reaching in and picking the photo up. I stare into Aunt Mary's warm, smiling face. She has only been gone a few years and already my memories of her feel like wisps of cloud that I am struggling to hang onto. Will the same thing happen to my memories of Mom?

Anna is already pulling the next item from the box and holding it out for me to inspect. It's another photo. "Who are these people?" she wants to know.

I take it from her and study it. I have never seen this photo before. I recognize a younger Mom and Dad but not the man between them with an arm around each and a big, toothy smile.

***

Question 36:

How many new orphans (under age 18) are there annually in this country?

a) 25
b) 170
c) 400
d) 1,500
e) 5,000

Answer 36:

d) 1,500

There are around 1,500 new orphans every year. Many are taken in by family members, and the remainder are sent to government-sponsored boarding schools until they are of legal age.

***

I am curled up in an armchair in the main room staring at my tablet. The family cat, Tommy, is snuggled up beside me, his eyes squeezed shut and whiskers twitching. I wonder what he thinks of this stranger in his home. Uncle Al and Mr. Cameron are at the table talking farming, machinery, and storms, and Mrs. Cameron is at the sink washing dishes. Anna is drying them and putting them away and telling her mother about her newest best friend at school. I know they are all trying to give me some space and I appreciate it.

When Anna and I came out of the room together this morning, after Mrs. Cameron hugged me and fed me, they filled me in on some of the basics. Uncle Al told me that years ago Mom had asked him to be my legal guardian in case of an emergency and that those documents were in a file online. They had been in touch with Ms. Hunt and explained what had happened and promised to update her daily on my status. Uncle Al contacted his son, Chuck, who lives on a ranch in Montana and he will be moving there to help him out when things here are settled.

I check my inbox, and there are three messages from Lee and one from Phish. I want to video chat with both of them, but I'm also nervous and I don't know why. I tell myself it makes sense to read their messages first, anyway, before I call them.

The messages from Lee are all sweet but short:

I miss you. I'm worried about you.
Please come back to school! Soon!
It's torture not being with you. Call me!

Phish's message is longer:

I was so relieved when Mom told me you were back and then so shocked to hear about your mother. I can't even really believe it. I mean, I just assumed because she was in the hospital that eventually they would fix her. It's not right! Mom said they tried everything they could, but sometimes things are so bad that everything is still not enough.

She also told me about you saving Uncle Al and about Ruthie. She didn't seem to know much detail about any of it, though. I guess Uncle Al is not a big talker and you've kinda been in hibernation?

I'm sorry to have to make you think about anything else right now, but it is IMPORTANT! Right now you are reading this message in JONI'S inbox. (I hope you don't mind, but I let Lee in on the fake ID.) But there are messages piling up in your (Tic's) inbox. I know because I checked. There isn't anything super important, and no one will be surprised if you don't check on it for a little while, but eventually you probably should. There's a message from Ms. Hunt, and I know Mom is checking in with her daily so . . .
And yes, I checked and your messages (and most likely video) are still being monitored. I still don't know what that is all about?!?

You should be able to use either ID by powering your tablet off and on again and pressing your left thumb to the tablet for Tic and your right thumb for Joni. Try it and let me know if it works.

Xoxo, Phish

I had totally forgotten about my fake ID. My heart starts pounding like a hammer. I am sure whoever is spying on me is the same person (or people) who was at the barn. I try to clear my head and think. I am pretty sure that the last time I was signed in as myself I didn't give any clue that I was anywhere other than the hospital. I will double-check any messages I sent when I sign in as myself. The only video chat I had with Phish after I left ended when she cut me off before I said anything. So that means whoever is listening in doesn't know that I went to the barn and that I have Dad's box. I had a look through it and I think I found what it is that they were hoping to destroy. It looks like an old-fashioned computer memory card. I don't know how to use it, but I hope that Phish will.

As I am thinking about it there's something I don't get. If they think everything has been destroyed in the fire, why are they still spying on me? My fingers tug gently at Mom's necklace. I am totally lost in my head, trying to figure this out, and I can't make sense of it. When Uncle Al puts his hand on my knee I jerk, startling Tommy who jumps down and sideways and struts away from us with his tail swishing back and forth in reproach.

"You okay there, Tic?" he asks.

"Yeah," I say, spitting the pendant out of my mouth, not sure when I put it in there. "Yeah, I'm okay. What's up?" I look at his worried face and reach out and take his hand.

"I'm going over to the hospital for a check-up. They wanna look at the stitches in my leg, and maybe take another X-ray of my broken ribs, and who knows what all else they will want to check. Anyway, I thought maybe you would come with me, huh?"

I look over at Mrs. Cameron who is nodding with encouragement. "Sure," I say. I power my tablet off and slip it in my bag.

***

Question 37:

New-build cities _____.

a) Are laid out to maximize walkability
b) Are powered independently by renewable energy
c) Have a population between 80,000–150,000
d) Seek to balance safety with sustainability
e) All of the above

Answer 37:

e) All of the above

New cities are being built all the time to accommodate climate refugees, and advances in science are making them safer and more sustainable than ever before.

***

Above me the waxing moon and scattered stars are muted by the light rising up from Arquette. I take in the strange view from the rooftop. Strange for me, anyway. I guess I am a "country girl," as Phish would say. Roofs stretch off in every direction from here, the streets lit below them in a glowing grid. The buildings feel crowded together and I realize how much I miss the open natural space that surrounded our cottage and NESA. I suppose this is safe and efficient, but it feels alien to me and I wonder if part of my interest in the Change has always been driven by my deep connection to the outdoors.

Beneath me, Mr. and Mrs. Cameron are back in their own bed tonight, and I am supposed to be sleeping on a mattress with Anna on the floor of the main room. Her brothers are sharing another mattress nearby, and Uncle Al is snoring on the couch. Anna showed me earlier how to get up here. As much as I appreciate Phish's family, it feels just as crowded in there as it looks out here. At home it was just me and Mom in the same amount of space they have here for seven of us. I'm used to having a space of my own, and I just needed a bit of privacy before I could rest tonight. So here I am on the roof, walking between the solar panels that are laid out in rows and remind me of our garden beds back home. This garden is harvesting sunlight for energy. Our garden, our garden…our garden doesn't exist anymore.

I pull out my tablet and power it on, pressing with my right thumb and opening up Joni's account. I already checked the messages in my Tic inbox briefly this afternoon. Lots of condolences from classmates, which are nice, but they don't make me feel very good at the moment. The "sorry for your loss" sentiment just keeps reminding me that Mom is gone.

There's a message from Ms. Hunt urging me to take my time and consider all of my options. It's fairly neutral except for the line that says, "consider what your mother would have wanted you to do," which I am guessing is meant to guilt me into going back to NESA. There's also a message from Tate urging me to come back and hinting that he has some updates on my sea level rise project when I am ready to discuss it. I am curious to see what he has found out, and the impending doom predicted by my model is almost enough to pull me out of myself, my life, my problems.

I talked briefly with Phish earlier when she video chatted with her family, but I will have to talk to her privately soon. Now, though, I know it is time—probably past time—to chat with Lee. I sent him a quick message earlier telling him I would call after everyone here had gone to bed. He answers on the first ping.

"Hi," I say.

"Hi. Are you okay?" he asks and frowns. "Sorry, that was a dumb question."

"No, it's not. I am, I don't know. Not okay but not, not okay. Sorry, it's just--"

He just nods as if this makes sense. "Where are you anyway? It's pretty dark."

"Oh, yeah, sorry, it's—I'm up on the roof of Phish's house. Hang on, and I'll turn the flashlight on." I swipe up and select the light from the menu.

Lee gives me a half-smile. "So much better," he says.

I nod. "There's something I want to show you. I found this in my mom's jewellery box." I move the tablet so its camera is close to the pendant dangling at the top of my breastbone.

"Can you see it?"

"Yes." He hesitates and I can hear the confusion in his voice. "But I don't understand."

I hold the tablet up to my face and see that he is frowning. "Me neither," I say. "When I saw your tattoo I thought there was something familiar about it, but I couldn't place it. When you said your uncle designed it, I figured I was wrong. But my mom has had this necklace forever. I used to play with her jewelry when I was little even though I wasn't supposed to. She sold all of it off over time when we needed money. All of it except for this. I haven't seen it in about ten years. She never wore it so I forgot about it until now."

Neither of us says anything for a minute. I look up at the moon and remind myself that it is the same moon that is hanging over NESA right now. The same moon shining over Lee.

"Shit. I really wish I had pushed my father or my uncle harder to tell me what it is or what it means," Lee says.

"Maybe I misunderstood. It just never really seemed important enough to fight with them about and that's what I figured it would have turned into. Neither my father or my uncle are easy to talk to or to get answers from." He looks at me quickly and then looks down so that I can't see his eyes at all. "The men in my family are really screwed up." He says this with such quiet anger I can tell it's not the first time he has thought this, and I wonder if he is trying to warn me.

I push him anyway. Right now I don't really care how dysfunctional his family is. I need to understand—to know—anything and everything about both my parents.

"You said your uncle said something about the tattoo and you being saved?" I remind him.

He shakes his head and shrugs. "I'm sorry, Tic, but I don't know what he meant or if I even remember it right. I was pretty young. Let me work on it, okay? Maybe I can get my mother to open up." He sounds doubtful.

"Sure. It's just weird, right?" And then I say it quickly, like taking off a Band-Aid, before I can chicken out: "You don't think we could be related, do you?"

"Shit," he whispers, shaking his head. "I don't think so. Chris is my mother's older brother, and they don't have any other sibs. My dad has a younger brother, Charlie, who is married with five kids and lives in Arkansas. That's it—that I know about, anyway."

We both don't say anything for a while. It's starting to get pretty cold up on the roof, even in the big wool sweater I borrowed from Phish's drawer.

"So, you are coming back here, right?" Lee asks. He is trying to control his voice, to sound cool and casual, but he doesn't fool me for a minute. I see the fear in his eyes.

I shrug. Of course, looking at him this minute, I want to go back to NESA. I want to be with him. I do. But I know I am not ready to decide anything yet. "I have a few things to take care of," I hedge. "For one thing, I want to decide what to do with my mom's—her remains," I say quietly. I have never said it out loud before. Remains. All that is left of her. Ashes in a canister.

"Oh," Lee says.

"I just don't know what to do. With them, I mean. I never thought about it, but if I had thought about it, I would have thought maybe scattered in our garden or under my tree." I have to stop talking to wipe my cheeks and take a deep breath.

"What does your heart tell you?" Lee asks.

I search inside me for some answer that makes sense, that feels right. "Whenever I could get anywhere near the Edge, I would look out at the water and think, *That's where my dad is. He's somewhere out there.* You know? Do you think maybe she would want to be out there too? They could sort of be together again."

***

Question 38:

A critical moment in a complex situation in which a small influence or development produces a sudden large or irreversible change is called a _____.

a) Point of no return
b) Breaking point
c) Tipping point
d) Turning point
e) Crisis point

Answer 38:

c) Tipping point

Tipping point is the term that refers to this critical moment and is applicable to both physical and social science phenomena.

***

The noisy chaos of this morning has disappeared, and Mrs. Cameron sits across the table from me idly turning her almost-empty coffee cup in a clockwise circle. Anna and the twins have gone to school, and Uncle Al went downstairs to hang out at the shop with Mr. Cameron. I know she needs to leave soon to start her shift at the camp, but she seems to be waiting for something. I take another tiny sip of my cold coffee.

"I washed your clothes and put them in Alex's drawer," she says, pointing to a dresser in the corner. "You are welcome to wear her stuff too. I know you didn't pack that much so..."

I nod. "Thanks."

"Tic, can I ask you something?" she says.

I figure it will be about the big decision I have to make soon and I feel badly that I still don't have an answer for her. Should I go back to NESA? A part of me wants to go back to my friends and routine there. It was my dream for so long that I can't imagine my life without that dream. But Uncle Al is the only family I have left. How can I let him go so far from me? How can I not go with him?

"I know you have only been at NESA a few months now, but I figure you probably understand more about the Change than I do. I see the results come pouring in to the camp on a regular basis, and I follow the news videos when I'm not too busy, but what I want to ask you is—" She stops and reaches her hands out across the table to me.

I take them, and she gives my fingers a gentle squeeze. "As a mother, I am really worried about the future. Not so much for myself, but for my kids, and for everyone else's kids too. Is it really as bad as it seems? Are we going to beat this thing?"

I am surprised by her question, but given where she works and what she sees, I guess she must think about it a lot. I understand what she is asking me, but I don't have a yes or no answer for her. I have felt both hopeful and hopeless about the Change and never more so than since I started at NESA. I want to answer her as truthfully as I can.

"I don't know, but maybe it's like a code blue in the hospital when someone is dying and they try to resuscitate them."

"How do you mean?" she asks, staring at me.

"It feels like the planet is right on the edge. Well not the planet, but human life on the planet, because the planet can easily go on without us. It seems possible that if we do everything, or do the right things, then maybe we can save ourselves. It also seems possible that if we don't, or even if we do, it might already be too late. Like a code blue."

She listens, nods, and squeezes my hands before letting go. "Thank you, Tic."

"Sure," I say.

"I better go or I'm going to be late," she says. "Are you sure you'll be okay here today? You know the men are just downstairs if you need anything, right?"

"I'll be okay," I say.

After the door closes behind her, I take our mugs over to the sink and wash and dry them. Tommy the cat is stretched out in a patch of sunlight on the floor by the window. He rolls over to look at me as I approach. I stare out the front window at the cement buildings across and along the street. Solar trees line the street, but there is nothing green as far as my eye can see. It's all cement: heat-reflecting, water-repelling cement. It's not good.

I pull out my tablet and go to the message with the link that Phish sent me. She is nothing if not persistent. It's definitely going to be the strangest video call I have ever made, but what have I got to lose?

A woman with a slash of bright-red lipstick and hair slicked back in a tight bun answers. Her navy-blue uniform is ugly and unflattering, and I can't make out the name on her badge. "Central East Correctional Facility. Officer Renfrew speaking. What is the nature of your call?"

***

Question 39:

Which word below means "to use destructive or obstructive actions to harass people or organizations who are harming the environment":

a) Ecocide
b) Ecotage
c) Blockadia
d) Tree-spiking
d) Terrorism

Answer 39:

b) Ecotage

A combination of the words prefix eco- for the environment and sabotage. Tree spiking is one example of ecotage, whereby nails are placed in trees causing no damage to trees but lots of damage to logging equipment if trees are cut down. Blockadia is a term for loosely affiliated networks participating in ecotage. Historically there have also been organizations like 'Earth First!' who's focus is ecotage. Ecocide is the extensive destruction and loss of ecosystems.

***

After almost thirty minutes of waiting on the video call I hear the sound of a door opening and feet shuffling. The screen on my tablet still shows an empty chair in a grey room, but now I can hear voices as well.

A man's gruff voice says, "Ten minutes maximum, and remember I will be right here watching and listening."

"Yessir," answers another voice.

He sits down in the chair and he looks...ordinary. He has brown hair cut short, wire-rimmed glasses, and a clean-shaven square jaw. He doesn't have any tattoos and, except for being more muscled than I would expect of a man the same age as my parents, he just looks normal. I thought someone in prison would look different, scarier or something.

"HOLY SHIT!" he says loudly, staring right at me through the screen. That does scare me.

"Keep it down *now* or this call is over!" says the voice off-screen.

"Holy shit," he says again quietly. "You really are her? Atlantic Brewer? No fucking joke?"

I swallow and nod. Even though I initiated the call, I still can't believe I am talking to Matt Haley. "Yes."

"Sorry, man. It's just so fucking hard to believe. They told me when they were bringing me here, but I thought they were shitting me. You are Sarah and Jim's kid." He shakes his head and seems to be calming down. "I'm sorry about your dad, eh? He was a great guy. He was so goddamn smart."

He knew my dad. Aside from my mother, I never knew or talked to anyone who knew my dad. I have a million questions I want to ask him, but the clock is ticking and he keeps talking.

"So how's your mom doing? Does she know you called me?" he asks.

I shake my head. He doesn't know. Of course he doesn't know. I haven't had to tell anyone yet. I haven't had to say it. Everyone else around me has done the telling. Now it's my turn. "She's dead."

"Motherfucker!"

"*Hey*! Clean it up, asshole. That's a kid you're talking to," says the voice off-screen.

"When?" he asks, and it is gratifying to see that he looks so upset.
"Three days ago," I explain. "She was hurt in the last four and made it to the hospital, but they couldn't save her."

"She was so beautiful. God, she was stunning. We were all in love with her," he says, looking down at his hands.

I don't know what to say. I want to ask who he means was in love with her, but I am waiting for him to look up at me again.

"Six minutes," says the voice.

He looks up. "So?" he asks.

"So, why did you call me, Atlantic?" Before I can answer, he has more questions.

"And seriously, *that* is your name? People call you Atlantic? I guess your mother was still pretty upset when you were born, huh?"

I feel like I have been insulted. I can't help getting just a little defensive and it comes out in my voice. "People call me Tic, actually, and I called because I found a message on the back of the picture you took of my parents a few days before my dad died and I thought maybe you would know something about it."

He looks curious and, for the first time since we started talking, he seems to be really paying attention to me for who I am and not just for being someone's daughter.

"It says, 'Just in Case, 95-19-4, Leaf.' Does that mean anything to you?"

He rubs his chin and frowns. "Listen, Tic, I know that your dad was working on something that had him worried. Really worried. He wouldn't tell me what, but it had to be something big, right?"
"I guess," I say.

"Sure. I think he knew that something might happen to him on his trip. I think that's why he wrote 'Just in Case' on the photo. That's why I...never mind."

"Is that why you broke into his office?"

"I never admitted to that. I pleaded not guilty to everything. Not that it did me any fucking good. The judge had already made up his mind that I was going away for life. I think

243

someone helped him with that decision, probably the same person who set fire to the Wincor office."

"So, you didn't break in to his office, and you weren't a member of Greenleaf?" I ask.

"Look, kid, the trial is over so stop interrogating me, all right?" he says.

I would love to ask him more about this, but I don't want to upset him more than I have already. I need his help. "I think I found something else. Something of my dad's." I hold up the old computer card.

Matt starts to blink and takes his glasses off and puts them back on. "Fuck," he says so quietly I can barely hear him.

"One minute," says the voice.

I feel desperate for more information. Matt is talking fast and low. "Maybe this is old news and I am worried for no reason, but I think this could be dangerous. Be careful, Tic." I think about Uncle Al's barn and nod in agreement. "I know. I also found this in my dad's stuff." I hold up the picture. "Do you know who that is standing between them?"

"That's Chris," he says, and the look in his eyes is hard and angry.

"Chris?"

"Chris Mayer. Son of a bitch was our roommate at Midhurst. It was him, me, and Jim. He met your mom first, in a comparative religion course they were both taking. He had her over to our place to "study" as often as he could. Mostly they just sat around talking about religion, politics, and stuff. Like I said, we were all in love with her."

"Time," says the voice.

***

Question 40:

How many people were killed by the Faithful Few during the Heretic Wars?

a) 2
b) 36
c) 305
d) 861
d) 1,204

Answer 40:

d) 861

The Faithful Few killed 861 people and injured over 4,000 during their fifteen-year reign of terror.

***

I will call the prison back tomorrow, and the next day, and the next, and as many times as it takes to get the answers I am desperate for. Chris Mayer, Lee's uncle, head of Alpha-Omega, went to school with my parents. WTF! I am agitated

245

and restless, stalking the small apartment, and I am overdue for a private talk with Phish. We have a lot to catch up on.

"Hey," I say.

Even dressed in first-year blacks, Phish looks like sunshine today. She is her usual energized, smiling self. "Hey back," she says. "Are you surviving my fam? Do you miss having your own room and your own bed yet? Is Anna kicking you in her sleep?"

"Your family is awesome, and yes she kicks a little, but I don't mind." I smile and actually feel myself smiling and wonder how I can be smiling. As soon as I wonder, I stop. "I just spoke with Matt Haley," I tell her. "He thinks my dad knew he was in danger, thinks he was working on something big."

"Fact," she says, clearly impressed.

"Anyway, I wanted to show you something, K?" I ask.

"Course," she says.

"I found this in a box of my dad's stuff." I turn the camera so she can see the computer memory card on the table clearly.

"Now that's a real antique. I'd put it at twenty years old, give or take five," Phish says.

"I think it might have something important on it," I explain. "Any idea how I can access it?"

Her face loses some of its shine as she considers. "Yeah. My ex is really into vintage stuff. I'm sure she has something that would open it. I haven't talked to her since I got in to NESA. She was kinda pissed at me for ditching her, but this is important, right? I can call her and see if it's okay for Anna to bring you over to her place after school."

I didn't know Phish had an ex. For all she talks, you'd think she would have mentioned something. I can see Phish isn't super happy about the idea of being in touch. "Thanks," I say. "Are you sure?"

"Yeah, I'm sure. Asker is chill. It'll be fine."
"Sorry, what did you say her name was?"

"Asker."

"Ask her? You're not going to tell me?"

"No, that's her name—well, her nickname."

"What is?"

"Asker," she says. Phish starts grinning, which makes me feel better even as I remain extremely confused. "Her name is Jules, but everyone calls her Asker because she is a real know-it-all and if you wanna know about anything you just ask her."

Now I am smiling too. "Cool," I say.

***

It's late afternoon, and Anna and I are at another concrete box of a building about a dozen blocks away. A girl with long, straight, blue hair and blue contact lenses opens the door and invites us in.

"Hi, Anna-banana," she says.

"Hi. This is Tic," Anna says.

"Yup," she says, looking me over and then turning away. "Let's go up to my room."

We follow her and end up in a small room that feels even smaller as it is stuffed to the max with stuff.
"Make yourself at home, kiddo," she says to Anna, who plops into an amorphous blob of a chair. Asker goes to a set of shelves and drawers that runs across one wall and pulls out a sheaf of papers with coloured pictures in boxes and words and tosses it to Anna. "Have a look at that and let me know what you think. It's an antique—a comic book," Asker says before turning to me. "So, what have you got?"

I pull out the computer memory card and hand it to her. She looks at it for maybe five seconds before heading back to the shelves. She opens and closes a few drawers and pulls out a machine that she sets up on the desk. She opens it up and there is a screen and keyboard. After a few keystrokes, it slowly hums to life. We wait in silence.

A few minutes later she pops the memory card into a slot on the side of the machine and starts typing. "We might have an issue," she says to the screen. "Looks like the files on this need an ID and password to open. I have programs that can crack it, but given this vintage I am not sure they'll work. You might have to leave it with me for a few days."

"I know the ID and password," I say.

"Really?" she says, turning to look at me as if she is reconsidering something.

"I think so," I say.

"Okay. Let's try. What's the ID?"

"95-19-4."

"And the password?"

"Leaf."

"I'll try, but I doubt it," she says, chewing her bottom lip. She types and hits enter. As she predicted, it's rejected.

"Passwords from back then usually needed to be at least nine characters long, typically with a capital or number or something. Any other ideas?"

I pull the photo out of my bag and stare at the neat, green writing. "Try G-r-e-e-n-l-e-a-f."

Asker types as I say it, and we both stare at the screen as pages and pages of documents open up. I lean in closer, over her shoulder, to read as she scrolls around the info. At a glance I see that my father was researching interactions between carbon dioxide and water in different states of matter. There's some chemistry that I recognize and more that I don't. He has tables of measurements of glaciers, water, and permafrost at different depths and temperatures. I am totally absorbed in it until I realize that Asker is staring at me. I back away and smile in what I hope is an apologetic way.

"Do you want me to send it to you as a file you can open on your tablet?" she offers.

"That would be great."

"KK. Hang on, I have to convert it to a newer format." She types away on the keyboard. "This might take a few minutes," she says, sitting back while a bar slowly fills in at the bottom of the screen: 10%, 20%, 30%. "Where'd you get the retro necklace?" she asks.

"It was my mom's," I say, reaching up and rubbing the pendant between my finger and thumb.

"Fact?"

I nod and she lets out a low whistle.

"So was your mom a member then?"

"A member of what?" I ask, confused.

"The Few," she says.

"*No*," I say, feeling a mix of anger and horror churn inside my head. "What? Why?"

"Well, the symbol on it is for a secret sect that was either part of the Few or broke off from them completely. They were the super rich and super powerful mega elite twenty or thirty years ago. Anyway, lots of important people were suspected of being members but no one can say for sure. Then they more or less disappeared from view. Secret sects tend to do that, if they're any good at being secret, if they even still exist."

I look away from her and see Anna reading, politely trying not to hear us but clearly listening.

"And zip your file is ready. Tell me where you want me to send it and we're set." She touches the side of the computer and the memory card pops out. She holds it out to me and I take it.

"Um, send it to this account at NESA," I say and scribble down Joni's contact information.

"Who's that?" she asks.

"My alter ego," I say.

She looks at me like she thinks I am being rude.

"Just kidding, it's a secret account that Phish set up for me. Someone was tapping my other one."

"Sure they were. Whatever. Any interest in selling the necklace?" she asks. "It's pretty rare and I could get a stellar price for it on-line? We could work out the split."

I can't imagine that it is valuable. Did my Mom know that? Why did she choose to hang on to it and not sell it off with everything else? Could there be a sentimental reason? Lee's Uncle Chris must have given it to her I assume based on the fact that he's responsible for Lee's tattoo. Matt said they all loved Mom. Did she have a thing with Chris? For right now at least even though it's creepy to think what the symbol means and how my Mom came to have it the pendant connects me to her and also somehow to Lee. I clasp my hand around it and shake my head.

"Nah, but I'll keep it in mind. Thanks for everything," I manage. "We should get going."

***

Question 41:

Food security is achieved through which of the following?

a) Growing all food inside level-five safety bunkers (fire-, storm-, and earthquake-resistant)
b) Growing food close to where it will be consumed
c) Having paid security at growing facilities
d) a & c
e) All of the above

Answer 41:

d) a & c

It is not feasible to grow food in close proximity to all consumers as the facilities are expensive to build and maintain and are most economically build in areas without risk of severe drought.

***

While we walk home I forward the file to Phish and Lee and ask them to send it on to Tate to look at. I don't want him to contact me about it through my personal account, though, in case it's still being monitored. In the same message I also ask Phish to explain the Joni account to Tate so that he and I can message and chat freely.

I can feel my friendships like long threads tugging me back to NESA. I can only sort of imagine moving west with Uncle Al. I can imagine what a day there would be like—riding horses, helping with the cows and the gardens—but I can't imagine lots of days strung together into weeks and months and years there. I guess I would finish high school there in two years and then what? Apply to university? I have the money to go almost anywhere thanks to Mom, but if I am just going to be there for two years and then leave anyway, does it really make sense to go? I know Uncle Al will wait for me to make a decision for as long as I need, but will Ms. Hunt? And what about Phish's family? How long can I continue to impose?

When we get back, the scene of domestic bliss is inviting but foreign. There are seven of us and the cat all in the one main room. Uncle Al is playing cards with the twins, and the table is set for dinner. Mr. Cameron is watching a news video on his tablet, and Mrs. Cameron is washing a big pan.

As soon as we arrive, dinner is served: a hearty vegetable stew with bread and butter. Mrs. Cameron is a good cook but, just like at NESA, I can taste the difference. It's not what I grew up with. The vegetables have a uniformity of shape and consistency. Even the flavours are flat and almost indistinguishable. I can only tell peas from carrots by looking at their overly bright colours. I have to remind myself that this is what most people eat if they are lucky enough to afford it: fruits and vegetables, bread and pasta, and rarely meat. It's all scientifically modified to grow in bulk as quickly as possible in indoor shelters. At school, the sheer quantity and variety is a testament to the investment our society is making in us and compensates for the lack of flavour. Here, the warm company and lively conversation provide distraction from the meal. As I look at Uncle Al across the table, it reminds me of all the simple but amazing meals we shared with Mom at our house, with produce from the garden and dairy and eggs from his farm.

After dinner, Lee calls to video chat. He asks if we can speak in private. For all his sweetness, for all his begging me to come back soon, Lee hasn't said those three words and I wonder if that's what is coming next. Has he decided he needs to say the L-word to get me to agree to come back to NESA? And if he says it will I say it back? Mrs. Cameron indicates I can use her bedroom to continue the video chat. As soon as I close the door, Lee speaks.
"I need to tell you something."

I sit down on the floor and lean my back against the bed.

"I thought about what you said yesterday about wanting to take care of your mom's remains and all, and I got in touch with some of the guys I dived with last summer. Long story short, Big Rob is crewing for a ship going to the North Atlantic for a quick research trip. Six days there and back. Thing is, it leaves tomorrow."

"Tomorrow?" I say, my breath catching in my throat.

"It'll be November in two days and they don't usually go north much after that. I told him your situation. He's a real marshmallow and was on board with you going but said he'd have to clear it with the captain. I told him he could offer the captain some extra incentive. The captain said yes. And Tic, don't worry about the money. I got it covered."

"I don't know. I want to. I'm just . . . it's just . . ." I sigh.

"You don't have to. It's only if you want to, okay?"

I close my eyes and try to listen to my instincts, my gut, my heart—whatever it is inside me that is supposed to tell me what the right thing is to do. I'm afraid. I don't know why but I am. I can't think of a good reason to be afraid. I have always wanted to go to the North Atlantic. When will I ever have the chance again? I can picture myself standing at a ship's rail with my mom's ashes. Maybe I would be better able to move on if I did this. I open my eyes. "Yes."

"Cool," Lee says, smiling.

After we work out some details, including that I have money I want to use to pay the captain, I tell Lee about his uncle having gone to school with my parents and my sense that there was something possibly romantic going on. It could explain the necklace if Chris gave it to my mom as a gift. "Also,"—and here I try to pick my words carefully—"I found out something about what the symbol means, maybe."

"Oh yeah?" Lee says.

"Yeah. Well, I met Phish's ex—interesting girl, by the way, though I am not sure she likes me—and she said...um, well, she said it is a symbol for a secret sect that was a part of...a part of the Faithful Few." My voice has dropped to a whisper as if saying the name could invoke them.

His hand unconsciously goes to his chest, a closed fist resting on his breastbone. "Do you know anything about this secret sect?" he asks. His eyes have gone dark and hard as stone.

I shake my head.

"Really?!" He sounds pissed. Does he think I'm lying? Why is he angry with me? Is it because I have implied that his uncle and maybe his father are involved in something so extreme? They are his family after all. I feel super uncomfortable.

"I gotta go," I say. The noise of the family just on the other side of the door penetrates my consciousness, and I feel like a terrible guest. I know I should go back in there and spend some time with them before bed. I also know they are so understanding that if I don't it would still be okay. I listen for a while to the rise and fall of voices, but I can't make out any words. I think I can make out Uncle Al's low rumble though and it gives me comfort. I make one more call and then I force myself up on to my feet and methodically put one foot in front of the other until I have crossed the floor of the dim bedroom. On the threshold my hand pauses on the door knob. I stand still and wait for nothing. Then I take a deep breath, open the door and rejoin the family.

Later, lying in bed, I think about my dad's files. I need more time to look at them and hope that I will be able to while I am travelling. I can't sleep, so I find myself up on the roof again, alone in the dark, open air. I try to video chat with Tate but he doesn't answer. I hope he got the file. I hope so much that it means something important, that it was worth Uncle Al's barn burning, worth Ruthie, worth possibly my dad's life. But how could it be? How could it be worth losing any of those things? And I wonder if I am doing the right thing, leaving tomorrow.

***

Question 42:

Ocean acidification _____.

a) Is a result of increasing levels of CO_2 in the ocean
b) Is a result of the increased temperature of the ocean
c) Has resulted in ocean deserts
d) a & c
e) All of the above

Answer 42:

d) a & c

Ocean deserts, or dead zones, have expanded by over 1 million square km in the last decade alone.

***

I can smell the ocean, even though I can't see it yet. Billy Williams drove like crazy to get me to Gloucester, with less than an hour to spare before the boat leaves, just like he promised he would when I called him yesterday. Gloucester used to be a fishing town, but it's been years since the oceans have had enough fish to make it worth anyone's while to fish commercially. Fish are now grown in huge indoor tanks and harvested at maturity.

I am glad I still had Billy's card in my bag. My bag now has what I have come to think of as my three essentials: my tablet, my pocketknife, and the picture of Mom, Dad, and me. At the last minute I decided to put the other picture in too. I thought I might want to study it more on the trip, and it's not like it takes up any room. I borrowed the warmest clothes I could find from Phish's drawer.

I touch the necklace, which I haven't taken off since I found it, and wonder if I will have the courage to toss it in the ocean with Mom's ashes. Now that I know what the symbol on the pendant represents—a group that is excited for the end of the world, the apocalypse, to come so that God can "save the righteous"—it feels uncomfortable against my skin. At least I can throw it away, but the tattoo--I want to believe that he is as horrified as I am. There's a tiny bit of my brain that's afraid though. What if he already knew about the secret sect and was pissed that I had found out? I close my eyes and try to recall every detail of his expression last night. Amazingly, when I open my eyes, he is there on the dock as we roll to a stop.

I step out of the car, and he grabs me in his arms. I am confused and worried. I try to wiggle out to ask him why he's here, but he holds me so tight I can't move and kisses me so hard I can't think, and all I can do is melt and kiss him back. Finally, we come up for air.

"What are you doing here?" I ask.

"I couldn't let you go alone. I'm coming with." He wraps an arm around my shoulder and steers me towards the boat.

A part of me questions why he is coming with. Is he still upset about my discovery around his family secret? Or is this him wanting to take care of me, and why does he think I need to be taken care of? But another part is glad that he is here. This is going to be hard, and it is amazing that he would do this for me. I hope that he isn't in trouble with anyone for it.

"Tic!" Billy calls, walking towards us. "Don't forget this."

I turn and see he is holding out the canister of Mom's remains that I had put by my feet on the floor of the car. I shrug Lee's hand off my shoulder and go back to meet Billy. "Thank you," I say, and then I hug him. I don't know why, except maybe that I wish I could have hugged Uncle Al this morning before I left. I lied to Uncle Al and told him I was going over to Asker's to hang out for the day. If I had hugged him, he might have been suspicious. I will message him once we are under way and tell him the truth, but I know he would never have agreed to let me come if I had asked. Billy returns my hug, and when we let go of each other he seems both happy and embarrassed.

I turn back to look at the boat that will take me, take us, to a spot I have wondered about my whole life: the North Atlantic. It is grey with a single red stripe running its length. It looks bigger than I thought it would. There are only a few men on the dock, but the boat is swarmed with them. Some move crates around, some tie things down, and others are checking equipment. We climb a plank from the dock up onto the deck. We thread our way through the bustling men. Lee keeps his head down to avoid obstacles, and I do the same. We come to an open hatch and climb down a ladder into a room with a table, chairs, and bunks lining the walls. One man is here, and he is occupied looking back and forth between an open drawer and a checklist. He doesn't look up as we make our way to the back of the room and through a door that leads to a small room with no windows. It is bare except for a beat-up mattress that covers ninety percent of the floor.

Lee kicks off his shoes and sits down. I do the same. If I stretch my arms I can almost touch both side walls, and I am sure if Lee lays down, his head and feet will touch the front and back of the room.

"Our spot for the next six days," Lee says.

"Sweet," I say. It may not be pretty, or very clean, or even comfortable, but it is private and that in itself is a luxury.

"I missed you," he says, reaching up and gently caressing my face with both hands.

I lean in, my forehead resting on his, and let go of the misgivings I have had since I told him about the Faithful Few. Then I kiss him soft and slow. Our hands explore one another, checking, remembering. He climbs on top of me and the boat's engine shimmies awake, a low thrumming that pulses up through the floor, through the mattress, and through me before it reaches him.

A few hours later when we are calmer, our touches lighter, less urgent, and more soothing Lee finally pulls away. He gets dressed and leaves me to go find his friend Big Rob to see what's what. I feel more relaxed than I have in a long time. I'm at peace but wide awake and alert. I pull my tablet from my bag. There's a message from Tate. I am dying to know what he thinks of my dad's files, but first I message Uncle Al.

I am not at Asker's, but please don't worry, and please don't be mad at me. I am on a boat called the Joshua. *A friend from school is with me. We are going to the North Atlantic to scatter Mom's remains. I am as sure as I can be that it's what she would have wanted. I will be back in one week. I am sorry I didn't tell you before.*

Xo, Tic

With that sent I am free to open Tate's message. It is a long, detailed, and compelling analysis of my dad's files. My dad was studying the interaction between glaciers and carbon dioxide. People had been taking core samples of glaciers for years. From these they could determine the carbon levels in the atmosphere, temperatures, sea levels, and other factors from hundreds and even thousands of years ago. But my dad really focused in on the carbon in the glaciers and, after checking the results of many samples from different places, as well as performing complex calculations well beyond my understanding, he came to believe that glaciers are more than just maps of history. Glaciers themselves store carbon. They are carbon sinks. When they melt, the stored carbon is exposed to atmosphere and released as carbon dioxide. The more carbon dioxide they release, the warmer the atmosphere gets and the more they melt and release in a vicious cycle.

I wonder if that could explain my mathematical finding that everything seems to be melting quicker than anticipated in the established literature. I will see if I can understand his formulations and plug them in to my equations, but I will also ask Tate his opinion because I respect and value it.

I am still reading the message when Lee returns with two sandwiches and a bottle of water.

***

Question 43:

Until recently, the Greenland ice sheet covered _____.

a) 1,700 square km
b) 170,000 square km
c) 1,700,000 square km

e) None of the above

Answer 43:

c) 1,700,000 square km

In 2015, the Greenland ice sheet was 1.7 million square km, the second largest in the world after the Antarctic ice sheet. If it had melted entirely, it would have raised sea levels by twenty-four feet.

***

The sky is cloudy, with no stars to light our way. We catch the briefest glimpses of the almost-full moon as it is veiled by drifting smoky-grey curtains. The deck is dark except for a single light on the bridge behind us. I lean against the rail, and Lee wraps his arms around me from behind. The wind whips my hair back against his chest as the boat speeds along, cutting across the black, barren plain.

The captain wasn't interested in meeting me. Lee gave him the roll of bills I had brought along, and he instructed Lee that we were to stay out of the way as much as possible, preferably in our room where he wouldn't have to worry about the safety of two unauthorized passengers. He didn't say we weren't allowed out; he just made it clear we should be spending most of our time below deck. We should reach the destination in the North Atlantic, a group of glaciers, the morning after next. The three researchers on board will be working there for two days and then we'll head home.

"Do you want to go back down?" Lee asks.

"Soon," I say, savouring the fresh air even as it bites my nose and cheeks. "I spoke to Matt Haley again this morning before I left," I say.

"Yeah?"

"Yeah. He told me more about your uncle Chris and my mom and dad."

I can feel Lee's body tense up behind me, but he says nothing.

"Matt, Chris, and my dad were roommates, right? And Chris and my mom met in a religion class halfway through their second year. I guess they were both pretty opinionated, and Matt was too. She'd come over and they'd all debate stuff, all except my dad who mostly just listened if he wasn't off studying. By the time that semester had ended, she was friends with all three of them and was at their place lots.

"Chris made it clear to Matt and my dad that he was interested in my mom. Matt said he and my dad could respect the fact that since Chris met her first he should have the first shot at her." I stop. It feels really weird talking about my mom this way. It was awkward enough listening to Matt tell it. She would have been only a few years older than I am now, and I can't imagine having three guys talking about me behind my back like that. It's creepy. "Anyway, I guess he asked her out at the beginning of third year and my mom turned him down. Said she just wanted to be friends or some BS like that. He told her that was fine and they could still be friends, but privately he told Matt and my dad that he was going to get her to try to change her mind. So Chris was still inviting her over a lot. Matt said one night when they were drinking he tried to "make a move on her" as well, whatever that means, but she turned him down too. He doesn't think Chris ever knew about it, and he says his feelings weren't hurt and he and my mom were still friends after.

"So one day she came over when Chris and Matt were both out. She and my dad didn't have that much to talk about at first since he was into physical sciences and she was studying social sciences, but it was raining out and she stayed. They put on some music and turned the lights off. There was a fish tank, and they just lay there, watching the fish, listening to music, and when the music ended, they listened to the rain. Later, my mom told Matt that by the time the rain stopped, she was in love."

"Sorry, but if they weren't talking, and I am assuming from what you have said they weren't--you know," Lee says, snuggling his face down into my neck, tickling me behind the ear with his tongue in a way that makes me gasp, "then how did she fall in love?"

"I wish I knew," is all I can say.

I wish she had told me all of this—any of this—herself. I really do wonder how a person falls in love. Are Lee and I in love? I lean into him and think I might be. When did it happen, though? When I saw him on the dock two days ago, or during our escape from the fire? Did I fall in love that first day when his hand covered mine on his chest and I felt his heart pounding beneath it because together we had just risked our futures trying to help someone?

"Matt said that once my mom and dad were a couple, Chris was still super nice to my mother, but he was royally pissed at my father. He would fight with my dad, arguing and trying to convince him that he should dump my mom. He would say that my mother should be with him instead because they were the same race and religion."

"Uh-huh. That sounds like shit he would say," Lee mumbles to himself.

"The tension in their apartment was bad, and Matt said he started spending as much time away from there as he could, hanging out with other friends instead. By the time third year ended they agreed that the three of them shouldn't live together for their last year at Midhurst."

Suddenly a beam of light from the bridge sweeps over us and back, stopping on us. Clearly we have been spotted from above, and I personally feel pinned in place by someone up there.

"I'm getting cold. Let's go below. I can show you a picture I found of your uncle with my parents."

***

Question 44:

What is the term used to describe a piece of glacier breaking off and becoming an iceberg?

a) Spawning
b) Calving
c) Fracturing
d) Cracking
e) Splitting

Answer 44:

c) Calving

Calving occurs when a piece of glacier breaks off to form an iceberg. Calving of glaciers as large as 66.4 km² (25.6 sq. mi) in area (equivalent in area to approximately 11,000 football fields or slightly larger than the old city of Manhattan) have been occurring with increasing frequency.

NOVEMBER

Later this morning, we will arrive at our destination. In the meantime I reread a message from Tate this morning asking permission to discreetly share Dad's research with a few people. I told him that was fine.

The deeper we read into my dad's work, the more fascinating and scary it is. He discovered that the fracture resistance of ice is decreased significantly under increasing concentrations of carbon dioxide molecules, making ice caps and glaciers more vulnerable to cracking and splitting into pieces. The strength of hydrogen bonds—the chemical bonds between water molecules in an ice crystal—is decreased under increasing concentrations of carbon dioxide. This is because the added carbon dioxide competes with the water molecules connected in the ice crystals. The carbon dioxide molecules first adhere to the crack boundary of ice by forming a bond with the hydrogen atoms and then migrate through the ice in a flipping motion along the crack boundary towards the crack tip. The carbon dioxide molecules accumulate at the crack tip and constantly attack the water molecules by trying to bond to them. This leaves broken bonds behind and increases the brittleness of the ice on a macroscopic scale.

Lee comes in with our breakfast.

"Did you see them?" I ask.

"Uh-huh. I think so, anyway. They look like white clouds touching down at the horizon, which I guess they could be, but, no, I'm pretty sure I saw the glaciers."

"Huh. I can't wait to see too," I say.

Lee and I were out on the deck for fresh air and to stretch our legs twice yesterday for a total of maybe twenty minutes. The curious stares of the crew following us around made me uncomfortable, and aside from Big Rob, no one talks to us, so it's awkward. I console myself by reasoning that there hasn't been anything to see anyway except the grey water and grey sky. Also, it's been getting super cold out. Mostly we have happily hung out in the converted supply closet, AKA our room.

We eat breakfast in bed--scrambled eggs and toast—and then I put on the long underwear Lee brought for me, my track pants and top, Phish's cream wool sweater, and a black insulated vest, also courtesy of Lee. I tuck my hair up under a wool cap that pulls down over my ears. Lee and I both drape our messenger bags with our tablets over our shoulders and across our chests. The supply closet doesn't have a lock on it.

We enter the main room, which is bustling. There's a hatch open to the hold below us, and men are passing up pieces of equipment. Some pieces are being stacked inside at the direction of one of the researchers, but most are heading to the deck. As we wait for an opportune moment to climb up the ladder to the deck I look at the equipment and try to imagine what the different tools are used for. I wonder what the research is, but Big Rob—a truly large man in every direction—doesn't know and the three men who he pointed out to us as the "research team" don't even talk to the crew, never mind Lee or me. When there's a break in the unloading Lee and I go up on deck. The boat has slowed considerably, and in the distance I can see a range of what appear to be white mountains.

Lee and I find a spot by the railing on the port side and watch in awe as the mountains grow ginormous before us. They rise straight up out of the ocean, dark black water transforming to variegated white ice that towers above us, larger than any building I have ever seen. As we draw closer I can see that some of the vertical surfaces are flat and smooth as glass and others are craggy, folded and wrinkled. I sense my physical insignificance not only in size but in terms of time. How old these giants are. It's beautiful almost to the point that it feels unreal, like we are moving into a painting or a dream. I can't reconcile what I am seeing with the calculations showing that all this will be gone in five years. It feels impossible. I squeeze Lee's hand tight. The boat stops and there is an eerie silence broken by deep groaning coming first from one direction and then another; coming from the glacier.

"I can't believe…" I whisper.

"I know. Me too."

What else is there to say really? I am so in awe, so grateful to have this chance to see these monuments to Earth's history and unbearably sad to think I will probably never get to see them again.

Behind us, on the largest and most open part of the deck, one of the researchers is assembling equipment and checking it. The third is up on the bridge with the captain, presumably directing him as we come ever closer to the glacier. I imagine my father working like this: precise, absorbed, oblivious to everything and everyone around him, and so committed he was willing to risk his life.

All of the researchers go below deck, and Lee and I take the opportunity to inspect the equipment more closely. Some of the crew watch us, but if they aren't going to tell us to stop, then why not? There's some lighting equipment and what I think must be drills for samples. The smallest one is easily handheld, and the biggest one is almost twenty feet long. While we are walking around the large one, the researchers come out in wetsuits. All it takes is a glance from them and we back off. Soon all three of them are in the water. They have searchlights and small drills.

"What are they doing now?" I ask Lee as the men in the water pull on tubes snaking between them and the boat.

"Checking their O_2 lines," he explains.

"But they have tanks on their backs."

"Those are probably just for backup. If they are going to be under for a long time, they use the tubes so that they don't have to worry about stopping in the middle of working to come back up if the tank is running low."

In a moment, all three disappear below the surface. The oxygen lines coil out from the boat smoothly. Most of the crew are relaxing on the deck. The sun has finally made an appearance causing the ice to shine iridescent in spots and milky in others. The sky is a brilliant blue, and the mood is light as the crew will have a rest for the next two days while the researchers work.

I didn't bring my mother's remains up with us. I wanted to check out the situation first, but now I feel like my mom would love this bright day, and I don't really want to wait anymore. As much as it is a crazy hard thing to do, I want to just do it.

Big Rob wanders over. He is at least three hundred pounds, but he moves with a grace and ease that speaks of a thick layer of muscle beneath. His smile is easy and makes him look like a little boy looking for fun and adventure.

"So, kid, was it worth it?" he asks Lee, cuffing him on the shoulder.

"For sure," Lee replies, smiling back.

"You're going to catch heck back at home, ya know?" Big Rob chuckles.

"That's assuming they figure it out," Lee counters.

I don't believe for a second that he will get away with it, but he seems to think it is possible. He told Ms. Hunt he was going home for a family emergency and had his sister send a forged letter with their chauffeur, who came to pick him up.

I worried about the risk he took in coming until I realized there was nothing I could do about it anyway. As much as I am sure I would have been fine hanging out by myself in the cabin it was nice to have the time alone together these past few days.

"Your folks are going to figure it out, son, you wait and see," Big Rob says.

"As long as they think I'm at NESA, which they do, why would they? Like I said before, they are not overly interested in me and it's not like Manny hasn't kept secrets for Eva and me before." Lee changes the topic, asking Big Rob about some of the features of this boat, and I excuse myself to go below and get Mom.

***

Question 45:

What is the most abundant greenhouse gas?

a) Water vapor
b) Methane
c) Carbon dioxide
d) Nitrogen oxide
e) Carbon monoxide

Answer 45:

a) Water vapor

Water vapor, with a concentration of between 10,000–50,000 ppm, depending on location, is the most abundant greenhouse gas.

***

I descend to the main room, which is messy and empty, and I stop and really look around. I've been on this boat for forty-eight hours, and the temptation to look around now that I have the opportunity is irresistible. I am not interested in going through the crew's stuff, but I do take a snoop around the kitchen, looking in drawers and cupboards. There's a refrigerator and a propane stove but not much counter space. Whoever has been doing the cooking, the food's not bad. I can't imagine cooking for sixteen people in this cramped space that also serves as living room and bedroom.

I turn slowly, hands on hips, scanning the room, wondering if there is anything else interesting to see before I get the canister and head back up. Am I stalling? Maybe, but I'm also curious. I always have been. My eyes land on the hatch leading down to the storage hull where the researcher's equipment was. Do I dare? They'll likely be out for hours. My feet lead me to the ladder.

It's dark below. The only light comes from the open hatch. I stop at the bottom of the ladder and survey. The floor space seems to be divided into caged-off sections, most of which have bare light bulbs hanging from the ceiling. I don't bother turning the lights on but pull out my tablet and use its flashlight instead.

The cage closest to the landing appears to have more food supplies. The next cage has life vests, extra dive suits, a first aid kit, flares, and inflatable rafts. As I move farther towards the back of the boat, the next few cages are almost empty. I assume these are where the research equipment was stored. Beside these are three huge tanks. Each has a pipe leading up along the wall. On the side of each is the symbol for flammable contents. The last cage is full of crates. Two are open, their lids on the floor; one is empty, and inside the second are four small tanks, like the ones the divers are wearing on their backs. I wonder if all the crates hold the same thing. That would be a lot of backup tanks. I'll have to ask Lee what he thinks. I remember that Lee is waiting for me up top and probably wondering what is taking me so long.

I am relieved to find the main room still empty. I quickly pop into our room to grab the canister and then head up top. Lee is still talking to Big Rob but sees me immediately and comes over, putting an arm around me.

"You okay?" he asks.

I nod.

Big Rob gives us a smile and wanders off.

"Yeah. I was actually just exploring a bit down below."

"Oh?"

"Uh-huh. Do you think it would be okay if I took some pictures of the glaciers with my tablet? I know it seems like you could never forget seeing this, but if it's the spot where I am doing this"—I hold out the canister of Mom's remains—"I just want to have something, some insurance that I will always remember this exactly."

"I don't see why not," Lee says.

We walk along the railing, taking pictures along the way. About halfway around, a few of the crew get up and go over to the guy manning the oxygen line. Something is happening, and we stop and watch. The lines are being pulled in and wrapped so they don't tangle. Soon the black wetsuit heads of the researchers pop up, tiny in the grey water. They swim over to the boat and climb up a side ladder. Their small drills are holstered to their sides.

After conferring they strap the big drill into a lift. Two go back in the water while one stays on deck and monitors as the crew hoists this big tool up and gently rolls the lifter towards the side rail. They slowly and carefully lower the drill into the water. While the two in the water unstrap it, the third uses his feet to kick three medium-sized canvass sacs over to the edge. They make loud clanging noises as they jostle each other. He climbs down the ladder and directs a crew member to toss the bags overboard to him one at a time. He then swims over to his colleagues, passing each one a sac. When they indicate they are ready, one dives under ahead and the other two follow, guiding the drill between them. The tubing is slowly unrolled again and some of the crew head inside.

Lee and I stand together, staring at the spot the men disappeared.

"Do you want me to leave you alone to do this or stay?" Lee asks.

"I--I don't know." I hesitate. Now that it is coming down to it, I am picturing the divers' black heads popping up through the scattered ashes and it doesn't feel right. "I don't think I'm ready yet," I say. "Is that okay?"

He hugs me tight, and I lean my head on his chest, feeling the rhythmic rise and fall of breath, trying to steady myself, trying not to cry.

"Shh," Lee soothes as he rubs my back. "Hey, I've got a little surprise for you, okay? Can you give me five minutes and then come down to our room?"

"Sure," I say, snorting up some snot that wants to drip out my nose and onto his vest.

He disappears down the hatch, and I stare out at the water. Maybe I will scatter her ashes tomorrow night. The diving will be all finished by then—and we will head back the next morning. Then it will feel more like she is resting in peace, not being disturbed by the divers. I nod to myself, satisfied that it feels right, and head in.

Lee is sitting cross-legged on our mattress and grinning shyly. He holds out a small plate with a chocolate cupcake. I put down the canister of Mom's remains and he passes me the plate before flicking a lighter. He lights the pink candle nestled in the white icing.

"Happy Birthday," he says.

Question 46:

Which gas is inert and will not take part in a combustion process?

a) Oxygen
b) Nitrogen dioxide
c) Carbon dioxide
d) Methane
e) None of the above

Answer 46:

c) Carbon dioxide

Carbon dioxide is inert. The other gases listed will, under the right circumstances, ignite.

***

I want to laugh and cry. Instead, I blow out the candle. Is this love?

"I can't believe I forgot," I say.

"Well you have had a lot going on, and I didn't know if you would feel like celebrating," he says.

I smile. Even though he wants me to eat it all, I insist we split it.

"What do you want to do now?" Lee asks. "Do you want to go back up top and see what's going on or--?" He has the faintest smile and raises his right eyebrow slightly, looking from me to the mattress and back again.

"Actually, I have another idea," I say as I give voice to the confusion and curiosity that has been nagging at me since exploring the hold. I tell him about it, and he agrees it seems odd that there would be so many reserve tanks.

"Let's check it while the researchers are still out, huh?" he says.

While we were in our cabin, a few of the crew came down to hang out in the main room. Big Rob and two other guys are playing a card game at the table. Big Rob lets out a belly laugh, and one of the other players snickers as the third swears and drops his cards face up on the table. One man is reading on a bunk bed, and another is buried completely under a pile of blankets, presumably asleep. The card players watch us cross the room and head to the hatch leading down to the hold. Big Rob raises a quizzical eyebrow, but no one says anything, and we don't either.

I lead the way to the cage with the crates, and Lee turns on the dangling overhead bulb. I count four piles of four crates stacked and closed. There are another two stacked in a shorter pile, and then the two side by side on the floor brings it to twenty in total. Each crate has the same series of nine numbers on it followed by three letters. Lee has pulled one of the tanks out and is looking at it.

"What do you think?" I ask.

"I don't know. Looks like an oxygen tank. I would guess these would fit ten to a crate. How many crates?"

"Twenty," I say.

"Two hundred spare tanks," Lee says, shaking his head. "That doesn't make sense."

"That's what I thought."

Lee tries to lift a crate but can't quite do it.

"Do you think they're all full of tanks?"

"I don't know. If they all have identical markings, chances are they have identical contents. Some could be empty, but we won't know unless we unstack and open them--but then we would have to close and restack them. If we pull on the top ones and they are heavy maybe we can assume they are all full."

We try pulling and confirm that each crate in the top row is heavy. Lee opens one of the two tanks just a little and a small hiss of gas escapes. I am thinking, staring at the three big tanks.

"Look," I say, pointing at them.

Lee glances over at the big tanks and then back at me. "Those are what the hoses are connected to, one for each diver," he explains.

"No, I know. I mean, I figured that, but look, "I say again. "Those tanks each have a symbol on the side that means the contents are flammable."

He looks down at the tank in his hand as comprehension dawns on his face. "And these don't," he says.

"So maybe these contain a non-flammable gas?" I suggest, thinking of my message from Tate this morning about my dad's research.

"Let's test it out."

"What? How?" I say.

"Chill," he says, smiling now. "I will just let the tiniest little stream of gas flow over a flame. If it catches, I will shut the valve immediately."

I am still shaking my head. I do *not* think this is a good idea.

Lee reaches into his bag and pulls out a small, black lighter with a grinning skull on it. "Big Rob's," he explains, "for the candle." He puts the lid back on the empty crate and stands the tank on top of it. With one hand already on the valve he flicks the lighter on with the other. A small flame dances up, and I hold my breath. I can just picture the oxygen from the tank turning the little flicker into a giant flame, leaping from his hand to touch anything and everything in the hold. I have had too much bad luck with fires. I really don't think this is a good idea.

Lee turns the valve a fraction of an inch and then places the flame in the path of the escaping gas. Nothing happens.

He brings it closer. Nothing.

He opens the valve more and more until the force of the escaping gas puts out the flame. He turns the valve closed.

"Whatever is in here, it sure isn't oxygen," he says.

Suddenly, we hear more feet moving around above us and from close to the hatch Big Rob's voice booms, "Divers'r back, everyone!"

We quickly put stuff back where we found it and scramble up both ladders to get topside. We arrive in time to see the divers still in the water replacing the big drill in the hoist. Once it's lifting they climb out. Their sacs are clipped to their belts, dragging on the deck behind them, empty. They unclip them and throw them in a heap. The big drill comes apart in three pieces, and some of the crew carry these down to the hold. The researchers follow. There is nothing I see that suggests they have returned with frozen core samples and the hairs on the back of my neck are standing up.

Big Rob comes over and puts an arm around Lee's shoulder and another around mine. He gives what is I think meant to be a gentle squeeze and chuckles. "How are my two favourite snoops doing?" he asks in a tone that suggests he find us amusing.

"All right," Lee says. "Hey, Rob, can I ask you something?"

"Anything, but I can't promise to answer," he says, smiling and letting go of Lee. He keeps his arm around me though, casual, as if we are old friends. I find I don't mind.

"Anything about the researchers or about this whole trip seem strange to you?"

"Nah, I've been on trips like this one at least two dozen times over the years."

"Really?" I say, surprised. I guess I had the impression that this was more unique.

"Oh, sure, yeah. Usually real early or late in the season like this," Big Rob says.

"Who's running this show?" Lee asks.

"That's an easy one, bud. The Cap always runs the show."

Lee shakes his head. "No, that's not what I mean. This isn't R-dubs, right? I mean, who pays for it all? Who signs the cheque?"

"Nah, it's not R-dubs, though lots of the guys here do crew for R-dubs too. It's a big company, and they pay big too, called Alpha-Omega."

**

Question 47:

What was the slogan of the Faithful Few?

a) The meek shall inherit the Earth
b) As it was in the days of Noah
c) And there will be signs in the sun and moon and stars
d) Rule over the fish of the sea, and over the birds of the sky, and over every living thing that moves on the Earth
e) God has a plan

Answer 47:

b) As it was in the days of Noah

"As it was in the days of Noah" was the slogan meant to imply that the world was full of sin and God was planning to destroy all humans as he did in the Bible.

***

I look over at Lee, who is sleeping, curled on his side away from me. We talked until I don't know how late, and at some point we both dozed off. I feel the ship's engine vibrating as we move steadily on across the water, headed off to another glacier we'll reach tomorrow morning.

A breath later, there are three sharp knocks on our door and then it swings open. A crew member stands framed in the doorway. I shake Lee's shoulder and he groans and rolls over, rubbing his eyes. The main room is dark, and I guess it's still the middle of the night. The man at our door has a flashlight that he shines in on us, its light startlingly bright.

"C'mon, you two. Captain wants to see you in his quarters, and be quiet, would ya, the guys are sleeping."

I wonder if we are in trouble for spending so much time on the deck today. Or maybe someone reported us coming out of the hold. I am guessing the fact that he wants to see us in the middle of the night can't be good.

We are both in our long underwear, so we shimmy into pants. We don't bother with any other clothing as the man sent to fetch us seems impatient. I grab my messenger bag and sling it over my shoulder as we follow the crew man up the ladder and onto the deck. The glacier is slipping slowly by on the right. It's so cold out I feel my cheeks going numb even though we are outside for less than a minute. He leads us to a door tucked right under the bridge. He knocks once then pulls the door open and motions for us to go in. As soon as we do, he pushes the door closed behind us.

The room is warmly lit and has light wood paneling all around. There's a single bed, neatly made up, against the wall to my right and a few curtained windows. A big desk sits up against the wall directly in front of us. A chair is pulled up to it, and a man sits with his back to us. He has broad shoulders and short blond hair. He holds up a hand, indicating he is aware of our presence, but continues to type on a tablet with his other hand. As we wait, I look at the overhead light, which has a stained-glass cover on it. There are lots of greens and purples and oranges, but I am not sure if the design is random or meant to be something. His chair scrapes back and my focus shifts to the man as he rises and turns.

"Fuck," Lee whispers.

"Nice to see you too, nephew. And how nice to finally meet Sarah's daughter."

Chris Mayer stares straight at me as he takes two steps across the room, his hand out for me to shake. I recognize his sharp, blue eyes and cold smile from the photo, although his face is leaner now than in the old picture. Inside I am shaking like a leaf, but I pull my spine up straighter and force myself to meet his stare.

"And Jim's daughter," I say as I shake his hand.

He tilts his head slightly and licks his bottom lip. He still has my hand.

"What's going on?" Lee asks, not even trying to mask the anger in his voice or face.

Chris doesn't bother to look at him but silently stares at me for another moment and finally drops my hand. He motions to the bed. "Why don't you both sit down? I think it's time we had a little talk."

We look at each other and silently agree to comply with his request, which sounds more like a command. He paces the small room and comes to a stop by a window. He pulls the curtain back enough to peek out and then drops it and looks at us.

"I was surprised to get a call from Captain Huron earlier this week telling me there was a request for two young people to come on this research expedition. Alpha-Omega has been sponsoring and conducting research for nearly twenty years, and Luke—Captain Huron—has been a loyal employee all of that time. A request like this was a first, and I couldn't imagine why he would even consider it, never mind insist on speaking to me about it." He starts to pace again, hands clasped behind his back. "And then he told me who wanted to come on our little research trip and—"

"What kind of research are you doing here?" I ask. I don't know where I got the guts to interrupt him, except he keeps saying the word *research,* and I am pretty sure that is not what is going on here. Who knows if it ever was?

He glares at me, and I think I see his shoulders twitch, but his hands remain behind his back. He comes to stand right in front of us so that I have to crane my neck back to see him. "Let's be clear, kiddo, I'm the one who will be asking the questions. Got it?"

Lee stands up, coming between his uncle and me. His chest bumps his uncle's and Chris backs up a step. Chris walks over to the window and peeks out again, then leans against his desk. Lee remains standing beside the bed.

"Tic, I know all about you. I know about your science project, and I know you have been very curious about Jim's death. Did you find out something new that I don't know about? Why the sudden request to come on the expedition?" His voice is low and rocky, and he rubs the stubble on his cheek. "Is it to spy on me?"

It clicks now. Of course he knows all of that. He was the one spying on me. But the discussion to come up here with Lee happened on Joni's account, so he doesn't know I came up to scatter Mom's ashes. It *is* why I came up, even if I did do some snooping in the hold.

"No," I answer.

He comes at me with his right hand raised, ready to hit, yelling, "LIAR! LIAR!"

Lee is in front of me and grabs his uncle's arm in mid-air, blocking the strike. I scream and back up against the wall. The door to the cabin opens and a rush of cold air comes in with the two men who grab Lee, one on each side, quickly securing his arms. They back him up against another wall. He struggles briefly before stopping and looking first at his uncle and then at me.

"Are you okay?" Lee asks me.

"I'm asking the questions, remember?" Chris says and punches Lee hard in the gut. He buckles forward but the men holding his arms keep him upright. I fling myself at one of the men, the one who summoned us up here, and try to pull him off Lee, but he fends me off with one hand. Chris wraps me up from behind. I struggle to get free, but he tightens his hold. I can't outmuscle him, so I let myself go limp instead. I take advantage of his surprise and the fraction of extra space this gives to slide through his hold and down to the floor. I don't waste time standing up but scurry on all fours to the door.

I'm not fast enough. Chris lunges, grabs my left foot, and yanks back hard. He's down on the floor now too, and I try to kick him, but he twists my leg around so that I have no choice but to flip onto my back. He sits straddling me, pinning my arms with his knees. Lee is yelling at him.

Chris barks, "For Christ's sake, shut him up!"

I can't see anything except Chris's chest and neck and face, and Lee's voice is quickly muffled. Chris looks down at me. I have never felt such hatred in my life.

With a feather touch, Chris runs his finger down my cheek. "I never loved anyone else," he whispers.

***

Question 48:

Look at the three words below and find a fourth word that is related to all three.

Knife Light Pal

Answer 48:

Pen

***

I am gagged, and even though I know I can breathe just fine through my nose I still feel panicky. The only thing keeping me from freaking out is staring into Lee's eyes. He is gagged too, and both of us have our ankles and wrists taped behind our backs. For the moment we are alone, lying on the bed facing each other. I am trying hard not to cry. Chris will be back soon, I guess, and then--I don't want to think about it. More questioning. More beating. Worse.

Before taping our wrists, Chris had Lee get into a diving suit. If he decides to get rid of him—of us—he is going to make it look like an accident, like Lee went diving and ran into trouble. And what about me? Either he can't be bothered to waste another diving suit on me or he doesn't intend to kill me. But if he doesn't kill me and I know he killed Lee, how is he going to keep me from talking? Maybe he thinks no one would believe me. He could certainly pay enough "witnesses" to say Lee fell in. There's a crazy glint in his eye when he looks at me and mentions my mother. If he doesn't intend to kill me, does he plan to keep me hidden somewhere forever as a memory of her? I shudder. Too sick. I wanna hurl and then I have a thought that really makes my stomach drop. Probably he only intends to kill me. Lee is in a diving suit so that when he puts us both over, Lee, his nephew, his own blood will survive. He knows he won't talk. Why? Because they are family?

I shift and am aware of my bag pressed between my right hip and the mattress. I have an idea, but it means I have to trust Lee, to trust that he and I are in this together. Do I? I don't have a choice. I wiggle some more. Lee watches, his eyes questioning me. I shift until my bag is exposed on the mattress between us and gesture to it with my eyes. He seems to understand and rolls himself over so that he is facing away from me. His hands grope until they find the bag. I watch him struggle, but he finally pulls out the tablet and drops it between us. His hands disappear into the bag again and this time come out gripping the pocketknife. He drops that on the bed too and turns back to face me. We both look down at the knife. I nod and hope he can read my mind.

After a few seconds, we both roll over. Now our backs are to each other. I stare at the wall in front of me, the wood grain of the panelling a few inches from my face. I strain my trapped arms, my fingers searching until I feel the smooth wood of the knife. My initials are at the end away from the blade, so I am able to use those to orient myself. I squeeze. There's a satisfying click as the blade pops out.

I shimmy closer to Lee so that our butts and shoulder blades are touching. I feel around tentatively until I find the duct tape, and then I begin a sawing motion with the blade. I take it most of the way through and then stop. I would love to free Lee completely and then have him do the same for me, but if it's obvious we are free, we will lose any element of surprise we might have. We are going to need any advantage we can get. I am still trying to decide if I should finish the job when the door opens. I am so afraid I drop the knife on the bed between us.

I hear footsteps approach and then Chris is looking down at us. "Hmm, tired of looking at each other? What a surprise." I hear him pull the desk chair over and then I feel the mattress shift as he yanks Lee into a seated position on the side of the bed.

I roll over to face them and see only my tablet exposed on the bed.

Chris picks it up. "I will send this back to IT and see if there is anything else you have on here, Tic, that might be interesting to me. Let's get you sitting up too." He grabs my bicep to pull me up and is squeezing so hard that tears come to my eyes unbidden. He sits down in front of us so close that the rest of the room is blocked from my view. He rubs the stubble on his cheek with his left hand. "Here's the deal. The boat is stopped for now, and I sent the boys off to catch a few winks while we deal with some private matters. So let's talk."

Lee breathes out hard through his nose, and Chris raises a hand as if to slap him and could easily do it without even getting up from the chair but changes his mind. He puts his hand down and shakes his head. "I am going to ask you as many questions as I want, and you will nod yes or no answers. When we are finished I will decide whether one or both of you is going to have an accident tonight. Got it?"

He waits until we both nod.

"Tic, you said you came on this trip to scatter your mother's ashes?"

I nod.

"Good girl." He smiles at me, and I feel sick. "I believe you. I found them in your little love nest. I was naturally very sad to learn through reviewing the Arquette Hospital records that Sarah had died. I truly wish things could have been different. I wonder why she didn't use any of the money I sent her over the years to buy a better, and by better I mean safer, place for the two of you to live. As much as I loved her, and I did love her you know?" he says as he places a finger under my chin lifting my head so that he is looking me in the eye. "Sarah never made very sensible decisions. It wasn't her strong suit." He sighs. "I think I will hang on to the ashes. I think I would like that." He nods, smiling.

I look away. This is definitely not what I had in mind for Mom's ashes. Some creepy ex hanging on to her!

"Good. Moving on," he continues. "My men told me that they were surprised to find Al Savory in his barn. They told me what they did about the situation in detail, and I thought they handled it well. Next thing I know, though, surprise, surprise, Al is alive. He shows up at the Arquette camp hospital with you. Medical records suggest you suffered some minor smoke inhalation. Am I correct in concluding that you are the person who saved Al?"

I nod slowly. I hadn't expected him to know this much, but there doesn't seem to be a point in denying it.

"Brave, I guess," he says dismissively. "I wonder, though, did you save anything else from the barn? Anything I might be interested in?"

We lock eyes.

I consider.

I nod.

He seems genuinely surprised, whether it's that I did find and save my dad's work or that I admitted to it, I'm not sure. He grimaces. I wait.

"I'm going to take your gag out so you can tell me where it is, but don't even think about calling for help. Luke and Bruce gave everyone a little extra something in their dinner tonight to help them sleep through, and if you scream I will just shove the gag further down your throat before you can wake anyone who would care. So no yelling, okay?"

I nod.

He takes the gag out, and some spittle dribbles down my chin. I lick my sore, dry, stretched lips. He waits to see if I will scream, but I don't. I'm surprised they would drug the crew. Maybe he's bluffing, but maybe not.

"What did you find?" he asks.

"An old computer memory card." I say.

Lee is staring at me, surprised at what I am giving away. "And?"

"It had my dad's work on it. He found out that carbon dioxide molecules destabilize the bonds between water molecules in glaciers, making them crack and melt faster."

Chris is nodding. "Exactly right." He leans in close, so close I can smell his warm, minty breath. "So where is this card now?"

"It should have arrived at NESA yesterday," I say calmly.

"LIAR!" he roars and jumps up, knocking over the chair.

"I have shared the files with some other students already, and they have shared them with researchers outside of NESA," I say. I try not to sound too cocky, but even though I am tied up and this nutcase is probably going to kill me in the next little while, I can't help feeling triumphant. My dad's work is out there and will be, no matter what happens here.

"You think you're so smart. Just like your goddamn father!" Chris yells at me, his voice penetrating the sudden burning, throbbing pain in my cheek where his hand landed.

***

Question 49:

Who said the following quote? "Hatred is not to be carried in the name of God! War is not to be waged in the name of God!"

a) Buddha
b) Thich Nhat Hanh
c) Rabbi Eliezer Ben Kochot
d) Pope Francis
e) Dalai Lama

Answer 49:

d) Pope Francis

Pope Francis, the 266th pope of the Roman Catholic Church, was a key religious leader in the Change. His encyclical entitled "On Care for Our Common Home" was a milestone document.

***

Chris cut the tape off our feet so we could walk out onto the deck. I'm trembling from fear or cold or both. Lee still has his hands behind his back, but I wonder if he can break the last bit of tape whenever he wants. I'm not sure. I hope he can. I hope I sawed far enough down through it and he's just waiting for the right time to do something.

I am on Chris's right, my gag reinserted, and Lee is on his left. He has a strong grip on each of our biceps. We stop about five feet from the back rail of the boat. He lets go of Lee and, turning to me, reaches up his free hand and strokes the pendant dangling on my chest. He looks me in the eye, as if searching for something, and then grabs and yanks on the pendant hard enough to break the chain. I stumble forward, and he sticks his foot out to make me trip and fall. Unable to put my hands out in front of me to stop the fall, I land hard on my stomach, my forehead bouncing on the wood decking with a loud thonk.

"Mine," he says, pocketing the necklace. "I gave this to her."

I roll over and struggle to my knees, but my vision is cloudy and my head is spinning.

"You haven't stopped us, you know. Granted I may need to be more careful about my trips north. I may even have to stop coming up here to put carbon dioxide cartridges in the glaciers, but that's only one piece of it. We will prevail." His voice seems to me coming from high, high above me, but it sounds almost joyful now. "The end will come, and it won't be long now, five years at most. You wouldn't have survived anyway. You're not one of us." With a hand on each arm, he lifts me to my feet and whispers in my ear. "But at least this should be quick and painless for you, just like it was for your father when I pushed him in."

I start to struggle frantically against his grip. Adrenaline pumping, I kick at him and bang my head into his chest. I wrench from side to side but his hands are like vices on my arms.

"Stop!" Lee's voice is raspy but firm, and both Chris and I freeze. "Let her go," he says and his uncle obeys.

I sink to my knees, my head spinning and my heart pounding with relief. Lee came through for me.

He has a hand on his uncle's left wrist and is pressed up against him from behind. In his right hand he holds my knife up against Chris's throat.

"Calm down son. This is for the best, and you know it. I would never hurt you. You are of my blood and you are marked and you will be saved when He comes. And I know you would never do anything to hurt your poor mother, so ask yourself why you are holding a knife to her only brother's neck?"

For a moment, they are motionless statues on the ship's deck. Then Chris turns his head to the left and rams his right elbow back into Lee. Lee's knife grazes the skin on Chris' neck, a superficial cut, a bright-red line. Chris ducks his head under Lee's arm and turns, grappling with Lee, trying to wrest the knife away from him. I watch feeling horrified and helpless.

They spin in what feels like slow motion towards the rail. They are grunting and breathing hard. Chris has Lee's back up against the rail and pins him there with his body while his outstretched left arm slams Lee's right wrist into the rail. It hits so hard the metal rail rings and Lee drops the knife. Chris's eyes follow the knife as it falls into the dark water below.

I have been edging closer and closer to them on my knees. I can't say why. I have no hope of helping, but I can't just sit and watch. I am drawn to them. Lee takes advantage of his uncle's diverted attention to push off from the rail with his whole body heaving hard. To everyone's surprise, Chris topples backward over me. His feet fly up and he hits the deck head first. He lies still and motionless.

Lee and I glance at each other and then both stare back at him. I make a muffled moan, and Lee gets down on his knees next to me and removes my gag. He hugs me tight.

"I love you, I love you, I love you," he breathes into my neck.

"I love you too," I say, my cheek pressed to his chest. "Lee," I say, "my hands."

"Oh, yeah," he says. "I don't have the knife anymore."

"Go look for a scissors in the captain's quarters," I say.

"What about him?" Lee asks, indicating Chris lying face up on the deck.

I shrug. "He isn't going anywhere," I say. His chest is rising and falling, at least I am pretty sure it is, but I am no longer afraid of him.

Lee looks at Chris and back at me. "I'll be fast," he says before he goes.

I sit back on my heels and stare at Chris. I can't even begin to process what just happened, but my mind is jumping ahead like it doesn't matter. What next? Should we tie him up? Then what? He seems to be unconscious, but for how long? Is he still breathing? What if he dies? I am shocked to find that I feel relief at the thought. At least we wouldn't have to worry about him, but what am I thinking? We would be murderers! But it was self-defense so we had no choice. But still.

On my knees still, I shuffle over to him. I am on his right and can see that his neck is dark with blood from my knife. I want to gag. I look away and watch his chest instead. Is it moving? Holy shit, I don't think it is moving! I feel a desperate need to know if he is still alive. It's awkward, but with my hands still taped behind my back I kneel down across his body and lay my head on his chest to see if I can hear a heartbeat.

A siren scream tears the night air, rising high up from my throat before it is cut off.

Everything is cut off. No air. Just Chris's hands squeezing my neck tighter and tighter and tighter.

***

Question 50:

Name as many possible uses for a cast-iron frying pan as you can.

Answer 50:

Answers may include, but are not limited to, the following: cooking, shovel, head protection, paperweight, doorstop, bowl, hammer, weapon.

***

I am screwed! It's all I have time to think as the dark night around me turns even blacker and disappears.

And then, like a miracle, air rushes down my throat and into my lungs and my vision returns. I am lying on my side on the deck trying to make sense of what I see. A giant stands with his back to me, huffing and puffing. Sound comes rushing back in now too, and I hear a man's voice swearing.

"You asshole! You bastard! What the hell were you doing to her?"

"Rob!"

Big Rob looks up at Lee who is rushing towards us.

"Chris--" I have to stop and try to clear my throat, which throbs with every word I force out. "He was choking me."

Lee looks at Rob who looks down at the cast-iron frying pan in his right hand.

"I was just making eggs," he says.

"Eggs?" Lee asks.

"Just a snack," Rob says defensively.

"Okay," Lee says.

"I heard her scream, so I came. They were both there," he says, pointing to the deck at his feet where Chris's corpse lies. They both look at it, but my view is blocked. Neither says anything. "I guess I hit him in the face with the pan," Rob says.

"Fact," says Lee.

Again, I don't know what the hell is wrong with my mind. Why am I able to think ahead? Why am I thinking what I am thinking? Am I sick? "Atlantic," I say, as the pain from speaking brings tears to my eyes.

They both look at me uncertainly.

I point with my chin to the boat's railing, to the dark water beyond it. Despite the pain I speak again as slowly and clearly as I can manage.

"At-lan-tic"

"Are you sure?" Lee asks understanding dawning on his face as he looks deep into my eyes.

I take only a second to reflect. Here, somewhere, is where Chris did it. Where he ended my father's life. The father I never got to meet. I nod.

"Okay," Lee says to me.

"Rob, thanks for your help, man. I mean it," Lee says softly. "I got it from here."

"No problem, kid," Rob answers. "But I'll help ya. This guy looks like he might be a bit heavy for you to lift."

"Thanks."

"Can't say I recognize him, huh? Course it's hard to tell now cuzza the pan. Any idea who he was?" Rob asks as he scoops his big hands under Chris's shoulders and Lee lifts Chris's feet.

"My uncle," Lee says.

***

Question 51:

Do the Faithful few still exist?

a) Yes
b) No

***

The morning after Chris disappeared it was soon clear that none of the crew had heard anything the night before. I really do think that Bruce slipped them something. Lucky for me, the dose of whatever it was must have been too small for Big Rob. It also seems that no one aside from Captain Luke Huron and Bruce the cook, including the so-called research team, knew he had been aboard. As to why those two hadn't come to his help during the fight, we assume they were under strict orders to stay away from the deck because Chris didn't want any witnesses. These are clearly men who do as they are told, which just didn't work out in Chris's favour last night.

Lee and I went to lie down after the big fight, but neither of us could sleep, so we just held each other. Everything had happened so quickly, but I could still remember almost every detail of it, like watching a movie in slow motion. Out of all the events—the revelation about my father, the fighting, and both Lee and I almost being killed—the thing I still find hardest to accept is that someone would actively try to make climate change worse. He did get very rich as a result, but my gut tells me this wasn't his main motivation. He must have truly thought that when the world ended God would come and save him and other believers. Why would he—or anyone—even want to believe that?

I shudder, remembering Chris's look as he spoke about my mother. He was so intense you would have thought her rejecting him had happened last week or last month, not twenty years ago. He must have been crazy in love with her. Or just plain crazy. And what did he mean when he said, "This is just one piece," and "We will prevail"? Did he mean the Faithful Few? Could they still exist? I figure Lee and I can talk about all of that some other time.

A few hours after we lay down, a bang on our door and we are summoned to meet with Captain Luke Huron. It's morning, and the smells of eggs being fried and bread toasting make my stomach rumble as we pass through the main room.

"Hey Rob, save us some of that huh? We are just headed up to see the Cap. Be back soon." Lee says.

Rob nods and smiles, although I think maybe I see worry in his eyes. Or maybe it's just my own worry. Even though Lee and I figured this was coming and decided what he would say I am still feeling very nervous.

We enter the room where just a few hours before the Captain had left us alone with Chris. So much has changed, but the room looks just the same. Every detail of it, the wood paneling, the multi-colored light fixture, the dark curtains covering the windows is burned in my memory.

He is pacing the room when we come in. He doesn't invite us to sit. As we stand he pauses his pacing and faces us, staring at first me and then Lee. The silence drags on and on, and I wonder if he can see in our faces what has happened, what we have done. Is he waiting for us to confess?

"You wanted to see us?" Lee says, holding Captain Huron's gaze.

"Yes."

The Captain resumes his pacing and begins speaking to the walls, and to the floor.

"I have been at my job, this job for over twenty years. Do you know why?"

"You're good at it?" I venture.

"Yes. Exactly right. I am good at it, I'm very good at it. Sometimes I enjoy it and sometimes I don't, but I am always good at it. Do you know what makes me good at it?"

He still isn't looking at either of us, and I wish he would just get to the point and get this over with already.

"I'm good at it because I have been on ships my whole life. I understand the ocean and its moods better than I understand most people, probably why I don't get on with most people actually. But the sea's dangerous, and anyone who isn't afraid of the ocean is just plain ignorant. Heading out to the North Atlantic this time of year is especially dangerous; it's no milk run. What makes me very good at my job is that I don't allow myself to get distracted by anything."

He pauses and sighs. He looks at us both again and then resumes pacing. "So's I don't get distracted I don't ask questions about things that aren't related to me doing my job. Your uncle always appreciated that."

"My uncle has left us," is all Lee says but it is enough.

"I see," Captain Huron says. He pauses for a moment and then draws back a curtain and looks out a window as he continues. "I think then it's best to cut this research expedition short and head back. I have some money put away and a special beach in mind I'll want to spend some time at."

He turns around and barely looks at us. "Okay, I've got things to do now. Move on then you two." he says pointing to the door.

***

Today the fresh air feels sharp against my cheeks and tears sting the corners of my eyes, but they are being squeezed out by the sun and my smile. I hug the can with Mom's remains against my chest. I'm not sure what I will do with them, but it just didn't feel right to leave her in the North Atlantic any more. I suppose there isn't a rush to figure it out now or maybe ever. As we approach the dock in Gloucester Harbour, I can make out Uncle Al standing on the very end of the pier, his hand up to shade his brow, watching us, watching me. From our messages over the past few days I know he is upset with me for sneaking off, but I think—I hope—he understands why I did it.

Lee and I messaged Phish and Tate too, telling them about the carbon dioxide tanks and the drilling. We left out anything to do with Chris, though. It might have led to questions about where he is now.

We pull up alongside the dock, and the crew get busy tying up. I see that in addition to Uncle Al on the pier, there is a small crowd gathered on the shore. Seven men in suits stride briskly towards the ship. Uncle Al steps out of the way.

One man signals for a crew member to come closer and says with authority, "Special agent Peters of the ECU, I need to speak to the captain."

When the crew member hesitates, the man flashes a badge from his pocket. The crew member shrugs and goes to fetch the captain.

"We need to come aboard before anyone gets off," the agent states when the captain returns.

My heart is pounding in my ears like the ocean has gotten into my brain. Did they find out about Chris? Are we going to jail for murder? Who told? Is there any proof? I can't breathe. Oh shit.

They come aboard and speak to the captain out of earshot. I am frozen, staring at them. Are they looking at us? I don't think so, but most of them have sunglasses on, so I can't see their eyes. Then the captain points us out to them, and I squeeze Lee's hand so tight my knuckles turn white. They head down to the hold and everyone up on deck waits. No one talks, no one moves. We just wait.

Two agents come up the ladder followed by the three men on the "research team." Two more agents follow and handcuff the men. Another agent comes up and speaks with the captain.

"All right everyone, back to work. I'll let you know when you can go down to the hold again, but for now it's off limits."

An agent comes over and tells us we can get off the boat but not to go too far because they want to question us about the research team's activities. I glance over to the pier. Uncle Al has his hands thrust deep in his pockets and is staring up at me. When we lock eyes, he smiles and I wave.

Lee and I cross a plank onto the pier. Uncle Al wraps me in his arms, and I want to cry. His embrace feels so safe, like home, makes me sorry for any worry I caused him, makes me miss my mom so much. When we finally pull apart, I am pulled into another hug, this time from Phish. I am surprised that she came and even more surprised to look over her shoulder and see Asker smiling at me. When Phish lets go of me she takes a step back and grabs Asker's hand, pulling her into our circle. I look from one face to the other and their smiles just keep growing.

"Hey," Uncle Al says, "there's a few more folks waiting to say hi to you over there." He points to the shore where several cars are parked, and we head in that direction. Behind me, I hear him say to Lee, "I'm sure glad you went with her on this little adventure."

"Me too," says Lee.

As we get closer I see Billy Williams leaning against a familiar car. Tate is also here, leaning against a second car. He comes towards us, closing the distance of the last few steps. He puts out his right hand and I awkwardly do the same. We shake once and then he too pulls me in for a quick hug.

Stepping back, he starts an excited ramble. "I still can't believe it!" he says. "How could anyone want to melt the glaciers faster? It's crazy. It's just crazy!"

I smile and nod, thinking he doesn't even know crazy.

"Well, it could certainly explain the results of your project. You really think that someone has been doing this for the last sixteen years? I did some quick calculations and depending how many times, how many spots, I mean, it could, it just could—"

The back door of one of the cars makes a sharp noise which causes us all to look over. When we see the passenger who has emerged, Tate stops speaking.

"Tic, it's nice to meet you," Robert Sheffield says. He is even more magnetically handsome than I remember. He leans against the car and holds a hand out to me. I step forward and we shake hands.

"It's nice to meet you too, sir," I manage.

"Tate has been passing along your father's research, as well as all of your key findings both in your school project and on board the boat. What can I say? Excellent work. Really. The authorities will follow up on all of it, of course, but I can't help but think what a difference you have made. If there is ever anything I can do for you--" He smiles, and I feel like he and I are the only two people in the world.

I look over my shoulder at Uncle Al and Lee and Phish and Tate. They are only a few feet back, smiling encouragement and pride, and before I think any more I open my mouth again, "Well, actually," I say, "do you know anyone in the Department of Justice?"

He looks perplexed and I wonder what the hell I am doing asking for a favour from the chief scientific advisor, but I've already started now. "Or maybe just a really good lawyer? I've got some money from my mom, and the thing is, there's this guy, Matt Haley, who was friends with her and my dad, and he's in prison, but he was framed by the same person behind all of this. I am sure he was framed."

Sheffield smiles and considers before answering. "Well, you haven't been wrong yet. Let me see who I know and I'll have someone get back to you for more details, okay?"

I smile and nod. "Thanks."

"Sure," he says. "Now I have to get going, and if I'm not mistaken, you have some people waiting for you to decide where you are headed next." He indicates all of the people who have been discreetly watching and listening to our conversation: Lee, Tate, Phish and Asker, Billy Williams, and Uncle Al.

I realize he is right. I would ask for his advice—I mean, who better to get advice from? But I don't need it. I know where I am going: North East Science Academy.

***

Answer 51:

c) Maybe

About the Author

Marissa Slaven is an emerging author, practicing palliative care physician, and life-long reader of literature. She honed her writing skills at the Humber School of Writers where she was mentored by authors David Bezmozgis and Tim Wynne-Jones.

Born in Montreal and a graduate of McGill's prestigious medical school, Marissa completed her medical training in Boston, Massachusetts. A frequent speaker in medical circles, Marissa's career as a physician and science background fueled her research into climate change; a topic she has become both knowledgeable and passionate about.

Presently Marissa tries to keep her blog updated while she works on her next novel. She loves her wonderful husband, her three amazing children, her enthusiastic golden-doodle, and her tribe in Hollyrock.

CPSIA information can be obtained
at www.ICGtesting.com
Printed in the USA
LVOW03s0242260318
571117LV00002B/2/P